A Sinner's Saint

De Bellis Crime Family
Book 4

Kylie Kent

ISBN 13: 978-1-923137-08-0(ebook)
978-1-923137-51-6 (paperback)

Cover Illustration by Cover Kate Farlow – Y'all That Graphic

Edited By
Kat Pagan

Club Omerta

Are you a part of the Club?

Don't want to wait for the next book to be released to the public?
Come and Club Omerta for an all access pass!

This includes:
• daily chapter reveals,
• first to see - everything, covers, teasers, blurbs
• Advanced reader copies of every book
• Bonus scenes from the characters you love!
• Video chats with me (Kylie Kent)
• and so much more

Click the link to be inducted to the club!!!
CLUB OMERTA

Content Warning

Content warning. This is a dark mafia romance. Please read with caution. Topics found within these pages include but are not limited to: sexual assault, graphic violence, blood, death, and adult language.

This story involves child sexual assault/abuse and can be extremely triggering. Please proceed with caution. Your mental health is important.

Chapter One

My whole body is trembling. I try to fight it... the fear. They like it more when I'm scared. The sick fucks get off on it. I tried so hard this month. I thought if I was good, if I did everything right just like my father wanted, then he wouldn't bring me here. He wouldn't *make me do this. He wouldn't let these men do... this... to me.*

It didn't work. It doesn't matter how good I am, because I will never be enough. That's why he brings me here. Because I deserve the punishment.

When the door opens, the masked men walk in. They always wear masks. I have no idea who they are. All I know is that they want to use my body for their own sick pleasure. And if I scream, they leave quicker. Because they like it...

I've seen this one before. I recognise the skull tattoo on his hand. He has a Russian accent too. I close my eyes and take a deep breath. I used to fight back. But they're too many of them and they're all stronger than I am. Which means it only hurts more.

The door closes with a loud bang and I jump. I can't help it. As tough as I want to be, I'm not. I'm nothing but weak. A fucking kid. I have no doubt that I'll die in this room one day. At least it's me and not my brothers, not that my father would dare bring any of the others here.

No, he saves this torture for me. He says I deserve it. I'm the reason he had to kill my mother. I don't understand how. I was only a few months old when he shot her in the head—or at least that's what I've been told. I don't remember her. I have wondered if she did something bad, if it's her fault I am the way I am. The kind of son who is subjected to this by his own father.

The man is close now...

My body shakes. I can't stop it. I don't want this. I don't like it, and there's nothing I can do about it. Sometimes they give me something. A pill. I like the pills, because they make me not think. I'm numb when I get the pills.

Not this man, though. He likes me aware. He wants me to scream. I shake my head, and then his hand snaps out, wrapping around my throat so tight I can't breathe. My feet lift off the floor. His breath stinks of cigarette and alcohol.

"Did you just tell me no, boy?" the man sneers with that same thick Russian accent.

I can't move. I can't shake my head or nod. I can't say anything. Maybe this is it. The end. I'd welcome it. At least I might get some peace, because I know for sure I'm not going to the same place in hell these fuckers are spiralling towards.

My body falls to the floor when he releases me. I scramble to my feet, trying to get up, but I don't make it. The man forces me onto my stomach. He holds me down with one hand while the other slams onto my ass. Hard. I scream out in pain and he laughs.

I can already tell this isn't going to be a quick night. He's going to drag it out. And then I feel it... the tip of his cock at my ass.

"No!" *I cry out.*

I jolt up, the room dark and my body completely covered in sweat. My shaky hands reach out and flick on the bedside lamp. I'm alone.

Fuck, I hate these nightmares. It's still dark out, too early to get up, but I need to. I need to move.

I climb off the bed and pull on a pair of sweatpants, then pick up a shirt from my floor and bring it to my nose. I discard that one and go for another. As soon as I'm dressed, I head for my closet, where I grab the little metal box that contains the one thing that'll help me erase the memories.

I'm quiet as I walk out of my room. The last thing I need is to run into one of my brothers right now. I'm the youngest of four, and ever since my eldest brother finally put a hole in our father's head, my siblings have really upped the whole *overprotective* vibe.

Thankfully, Gio is a little preoccupied with his new girlfriend. I like Eloise. Not sure why. There's just something about her that's very maternal. Not that I know much about that either. And then there's Santo. I don't even know what to say about that one right now. He found his fiancée murdered, at the hands of our father, on the night before the wedding. It's fucked him up completely. I think he might even be more fucked up than I am, and that's saying something.

Gabe is the peacemaker of the family, the fixer. He's stepped up since Santo isn't himself right now, but he takes the whole fixing shit to the next level. There isn't a problem any of us has that he doesn't want to take on. Oh, and he's also hiding his relationship with one of Eloise's friends. Clearly, he's shit at hiding it, because I'm pretty sure everyone knows.

Marcel, the one who's closest to me in age, is mostly absent. He's at university and seems to take his studies seriously. Don't get me wrong. He's here when he needs to be, but if he's not needed, he usually finds a reason to be out. Not that I blame him.

Things are fucking weird in this house. For the first time in my life—well, that I can remember anyway—we have a female living with us. One who's not part of the staff. Eloise moved in, and it's as if she's taken over the entire family. I wouldn't be surprised if she starts calling all the shots soon. My big brother is a lovesick puppy around her. Actually, even when Gio's not around her, he's fucking pining for her.

Like I said, I love Eloise. She's brought something that we haven't ever had. She's making this place a home, and not just a cold-ass museum. And furniture. Thank fuck. Gio had this thing. He wouldn't furnish the house until he could get El to agree to move in. He wanted her to pick it all out.

Stepping onto the back porch, I nod at one of the soldiers standing guard. "Long night?" he asks me.

"Something like that." I sink to the floor, lean my back up against the wall, and open my little metal box. I pull out an already-rolled joint and a lighter and snap the lid closed.

"Have a good day," the guy says before walking away.

I haven't taken the time to learn all their names. I don't see the point. They don't work for me. They also all know I smoke. I think everyone does, except Gio. If he did, he'd probably kick my ass. My brothers are anti-drugs. I could easily go and help myself to a bottle of Cinque, the whiskey blend we all own a share of. But light up some of nature's best buds, and it's a fucking problem.

It's a fucking double standard is what it is. They really don't understand. *I need this.*

I shove the blunt into my mouth and use my hand to block the wind as I light the opposite end. Inhaling deep, I hold the smoke in my lungs for as long as I can before blowing it out. After just one hit on this thing, I can already feel my heartbeat calming down.

The nightmares fuck me up. It'll take a few of these and the usual morning routine before I can shake this feeling. Of being dirty... of being used and abused in the worst possible ways.

At this point, I'm wondering if I'll ever be rid of it, or if I'm destined to live a life reliving the torture of my youth. Two years. My father made me go to that house for two fucking years before it stopped.

Drawing in another lungful of smoke, I lean my head back on the wall and close my eyes. I have three hours before I need to start getting ready for school. Personally, I don't see the fucking point. I know how my life is going to turn out. I know my destiny. And no amount of education is going to change the direction I'm headed.

When I pull into the school's car park, Dash is already there. Leaning against his own car, right next to where I park mine. The moment I step out, I'm assaulted by the smell of smoke. "You know those things are going to kill you," I tell him.

"I'm already dying." Dash shrugs like it's no big deal. "We're all born to die, Vin."

I reach behind my left ear and grab the joint I stuffed there before leaving the house. "Sure. Start the day off all morbid and shit. What makes a Monday morning better than thinking about your imminent demise?" After lighting up the end, I inhale a lungful of smoke before passing the whole thing to Dash.

"There are worse ways to start a Monday," he says before passing it back.

"Like?"

"The English exam we have first period," he deadpans.

Fuck, I forgot about that.

"I'll meet you in there," I tell him, locking my car before walking off in the direction of the building.

I need to find Cammi. I know how she gets with exams. I don't know what it is about this girl, but I can't seem to *not* watch her. To not want to know more about her.

I find her at her locker with her friends. Leaning against the wall of lockers on the other side of the hall, I pretend to scroll on my phone while I continue to watch her. She's nervous. Her hands are shaking. Even from this distance, I can see her eyes watering. She gets like this before every exam. I'm not sure why. I've seen her grades. She's fucking smart.

The bell rings, and everyone starts moving. When I see Cammi step towards the classroom, I follow her. Taking the seat in the back, right next to hers. Her teeth dig into her bottom lip, and she pulls out a clear plastic pencil case filled with pens.

Ms Natt, our English teacher, walks into the room and closes the door. "Good morning. I hope you took time over the weekend to study and prepare for today's exam," she says.

I watch Cammi out of the corner of my eye. It fucking pisses me off how miserable and scared she seems. Her face pales. Her breathing quickens. Honestly, she looks like she's about ready to pass the fuck out.

Chapter Two

Cammi

I f there ever was a time for a sinkhole to open up and drag me in, I'd really appreciate it happening right now. Frankly, I'd take any kind of disaster really. Something to get me out of this damn classroom. What kind of evilness exists within Ms Natt that she'd purposely give us an exam first thing on a Monday morning? I imagine the devil hand delivered the papers she's putting on everyone's desks —you know, since she's besties with him, obviously.

I don't do well on exams. Never have, never will. I know that. But this is senior year, and exams are heavily weighted. I get stressed, beyond stressed. I can't help it. I have this fear of failing, of not knowing what's going to be asked and not understanding the content. I wouldn't say I'm an overachiever. I don't want to be the best or at the top of the class. I just don't want to fail. Give me an essay or assignment, and I'll get great grades. When it comes to exams, though, the nerves and the fear of failure get to me and I literally buckle under the pressure.

And then there's Vin De Bellis. The guy currently occupying the desk next to mine. That's a whole different reason to be nervous. He's not even trying to hide the fact that he's watching me. I have no idea why he does it. Why he watches me. I've never spoken to him, and he's never tried to speak to me.

Sometimes, when I feel him watching me, I almost think he hates me. For what, I have no idea. But he just keeps his distance and keeps watching. Except right now. When he sat next to me. I'm doing my best to not look at him. If I pretend he's not there, I can get through the next hour.

The thing is, pretending Vin De Bellis isn't there is impossible. He's noticeable, right down to that little dimple in his left cheek. Those dark, honey-coloured eyes and tanned skin. And don't even get me started on the lips. They look soft. I've lost count of how many times I've thought about what they'd feel like against my skin.

Nope, not going there. Reality never measures up to fantasies anyway, right?

When Ms Natt slams a paper down on my desk, I jump in my seat. *Shit. Get it together, Cammi. It's only an English exam.*

"Okay, you may turn your papers over and start," she says.

With shaky hands, I flip the test face up. My eyes water, blurring the words on the page, and when a tear lands on the paper, I swipe at my cheeks. *Great. Just great.*

A hand leans over, resting on mine. "Relax. You can do this. Just breathe." His whispered voice sends shivers down my spine.

And then I put the nail in my own coffin, so to speak. I look across at him. "Thank you," I mouth.

"Camile and Vincenzo, pack up your things and wait for me outside the door," Ms Natt says.

What? I look to the front of the room and all eyes turn towards us. Without a word, I pick up my bag and walk out of the classroom as quickly as I can.

The door opens and slams behind me. Vin slumps against the wall. So freaking close. He doesn't look at me, doesn't say a word. Just stands there. Silent. I don't know why he chose that moment to talk to me. During an exam. And now, out here, nothing. He confuses me, and if I'm honest, he also takes up way too much space in my mind. I don't understand what he wants from me. Or why he has a habit of watching me. I know it's not an attraction thing. The kind of girls I've seen him with at parties, well, let's just say I'm not one of them.

I'm short. Even now, standing next to his six-foot frame, he dwarfs me. I'm also a lot more conservative than the other girls around here. I wouldn't say I dress prudish, but I don't have my ass cheeks hanging out of my shorts either.

I open my mouth to say something, anything to break the silence, and then I close it again. *I don't need to break the silence.* Sliding down the wall, I sit on the floor and cross my legs. I can feel him looking down at me. I refuse to acknowledge him. If he's just going to stand there and not say a damn word, not even apologise for getting me kicked out of an exam, then he doesn't exist to me.

About five minutes later, Vin turns and walks down the hall. "Where are you going?" I call after him.

He stops short and glares at me over a shoulder. "Anywhere that's not here. Wanna come?"

"You're ditching?" I ask, even as I'm moving to follow him.

"We're already in the shit. It can't get much worse." He shrugs.

"Okay." I nod and take quick steps to close the distance before he heads towards the door again. I have to practically jog to keep up with his strides.

It's not until we've slipped out the back of the building and I watch him climb through a hole in the fence that I stop and question if I really should be following him. The fence leads to the park, a park where not much of anything good happens. "I... ah..."

"You're scared," Vin says. It's not a question.

"Should I be?"

"Of me? No." He shakes his head while holding the fence piece back, waiting for me to climb through.

"You taking me to the park to... I don't know... cut my body into tiny pieces?" I ask him.

"I'd need a saw or something to be able to do that. Which I don't have. You can either come with me or you can stay," he says.

Fuck it. There's a pull I can't deny, so I step through the fence and look up at him. "Just so you know, if you do cut me up, I'll come back and haunt you. I'll be your worst nightmare," I tell him.

Vin runs those honey eyes of his up and down my body. "You couldn't compete with my nightmares," he says, then turns and walks towards the park. "Come on."

Finding a spot he deems suitable underneath a huge old gumtree, he sits and pulls out a little tin box. I plop down in front of him. I don't make a habit of ditching school. I have ditched, just not as often as Vin has.

"So... how much trouble do you think we're in?" I ask him.

"You won't get into trouble. I'll fix it," he says.

"Just like that, you'll fix it?" I raise an eyebrow at him as he pulls a rolled-up piece of paper from his little tin. There's a floral outline detail on the lid, and the name *De Bellis* engraved on top. But the thing is old, worn, and looks like it could be an antique. "You always keep your weed in family heirlooms?"

"It was my mother's." He shrugs. "Considering she's the reason I smoke, I figured it's only fitting to use her tin."

"What did she use it for?" I ask, not broaching the fact that he just said he smokes weed because of his mother. I want to know, but I can read the room, and he's about as closed off as anyone could be.

"No idea. I didn't know her." He places the joint between his lips and lights up the end. After taking a puff, he offers me a hit.

I shake my head. "Thanks, but I'm good."

"Suit yourself," he says before bringing it back to his lips.

"Why'd you do that?" I ask him.

"Do what?"

"Talk to me during the exam?"

"You looked upset. I wanted to help. It's not a big deal, Cammi."

"Thank you." I sigh, unsure of what else to say. He claims it's not a big deal, but it is. To me. That he noticed and cared enough to want to help me.

"Why do you get so nervous during exams?" he questions.

"Why do you watch me all the time?" I counter.

"You're like a bright light. I can't help but notice you," he says.

Okay, well, that's... weird. I'm not sure why he'd think I'm a bright light. To be honest, Vin has always been a little strange. Standoffish. He has two friends he's always with, Dash and Marcus. He doesn't give anyone else the time of day, while people *give him* a wide berth when he walks by. Though that has more to do with the rumours that surround his family. That's to say, *I've* never seen Vin do anything that warrants the fear people have of him.

"You should go back, Cammi. You being here, with me—well, you shouldn't be," he says.

"You invited me," I remind him.

"A moment of weakness. You shouldn't be around me." He takes another puff of the joint and blows the smoke upwards. Away from me.

"Why? You said you wouldn't cut me up into pieces."

"There are worse things people can do to you than kill you."

"Are you going to do those things to me?" I ask.

"No. But if I were, it wouldn't be in my interests to tell you, now would it?" he fires back.

"So, you're not going to cut me up, or do anything worse to me. I don't see why I shouldn't be around you, then? Unless you just plain don't want me to be here. I mean, I can take a hint."

Vin stares at me, and for a moment, I think he's going to tell me he doesn't want me here, and then he shakes his head. "The problem isn't that I don't want you here. It's that I do."

"Mm, I'm not sure we have the same definition of the word *problem*." I smile at him.

Chapter Three

I told Cammi she wouldn't get into trouble because of the exam, and I made sure she wouldn't. I did have to promise Ms Natt that I'd bring my 'guardian' in for a parent-teacher meeting. My English teacher has never been subtle about her obsession with my big brother. Ever since the news of my father's death, she's been trying every-thing she can to get a meeting with Gio.

I may have told her I'd bring a guardian. I didn't tell her it'd be Gio. And when I showed up with Eloise, the look on Ms Natt's face was priceless. She was furious and tried to suspend me on the spot. I knew she wouldn't just accept that my brother's new girlfriend was my legal guardian, which is why I had adoption papers drawn up and filled out. I may have bribed someone down at the courts to expedite the process.

Eloise didn't even seem all that pissed off. Surprised, maybe. But she went with it. Especially after she picked up on how much my English teacher really just wanted a meeting with my brother. I'm glad Gio found Eloise. I really think she's going to be a great addition to our family. Plus, she seems to make him happy, which is no easy feat.

I know the moment I walk into the games room that I should have just stayed out. Gio is sitting on one of the black leather sofas. A glass of amber liquid in his left hand, his right leaning on the armrest of the sofa, fingers tapping. It's too late to walk out now. He'll just call me back in.

I walk over to the bar and pour myself a glass of Cinque. Gio waits until my body flops onto the sofa across from him to look up at me. "Want to tell me about the shit you pulled at school?"

"You need to be more specific. I pull a lot of shit at school, bro." My smart-ass remark does nothing but piss him off more, to the point that I see the veins in his forehead twitch.

"Cut the crap. What on earth made you think it was okay to have Ellie adopt you? Especially without her even knowing about it?" he grinds out.

"I figured you two were as good as married, which makes her my guardian just as much as you are. I want to live with her in the divorce, though—just putting that out there now." I smirk as I bring my glass to my mouth.

"There's never going to be a fucking divorce. And you're almost eighteen, Vincenzo. Grow the fuck up. Pull something like this with Eloise again, and I'll knock some fucking sense into you, got it?" he growls.

"Loud and clear, boss. Can I go now, or should we do some more bonding?" There really is no need for Gio to cop the brunt of my already foul mood. I'm the youngest, though, so I get away with giving him lip a lot more than the others.

"You need to apologise to Ellie. She doesn't need to get dragged into family shit, Vin," Gio says.

"Okay, got it," I tell him before pushing up from the sofa. I empty my glass and slam it down on the coffee table in front of us. "I have things to do."

"Where are you going?" Gio asks.

"Out," I reply.

"Out where?"

"Studying with a friend." It's not a total lie. I'm going to a party with Dash and Marcus, but I'll be studying the body of some girl before the end of the night. I'm certain of it. My head has been fucked up all week.

I never should have taken Cammi to that park. She's not the kind of girl I can lose myself in and then discard. She's the kind of girl you keep, and I can't keep anyone. Nobody deserves to be shackled down with my baggage.

Gio doesn't say anything else when I leave the room. And, thankfully, Eloise walks past as I do, which means my brother is going to be distracted for the rest of the night and won't be worried about where I am or what I'm doing.

I head straight for the garage, stopping by the wall of keys before I snatch the ones for the Tesla. I climb behind the wheel, press the button to open the garage door, and then I'm gone. The gates open as I approach, the soldiers currently on guard duty giving me a nod as I drive out.

Ten minutes later, I'm pulling up out front of Marcus's house. His parents are some sort of investment brokers, super wealthy, and Marcus is every bit the rebellious trust-fund brat. We've been friends since kindergarten, though, so I'm stuck with his snobby ass.

My family isn't short of a quid either. And, honestly, my trust fund is probably bigger. I just don't give a fuck, while Marcus is stuck under his father's thumb. The old bastard hangs that trust fund over my friend's head like a damn carrot, whereas my money ain't going nowhere. One more fuckup could see Marcus penniless with no parental money coming in.

Has that threat straightened out his crooked ass? Nope. He still gets up to as much shit as I do. He's just learnt to hide it better.

"Fucking finally. Where you been?" Marcus huffs while climbing into the passenger seat.

"Didn't realise I was an Uber service. Next time, drive yourself if you don't want to wait," I tell him before taking off down the street.

"Dash meeting us there?"

"Yeah, he's been there a while. Wanted to meet up with Kenzie."

Dash has been following that girl around for the past twelve months. I don't know what their deal is. They're the ultimate on-again, off-again couple. Last I heard, they were *off*. But if Dash is there early to follow her ass around, then they'll be *on* within the next few hours.

"Fucking Kenzie. He's never going to learn." Marcus shakes his head. "Bachelor life is the only life."

"Right, like your parents haven't already found someone to shackle your ass to." I laugh. I don't know if it's true, but I wouldn't put it past Marcus's parents to arrange his marriage. It'd be a business deal that benefited them, of course. Not that my parents were any fucking better. My father sold me out to benefit his deep-ass pockets.

Fuck, I run a hand through my hair. My right hand squeezes the steering wheel. Now is not the time to be going down memory fucking lane.

"Bro, take this." Marcus hands me a pipe.

I snatch it up and press the button for the window. Then I set the car to self-drive mode and reach into the centre console for my light. After two hits of the pipe, I hand it back to Marcus. "Thanks," I grunt out.

"Don't mention it," he says.

He knows when I need a hit and he knows when I'm about to lose my shit. We've been friends forever. He also knows something happened during those years when I was at my worst. But we have a very much *don't ask, don't tell* policy.

I'm relieved when I pull up to the party spot. It's at one of the jock's houses. His parents are out of town. The street is already lined with cars, and I have to stop a few blocks back. "Let's get fucked up," I tell Marcus before climbing out of the car.

"Behind you, bro," he says, handing me a bottle of Cinque.

"You buy that?" I ask him. "You do know I have access to warehouses full of those, right?"

"Of course I bought it. Gotta support small business and all." The fucker laughs.

"I'll be sure to let Gio know what you think of the family business," I deadpan.

"Nah, I know you want me alive. Who else is going to put up with your grumpy ass?"

The music blares from the house. Pushing through the front door, I glare at the fucker who steps right in front of me. He pales and steps back, practically running in the other direction.

Marcus's hand lands on my shoulder. It takes everything in me not to knock him off me. I'm not a fan of being touched by dudes. No fucking surprise there.

The house is crowded. I swear every fucking senior from school must be here. Walking farther into the house, I head for the back door while looking around for Dash. I spot him leaning up against a far wall.

"Did your cat die?" I ask him as I follow his line of sight.

It doesn't take me long to find the reason he looks so pissed off. Kenzie is dancing with Logan, an uptight preppy fucker who clearly doesn't know what's good for him. I'm surprised to even see the kid here, let alone dancing with Kenzie. Dude must have a death wish.

"We gonna fuck him up?" I ask Dash, because when it comes to fighting, I'll always have his back, just like he always has mine.

"Nah, let him have my sloppy seconds. I'm done with her anyway. What took you fuckers so long to get here?"

"Gio needed a chat." I roll my eyes.

Dash runs his gaze over me. "Well, you're not bleeding so I'll take it the chat went well."

I'm about to answer him when I spot her. Cammi. She's on the other side of the room, sitting around a coffee table with her friends. My brows furrow as I zone in on what's in front of her. "Are they fucking playing spin the bottle?" I growl.

"Seems that way." Marcus laughs.

"What are we? Fucking twelve?" I find myself moving closer to Cammi and her group of friends without realising I'm doing it.

Chapter Four

Cammi

I can feel him before I see him. You know that weird sensation you get when you know you're being watched? That's the only way I can explain how I always seem to know he's there. I have to crane my neck to see through the crowd before I find him.

Leaning against the wall. Wearing a pair of denim jeans, a black V-neck shirt, and combat boots. His hands shove into his pockets as he stares right back at me. My eyes drift down his arms. He really does have nice arms. Tanned, toned, and inked. The ultimate bad boy.

I know I should avert my eyes, look away, but I couldn't if I tried. I'd love to have those arms wrapped around me...

I haven't spoken to him since that day at the park. I'm not sure why he's gone back to staring at me from a distance. I could ask him, but that would mean I'd have to approach him myself. And, honestly, most of the time, Vin doesn't look very approachable. He has this permanent resting bitch face, or whatever the male version of that would be.

That day in the park, though, I saw a different side of Vin. A small glimpse of someone he tries really hard to hide from the rest of the world. I wonder what he's like at home, with his family. This whole *don't talk to me* thing he has going on could just be a front meant to intimidate outsiders.

Two guys walk up and stand next to him. His friends. Their mouths are moving, but I have no idea what they're saying. Vin doesn't pay them any attention. No, he's glaring at me.

"Cammi, come on. It's your turn, babe," Lauren says while shoving at my shoulder.

I look to her and then at the rest of the group gathered around the coffee table. I have no idea whose idea it was to play spin the bottle. I let Lauren and Elena drag me into the game.

"Okay, okay. I got this," I say.

My hand rests on the bottle and the tiny hairs on the back of my neck rise. He's still watching me. I know he is. Butterflies fill my stomach. Knowing he's here gives me a little thrill I didn't know I needed right now. I spin the empty bottle while praying it lands on one of my three friends, Lauren, Elena, or Devon. I can give any of them a quick peck and then it's over.

My heart pounds as the bottle slows. And then I swear the organ drops when the bottle comes to a stop. Aimed directly at Jye.

He smiles huge as he pushes up from the sofa. "Looks like it's my lucky night."

My eyes widen and I turn to Elena. "I can't kiss him," I hiss under my breath.

"Yes, you can. It's easy. Just close your eyes, kiss, and done. No big deal," she says.

"It is a big deal," I tell her. Jye is... well, let's just say he's kind of the class creeper. How I allowed myself to even be sitting at this table with him makes me question my own sanity.

"Just close your eyes and pretend it's a Hemsworth brother," Lauren chimes in.

"You're not backing out, are you, Cammi?" This comes from Dean, one of Jye's equally-as-creepy mates.

"Of course not," I grit out between clenched teeth as I slowly rise to my feet. By the time I'm upright, Jye is standing right in front of me, licking his lips. *Gross.* "Let's get this over with," I tell him.

"Come on, babe, don't be like that. You want this," Jye says.

Before I can respond, his body is flying backwards. And I mean literally flying. His feet leave the floor and then he's on his ass. "You'll stay the fuck down if you know what's good for you," Vin grunts while pointing a finger down at him.

Everyone is staring. Then the crowd starts moving back, giving room for the fight they expect to happen. I can't let Vin get into a fight because of me. I won't. I grab his arm and pull, but he doesn't budge.

He does turn around, though. He looks from my hand on his arm to my face, a frown tugging on his lips.

"Get me out of here, please," I ask him quietly.

For a moment, I think he's going to shake me off, ignore me. And then, without a word, he takes hold of the hand I'm offering him. "Let's go."

He steps in front of me and starts leading us through the crowd—they're all still staring at us like we're the most entertaining thing in the world. Which, I guess, Vin De Bellis holding the hand of a girl is new. I've never seen him with a girl. I've seen his friends in all states of undress at parties with girls, but Vin is usually just sitting around with that unreadable expression on his face.

That's not to say he doesn't or hasn't been with any of the girls at school. I've heard the rumours; girls like to chat in the bathrooms. Although I think a lot of them also like to make shit up, so I don't know if any of what they say is true.

Like, is he really hung like a horse? Who knows? Does he have a thing for tying you up? Again, who the hell knows? Do I want to find out? I think I do.

My mind is reeling with things I want to know about this guy, and then there's a tiny little warning flashing back there as well. Telling me to be careful, to watch out for whatever darkness lurks within him.

It's not until we're walking down the street that I dig my feet into the ground. "Wait! Where are we going?"

Vin turns back around to look at me. He tilts his head, and his hand squeezes mine a little tighter, as if he's afraid I'm going to run in the opposite direction. "You asked me to get you out of there. We're leaving. My car's just up here," he says.

"Okay. But if I come with you, you're not going to like drive me out to a deserted forest and cut me up into tiny pieces, are you?"

"Do you have some kind of weird fetish about being cut into pieces?" Vin asks.

"No." I shake my head from side to side.

"So, I just give off serial killer vibes, then?" Vin raises one eyebrow at me while the corner of his lips tip up.

"Well, I mean... you kinda do." I shrug.

"And yet, here you are, in the middle of a dark street, holding my hand."

"We all do reckless things when we're young. It's why so many teenage girls end up in a situation they'd rather not be in."

"I would never do anything to you that you didn't ask me to do," he says, then turns back towards his car and continues walking, with me in tow.

Vin opens the passenger's side door. "Nice car," I tell him. I know Vin's family is not short of cash.

Again, the rumour mill runs rampant when it comes to what people suspect his family has their hands in.

"Thanks," Vin says, closing the door once I'm fully seated in the car.

I have no idea where we're going. Vin's fingers tap on the steering wheel as he navigates us around the city. When he pulls into an underground car park, I decide I really should know where he's taking me.

"Where are we?" I ask.

"We have an apartment here. No one's home," Vin says.

"Okay." I look out the windscreen, staring at the cement wall in front of me. I'm about to go up to an apartment with Vin De Bellis. Alone.

"I can take you home, if you want. You don't have to come up," Vin says, as if reading my mind.

"No, I want to." I smile at him, trying to convey that I do want to be here. With him. I open the car door and climb out before pulling my phone out of my bag.

"Who are you texting?" Vin asks, walking around the car.

"My mom. I need to tell her I'm staying at Elena's tonight," I explain as I press send on my message.

"Elena, huh?" Vin chuckles, his eyes drifting to my hand. I hold it out to him on instinct. His much larger palm closes around mine, his touch warm, and bolts of lightning run up my arm.

"Well, if I tell her I'm about to walk into an apartment *with* a boy and *without* parental supervision, that wouldn't exactly go over too well," I say.

"Are your parents strict?" Vin asks.

"Not really, but they definitely still think I'm a virgin." I laugh.

Vin's hand pauses midair, hovering over the button to the lift. Then his gaze turns to mine. "You're not?"

I shake my head. "Are you?"

"Who?" he asks.

"What?"

"Who have you slept with?"

"Who have *you* slept with?" I fire back at him.

"I'll give you a list of names if you really want it." He shrugs.

"I really don't." I reach out and press the button myself. "Are we going to stand here talking about our pasts all night or are we going up?"

The doors open and Vin pulls me inside the lift. My back slams against the wall and Vin's mouth comes down close to mine. "Ask me," he says.

"Ask you what?"

"Ask me to kiss you, because I really want to fucking kiss you right now. But I need you to ask me first."

"Vin, kiss me."

His lips drop to mine as soon as the words are out of my mouth. My hands land on his chest, and he tenses momentarily before he tilts my face up and deepens the kiss. This isn't the sloppy, hurried kind of kiss I've experienced before. It's slow. The strokes of Vin's tongue against mine are gentle. Like he's mapping out every inch of my mouth, memorising it.

The lift starts to ascend. I don't remember either of us pressing the button to any of the floors, but Vin must have because he breaks our kiss and pulls me out of the open doors into a foyer.

"You know, I'll take you home or to Elena's whenever you want to leave," he tells me.

"Do you want me to leave?" I ask him.

Vin shakes his head. "Not even a little bit," he says, biting into his bottom lip.

"Okay, guess I'm staying then."

Chapter Five

My eyes flicker open and land on her. Cammi. I watch as her chest rises and falls with each breath she takes. I wasn't planning on falling asleep. I don't sleep next to people. I had every intention of sliding out of the bed and leaving the room. The last thing I want is to wake up screaming while someone else is in my bed.

Especially her. That's a part of me she doesn't need to see. I couldn't bring myself to leave her, though. Her naked body curled up around mine. There's something grounding about her touch. Something that calms my demons. It's different from getting high. Somehow, this girl's touch both numbs and sets something alive within me. Something I've never felt before.

I don't usually like when someone touches me. When I've slept with chicks in the past, I make a game of tying them down so they can't touch me. I didn't do that with Cammi. I wanted her to touch me, which made the experience all that much better. We didn't fuck last night. I wouldn't call it making love either, but it was something between the two.

When she fell asleep in my arms, so vulnerable, so trusting, I wanted to wrap her up and protect her from the evils of this world. Including the biggest risk to her right now. Me. I didn't do that, though. I'm not ready to let this go. Whatever this is.

She's good for me. For the first time in a long time, I didn't wake up with the need to light up. The nightmares didn't come. I shake the thoughts from my head. I don't even want to think about those demons while she's lying in my arms.

"You look like you have the weight of the world on your shoulders," Cammi says, her voice raspy and full of sleep.

"Anyone ever tell you you're beautiful when you're sleeping?" I roll over, my face close to hers.

"Only my parents," she says. "How long were you watching me?" Cammi asks while a small smile spreads across her lips.

"Not nearly long enough." I lean in closer. "Ask me."

She knows what I want—no, what I need her to ask me. I made her ask me all night. And when I finally got to sink into her, she didn't just ask, she begged me.

"Vin?"

"Yeah, babe?"

"Shut up and kiss me," she says.

Like a well-trained soldier, I follow her order. I kiss her. I consume her. If my soul weren't so fucking tainted, I'd meld ours together, so we'd be one. But I could never drag this girl into my darkness.

"Mmm, I could kiss you all day and not get bored," I tell her.

"I would let you," she replies, and then her stomach makes the most god-awful noise.

"What the hell was that?" I laugh, lifting the sheet and looking down at her naked body. Big mistake. My cock was already hard. Now it's just aching to get inside her.

"Sorry." Cammi covers her face with her hands, her cheeks pinkening as her stomach rumbles again.

"I think I need to feed you," I tell her.

"I can go. You don't have to feed me," she spits out quickly.

"You want to leave?" I roll over and begin to push off the bed.

Cammi's hands reach out for me, her arms hooking around my neck and pulling me back to her. "No," she says. "I don't want to leave. I *can* leave, though. I don't want to be a bother or overstay my welcome."

I cup her face with one hand and my thumb strokes up and down her cheek. "You would never be a bother to me. Ever," I tell her, kissing her forehead. "Let's shower, get dressed, and then I'll take you to get food. I doubt there's anything in the kitchen."

"Do you live here?" Cammi asks.

"No, I used to. For a little while, after our house

burnt down. But then my brother bought a big-ass place in the burbs. That's where I live now."

"Oh, nice."

"It's a house." I shrug, leaving out the part about how it's becoming more and more a home since El's moved in.

"Yo, Vin, where'd you disappear to last night?" Dash walks through my bedroom door.

Pressing the pause button on the console remote, I turn my attention to him. "Who the fuck let you up here?" I ask, knowing full well none of the soldiers would allow anyone upstairs.

"Gio." He smirks. "Your brother likes me." Dash plops down on the sofa and swipes up the second controller.

"My brother likes one person, and you are not her," I grunt while pressing the pause button.

"Come on, man, you're not gonna restart and play doubles?" Dash complains.

"Nope." I continue tapping on the controller, all

my focus on the imaginary enemies attacking me on the screen, until I finally meet my virtual demise and toss the damn thing aside. "What are you doing here?"

"Checking on your ass. Where'd you go after the party?"

"Did you grow a vagina overnight? What's it to you where I went?" I scowl in Dash's direction before pulling my tin from the pocket of my jeans.

"Well, I can see you're in one piece and in a fine-ass mood. I'll leave you to it." He stands and walks out the door.

The proper thing to do would be to stop him. Hang out with my friend. I don't do that, though. I'm really not in the mood for company. I woke up in the best mood. Spent the whole morning with Cammi before I dropped her off at home.

Then I came back here, and the ghosts started to invade my mind again. Every time I blinked, I saw them. It's as if they're making up for the brief reprieve I had last night.

I slide a sheet out of the packet and pinch the green herbs between my fingers, lining it up along the centre of the paper before rolling it up and licking down the edge to seal it shut. Then I lean forward, grab the lighter from the table, and walk over to the balcony. I don't smoke in my room. This shit stinks, and the last thing I need is my big brother storming in and lecturing me.

I drop onto my ass, lean against the balcony wall, and light up, enjoying that first hit as my lungs fill with smoke. After finishing and stubbing out one joint, I immediately roll up another one and light it. I need to numb my brain. I need to smoke *them* all out. It's the only way I'll get any peace tonight.

When I'm done, I shut the balcony doors and collapse onto my bed, closing my eyes. This time, I don't see them. I only see her. Cammi. Big, beautiful green eyes. Brown hair that never seems to end, and pale skin. Tiny freckles that spread across her nose and pouty lips that are as soft as pillows when you kiss them.

Fucking beautiful.

"Why me? I'm your son," I ask my father. He's brought me here again. I almost thought that maybe this month he wouldn't. That he'd stop.

He laughs at me, and then his hand snaps out, hitting me across my face. "Why you? Because everything is your fault, boy. You think you're my son?" He laughs again and then spits at me. "You're nothing to me, Vincenzo. Nothing."

He shakes his head and walks out of the room before the hard metal door slams shut. Leaving me alone in this living, breathing nightmare. But I know it won't be that way for long. They'll come for me. They'll do whatever they want with me, and I can't do a single thing to stop them.

I thought about telling Gio. My big brother would help me. At least, I think he would. Unless he already knows? What if he's in on it? He works so closely with our father. I mean, how could he not know about this place?

Sitting down on the filthy mattress that's the only thing left in the cement-walled room, I bring my knees up to my chest. I won't cry. No matter how much I may want to.

Men don't cry, *my father's voice echoes in my head.*

I don't understand why these particular men do this, though... I do know that when I'm older, when I'm bigger, I'm going to find them and kill them all. That day will come. I might not know who they are now, but I'll figure out a way to find them. And one by one, I will come for them.

If they don't kill me in this shithole first...

The handle on the door turns and my heart starts beating faster, as not one but two masked men walk in.

"On your feet, boy," the first guy says while the second one slams and locks the door. The noise makes me jump. "Look at that. We got a frightened little one."

"Good. I like 'em jumpy," the second guy says before stepping forward. "You deaf or just dumb, boy? On your fucking feet. Now."

I scramble off the mattress. I don't want to. But I also know if I don't, whatever they're planning to do to me will be much worse. I spent two weeks in a makeshift hospital bed last month. My brothers asked how my trip was when I was finally allowed to return home. They thought I went with a friend's family on holiday. I didn't correct them. I should have. I should have told them. Maybe if I had, I wouldn't be in the situation I'm in right now.

"You look familiar. Have I seen you before?" the first guy asks. He closes the distance before crouching down to meet me at eye level. I can feel his glare searing through the mask as he continues to study me.

I shake my head. I have no idea who these men are. I don't recognise their voices. When the second guy reaches out and places a hand on my shoulder, bile rises in my throat. I push it back down.

I am not here. This isn't happening to me. *I want to remove myself from my body. I want a pill. I don't want to be here.*

"Open your mouth," he grunts.

I do as he says, because not doing it is always worse. He drops a little white pill on my tongue.

"Swallow," he tells me, and I listen. *I know this pill will make me forget.*

"Now, on your knees," the first guy says.

My eyes widen. What? No, that's not how the pills work. They usually wait. I'm still lucid. I'm still me. When I don't move, his friend shoves me down. *I fall to the concrete, my knees hitting the ground hard. Then they both undo their belts.*

No! *I don't want to be here.*

I jolt up in bed. Covered in sweat with a silent scream trapped in my throat. Looking around my room, I take a mental note of everything. I'm okay. I'm alone. I'm not back there.

"Fuck." I run a frustrated hand through my hair.

Chapter Six

Cammi

Have you ever experienced something so life-altering you know it's going to be one of those moments that changes you forever? Except, you don't know it at the time, when you're living in that moment. That realisation comes later, when the moment's already passed, and you can't do a damn thing to take it back.

That's what Saturday night was like for me. A moment I know is going to change my entire life. Although, if I could do it all over again, I absolutely would. Just to experience it again. Vin was nothing like I expected him to be. He was caring, tender even. He touched me like I was precious. Like I was something worth millions.

Yep, a night I won't be forgetting anytime soon, if ever. I don't think anyone else could ever compare to Vin. I get it. I'm young and I'm sure I'll meet plenty of other men in my life. I also know that I'll compare every single one of them to him from this day forward.

I might have spent all yesterday contemplating if I should call him. Message him. Slide into his DMs. After a few hours, it finally hit me that I didn't even have his phone number. And when I went to search for him on social media, he didn't exist.

What kind of seventeen-year-old doesn't have socials? Vin De Bellis. That's who. Someone who doesn't care about societal expectations or social norms.

The guy literally moves to his own beat. Especially in bed. Boy, did he hit the right notes over and over again. And he never tried to tie me up, which makes me wonder if all the gossip about him is even real.

My stomach is filled with nerves. I don't know what to expect or what I should do today. How do I act when I see him? Is he going to go back to just staring at me from a distance? Should I approach him or wait for him to come to me?

It's not like I haven't had a one-night stand before. I know the drill. Don't get me wrong. It may have been only *one* one-night-stand. But trust me, these questions never popped up in my head afterwards. I didn't care if I saw the guy again.

Vin, though? I want to see him again. I want to talk to him. I want him to want to talk to me. Which is why I'm currently clenching my stomach as I walk through the corridor towards my locker. I feel sick with nerves. I hate it. The uncertainty of it.

I've never felt like this before. I mean, I've always been a little nervous when it comes to Vin. Those butterflies like to go wild in my stomach whenever I see him. But now, it's like those butterflies flew straight off the shelf of a Costco store, in bulk and super-sized.

Stopping at my locker, I dump all the textbooks I took home—the ones that didn't get opened once over the weekend—and pick up my English binder just as Devon and Elena come to a stop next to me.

"Explain," Devon says.

"Ah, explain what exactly?" I ask, looking from her to Elena.

"You were silent all day yesterday, and you followed Vin De Bellis out of the party without a word to us," Elena says.

"So?"

"So?" Devon gasps. "What happened? Did you...?"

I can feel my cheeks heat up. What do I tell them? Usually, I would have already called and spilled every single detail. It's different with Vin, though. I don't think I want to share him. I don't want everyone to know just how amazing he is. I also don't want to deal with the embarrassment after he doesn't acknowledge me today.

If I tell the girls I spent the night with him Saturday, and then he goes back to ignoring me...

Well, I just can't.

"Vin dropped me home," I tell a half-lie. I mean, he did drop me home. It just wasn't Saturday night.

"Really?" Devon frowns.

"He just dropped you home? That's it?" Elena asks with a confused look on her face.

Lauren pops up beside me, her arm snaking around my shoulder. "Don't look now, but lover boy is coming your way," she whispers.

My heart pounds in my chest. *Vin is coming this way?*

I turn and regret it as soon as my eyes land on Jye, who is very much not Vin and appears to be heading straight for me. "Argh, gross," I hiss to Lauren, turning back around while doing my best to ignore the creep and the sound of his squeaky shoes making a beeline for my locker.

A hand taps my shoulder. "Cammi?"

Taking a deep breath, I turn around again. "Jye? Can I help you with something?" I keep my voice neutral. Polite. I don't want to engage. I don't know why he's even talking to me.

"Yeah, you owe me a kiss," he says.

I laugh, and then stop when I notice he's not. "Oh my god! You're serious?"

"As a heart attack. A game is a game, and rules are rules." He grins.

"Yeah, well, I'm not kissing you. Now or ever."

Jye takes a step closer, forcing me to take one in the opposite direction. My back hits the cold metal of my locker.

"Whoa, back the fuck up." *This* comes from Devon.

"Stay out of it. This is between me and Cammi," Jye sneers at her.

Lauren looks past Jye and smiles. "Yeah, you might want to back away from her," she tells him.

"No, I don't think..." Jye's words are cut off when he's tugged away from me before I can blink.

Everything happens so quickly. One minute, he's right in my face. The next, he's on the ground and an extremely angry-looking Vin is on top of him, raining down punch after punch.

A crowd gathers. Idiots surround us, all chanting, "Fight, fight, fight!"

I need to stop this madness. I don't want Vin getting into any more trouble than he already has because of me.

Dash and Marcus pull Vin off Jye, whose face is covered in blood. "Let this be your only fucking warning." Vin points to the crowd and then at me. "Camile Taylor is mine. If I so much as see any of you fuckers think about touching her, I will kill you."

My eyes bug out of my head. What the hell? I wanted him to acknowledge me, sure, but he's just made a freaking declaration in front of the entire school. People are recording it.

Shit. They're all staring at me.

Vin doesn't seem fazed at all. He lifts his arm, an invitation for me to lean against him. "You okay?" he whispers into my ear.

I nod my head. Shouldn't I be the one asking him that?

"Vin, they're all staring," I whisper.

"Let them get a good look at their queen. We should get to class," he says. "You got everything you need?"

Again, I nod like an idiot, because I don't know what else to do. What else to say. When I look at my friends, their expressions tell me that the interrogation is coming. Just as soon as they get me alone. Thankfully, I have until lunch before I have to face them again.

"Later," I mouth in their direction.

"So, what'd you get up to yesterday?" Vin asks as we make our way to our English class.

"Not much. You?"

"Babysat one of my brothers," he says.

"Babysat? Aren't you the youngest?" I look up at him.

"Yep. But you wouldn't know it right now," Vin grunts. "What'd you really do? You can't expect me to believe you did nothing all day?"

"I... ah... Well, most of the day, I sat around debating whether or not I should call or text some-one. And then it occurred to me I didn't actually have their number anyway," I admit.

Vin drops his arm from my shoulder. "Give me your phone," he says.

"Why?" Even as I'm questioning him, I'm pulling my phone out of my pocket.

"I want to make sure you have my number. You know, in case that someone you want to sit around and debate on calling or messaging is me one day." He takes my phone from my hand, and I watch as he types in his number. "There," he says when he passes it back. "And for the record, don't ever sit around debating shit. Just call me."

"Okay. Thank you." My eyes drop to my shoes. I don't know why I'm feeling shy all of a sudden. He's seen me naked. We showered together, not to mention everything else we've done.

Whispers surround us as we walk into the nearly-full classroom, side by side. I don't blame them. I'd be curious too if I saw Vin De Bellis walk into class with the girl he just publicly claimed. He's never done anything like this before.

If I thought the whispers and stares would simmer down as the day progressed, I was wrong. If anything, they've gotten worse. After English, Vin walked me to my next class and then went on to his. I haven't seen him since.

Now, I'm walking through the cafeteria, wishing I'd chosen to eat somewhere else, anywhere else. Sinking into the seat across from Elena and Lauren, next to Devon, I look at my three best friends. And they all stare back at me like I'm a stranger.

"Okay, spit it out now or forever hold your peace." I wave a hand at them in gesture for them to get on with it.

"What the actual hell? Vin? Really? You're dating Vin De Bellis and you didn't tell us?" This comes from Devon.

"I'm just... shocked. Happy for you, of course... if you're happy," Elena says.

"How did this even happen?" Lauren adds.

"Okay, first... I don't actually know how it happened. It just did. Second, yes, Vin De Bellis.

And third, I didn't tell you because, like I said, it just happened," I explain.

"Don't look now, but lover boy is coming your way," Elena hisses.

Of course, I turn around and look. Thankfully, this time, it's Vin who's making his way towards me with determination on his face and his two friends flanking his sides.

He sits right next to me, leans in, and whispers into my ear, "Ask me."

I pivot in my seat and whisper back into his ear. "Vin, kiss me as if it's the first and last time you ever will."

"Oh, babe, it's never going to be the last time," he says right before his lips slam down onto mine.

Everything drifts away. The noise of the students, the sounds of the chairs scraping across the tiled floor. Everything except him. It all dies away when his lips are on mine. By the time we break apart, I'm breathless and horny as all hell. But let's not focus on that right now.

I turn to the very open stares of everyone at the table. "Well, this is new," Dash says, pointing from me to Vin.

"Not really. Our boy's been pining over this one forever," Marcus adds.

"This one has a name," Vin growls—yes, literally growls.

"Sorry, Cammi," Marcus directs to me. "Let me know if the animal gives you any trouble. I'll be sure to put him back in his cage."

"I'd likely jump in the cage with him if you did," I tell Marcus with a smile. And I mean every word.

Chapter Seven

Today has been fucking great. The more time I spend with Cammi, touching her, talking to her, the more I feel at peace. My head isn't weighed down by the nightmares. I don't even feel the urge to light up.

That good feeling dissipates when I get a text

message from my brother Gabe, asking me to meet him at the front of the school. Whatever he's here for, it's nothing good. He never comes to school. None of my brothers come here just for the hell of it.

Walking towards the vehicle Gabe is perched against, I notice mine isn't where it should be. "Where's my car?" I ask my brother.

"I had Jimmy take it home. Get in," Gabe says, walking around to the driver's side of his blacked-out SUV.

I'm not stupid. There's no point standing in the parking lot arguing with my brother. If he's telling me I need to get in the fucking car, then I need to get in the fucking car. I don't have to be happy about it, though. And I make it clear that I'm not as I throw my bag into the back before climbing into the passenger seat.

"Did someone die?" It's the only reason I can think of that would have him collecting me from school.

"No. Well, not to my knowledge." He shrugs.

I turn and stare at him as he pulls out of the car park. "Then why are you here?"

"I went to that house," Gabe says before clarifying, "The address you handed over to Gio."

I school my features. I knew what would happen.

I knew what they'd find, and I knew they'd have questions. Still, I did it because I thought maybe they'd also find what they needed. After my father died, we discovered he'd left three million dollars to an unnamed beneficiary. My brothers have been looking for that person ever since, trying to piece together the reason behind the giant payout.

I guess there was also a part of me that wanted to get the burden off my shoulders. Not that I want them to know what happened to me, just that the house existed. I always planned to go back, to exact my revenge. For the past three years, I've been plotting, planning, and not acting.

I knew I couldn't do anything while my father was alive. He'd kill me sooner than he'd let me interfere with his business. With his money.

But now Gabe knows... Because I can tell he knows. My pinkie finger taps along my leg, the only part of my body that moves.

"How did you know about that place?" he asks.

I focus on breathing evenly. I will not allow the memories to invade my mind right now. I lift a single shoulder. "Dad took me there a few times."

"Why?" Gabe presses.

"Why did that fucking asshole do anything he did?" I snap.

I watch as my brother's knuckles turn white while his hands grip the steering wheel. "Vin, did he... did you..." He shakes his head. "Why didn't you tell one of us? We would have stopped it," he says, his voice breaking.

Pity. Loud and clear.

I frown at him. "If I told any of you, he would have made you all do it too." That was my father's threat. He always said that if I told them, he'd take them there and make them do what he made me do. "I didn't want that to happen."

I can see the horror on my brother's face. His eyes water. I fucking hate this. I don't want to have this conversation. I don't want the nightmare to touch any of my brothers. It's bad enough I have to live with this shit. They don't need it. They deserve better.

"I'm sorry... I didn't know. I should have known." Gabe's words are choked out. There's so much remorse in his voice. I can hear it. He's the fixer of the family, now more than ever when everything feels like it's falling apart. He will go to any lengths to fix whatever problem we have.

"You weren't ever supposed to know," I tell him, doing my best to keep my tone neutral, remain unaffected. "This isn't your fault, Gabe. And I'd prefer if it stayed between us."

"You know we need to tell Gio," he says, which is the last thing I want to do. Our eldest brother has enough on his plate right now. He does not need my shit added to it.

"Why? What good will that do? He's finally settling down, finding happiness. He deserves that. He does not need to take on burdens that are not his to bear. Neither do you," I grit out.

"This... I think you should see someone," Gabe suggests.

I almost laugh at the thought of sitting on a sofa, complaining about my life to some fucker with a bunch of letters after his name. "What? Like a head quack? Pass. I'm fine. I've dealt with it." What I need is to change the subject. I haven't had a smoke all fucking day. I'm way too sober to be dealing with this shit. "Did you find anything there? At the house?"

"You mean other than a fucking child brothel and a heap of sick fucks? No. Not a fucking thing," Gabe growls.

"Where are we going?" I stare through the windscreen, trying to figure out where he's taking us. It's not in the direction of home.

"The warehouse. Marcel has that fucker Hamish hanging like the rotten pig he is," Gabe says, and I can feel myself pale. I don't want to be anywhere near the fucker who managed that house.

He never saw me. He didn't know my father was taking me there. Something I knew for a fact after I overheard a conversation I wasn't supposed to know about once. They were discussing Hamish—my father and someone else—talking about how they gave the old man the day off whenever it was my turn to make an appearance.

Does that mean I don't want to kill the son of a bitch? Fuck no. He sells little kids to sick fucks, allows them to use and abuse children for their own pleasure. I want to slaughter him like the filthy pig he is.

"Why am I here?" I finally ask Gabe when he pulls to a stop at the warehouse.

"Because I thought you'd want to do the honours." He smiles at me.

Does he really think he's doing me a favour? I don't want to face the man who benefited from the abuse of little kids. From my abuse.

I don't respond. I silently follow Gabe into the warehouse. I learnt from a young age not to ask too many questions. It's kill or be killed. Simple as that. I trust my brothers. I know they wouldn't put me in harm's way. But there's always that little doubt in my head. My own father sold me to my demons, after all. What's stopping my brother from doing the same?

The moment we walk in, I see *him*. Hanging from a rusty old butcher's hook that's hanging in the middle of the warehouse. I can't be in this room. I can't be around him, knowing what he's done, who he is. It makes my stomach turn.

So I do the only thing I can do. The thing that will get me out of here the quickest. I pick up a pistol, aim it right at the fat fucker's head, and pull the trigger. Then I turn back around and set the pistol on the table, knowing my brother will make sure any evidence I was here will never be seen again.

"It's done. Can we go home now?" I don't wait for an answer. I'm already walking out the door.

"Yep," Gabe says, and then I hear his footsteps behind me. As soon as we're in the car, he turns to me. "You good?"

Am I good? No. I'm not ever going to be good again. I will never get past this. I've accepted that. What I won't do is bring others down with me.

"Yep," I lie.

I can see he wants to push. He wants to continue the conversation. Thankfully, he gets a message telling him we need to get home. Santo is losing his shit. Again. Looks like we're on babysitting duty all night. My brother is not coping with the grief of losing his fiancée. Not that I blame him, or hold it against him. I will do whatever I can to help. I just wish I could ease some of his pain. I know I can't, though.

When we get home, I go straight up to my room. I need a smoke. I need to fog my mind as much as I can. Sitting out on my balcony, I light up a joint and scroll through my phone. There's a message from Cammi.

> CAMMI:
>
> So this is weird. For me anyway. I know you said I can call or message whenever I felt the urge. And, well, I feel the urge right now. Anyway, it's stupid and I don't even know what I want to say.

I smile and hit dial next to her name. She answers after the ringtone sounds out three times. "Hey."

"Hey yourself. What're you doing?" I ask her.

Just hearing her voice calms me more than anything I could smoke.

"Homework. I have a geography essay due at the end of the week," she says.

"Why are you studying geography?"

"I want to see the world one day, and I can't do that if I don't know where everything is, now can I?" Cammi says.

"I can show you the world. Name a place and I'll take you there," I tell her.

She laughs. I'm not joking, though. "I'll keep that in mind. What are you doing right now?" she asks me.

"Sitting on my balcony smoking a joint, wishing I was in bed with you instead," I admit.

"Maybe you should do something about that, then," Cammi suggests.

"Yeah? You want me to come and pick you up?" I offer.

"My parents are out. They won't be back until late. Why don't you come here?"

"Be there in twenty," I tell her. "And, Cammi?"

"Yeah?"

"Lose your panties. You won't be needing them," I say before cutting the call.

I stand, stub out my joint, and walk back through

the doors to my room. I spray a shit-load of deodorant all over my body so I don't stink like weed.

Then I walk into the bathroom and scrub my hands three times before I give up. They're never going to be clean enough. I shouldn't be touching her with these hands. The hands of a killer. If she knew, she wouldn't let me anywhere near her.

Chapter Eight

Cammi

I should have gone to his place. What was I thinking inviting Vin here? He shouldn't be driving if he's been smoking, but then again, when is he not smoking? I want to call him, tell him to wait for me to come to him. But it's already been twenty minutes since he hung up. He's probably already on the road, and if I call him now, I'd just be adding to the danger of him driving. I think.

This is insane. I don't know why I asked him to come over. I do know that I want to see him. He left school early. Without a word. Not that he owes me an explanation for his coming and goings. I just... thought I'd see him at the end of the day.

I pace up and down the foyer, waiting for him. When I spot a pair of headlights out on the street, I pull the front door open and run outside. I meet Vin halfway across the yard, throwing my arms around his neck.

"I'm sorry," I tell him.

His body stiffens and then he relaxes and tugs me closer. "What's wrong? What happened?" he asks.

"I made you drive here and I shouldn't have. You shouldn't be driving if you're high, Vin. Do you have any idea how dangerous that is?" I step back slightly, keeping my arms around him.

"I'm not high, and you didn't make me do anything. I wanted to come here." He smirks. "Were you worried about me, babe?"

"Not at all. I just don't want to be responsible for your untimely demise." This time, when I step back and drop my arms, Vin lets go. "Come on, let's go inside before the neighbours call my parents and tell them you're here."

"You know, sneaking around like teenagers is kind of fun." He laughs.

"We are teenagers." I turn back and frown at him. I can't pretend to know what kind of life Vin has led. I know that it's not all cookies and warm milk after school. People say the eyes are the windows to the soul. And Vin's? Well, there is a lot of darkness in them.

"Right. Lead the way." He laughs, but does little to hide the pain I recognise behind his façade.

I take Vin up to my bedroom. When I look around the space, trying to imagine it from his point of view, all I see is a mess. My bed is unmade, my pink-and-white polka dot comforter half off the mattress. The drawers on my white dresser are slightly ajar. I rush over to shut them.

"I'm sorry. I should have tidied up."

"It's... not that bad?" Vin says, but it sounds more like a question.

There's a pile of clothes covering the bedroom chair in the corner of the room and makeup scattered all over the top of my dresser. "It is. But thanks for pretending like it's not."

"So, this is you, huh? It's cute." Vin spins around, taking in my whole bedroom.

"Where did you go today?" I ask while plopping down onto my bed.

Vin looks away from me, his face closed off. "My brother needed help with something."

"Vin?"

"Yeah?"

"Come here." I pat the empty space next to me.

Vin looks from the bed to my face. "I shouldn't," he says.

I don't know what's going on in his head right now, but I can feel him distancing himself from me with each second that passes. So I push up and walk over to him. "Vin?"

"Yeah?"

"Kiss me as if it's the first and last time you ever will," I tell him.

"I thought I already told you there's never going to be a last time," he says. His hands cup my face before he brings his lips down onto mine. Gently. He's always so gentle with me. I don't hate it.

My arms wrap around his neck, pulling him closer. I already know that he won't do anything unless I ask him to. I learned that during our first night together. Which means I can't be shy when it comes to asking him to give me what we both want. "Vin?"

"Mhmm?" he mumbles as his mouth travels across my cheek.

I tilt my head as his lips travel along my neck. "I want you to kiss me..."

"I am kissing you," he says.

"Not there."

Vin lifts his face so his eyes connect with mine. "Where? Where do you want me to kiss you, Cammi?"

I walk backwards until I hit the bed. Then I lie across it and lift my knees so that my feet are flat on the mattress. My skirt creeps up my thighs and I know he can see my bare pussy. "Here." I point between my legs.

"Fuck," Vin hisses before stepping towards the bed. He drops to his knees, hooks his hands under my ass, and drags my body to the edge. "You sure you want this?"

"I want this," I tell him. "I want you."

His shoulders quiver before his tongue licks its way down the inside of my thigh. When he reaches my core, he flicks right up the centre, from bottom to top.

"You're the best fucking thing I've ever touched.

I've ever tasted," he says before his tongue pushes into my opening. Circling around.

My head tips back. "Oh god," I moan as pleasure starts to build in the pit of my stomach. Little sparks igniting all over my body.

Vin moves his tongue, flattening it out over my clit. He licks, sucks, and licks again. His fingers dig into the flesh of my thighs as he holds my legs down.

"Oh shit. I'm going to come," I tell him. "Don't stop." My hands land on the back of his head and he freezes.

He gently grabs my wrists before pinning them against the mattress as he continues to wring every bit of pleasure from my body. I come apart, screaming at the top of my lungs. And Vin... He continues to lick me until I stop shaking.

Then I feel the mattress dip as he climbs on next to me. "You good?" he asks.

"Uh-huh. You?" I turn my head, my eyes connecting with his.

"Eating you out is literally the highlight of my day, babe. No complaints here." He smiles.

"That's the highlight of your day?" I repeat.

"You *are* the highlight of my day."

I don't know what to say to that. I can tell that

he's not just saying the words. He means them. "What happened today?" I ask him.

"What do you mean?"

"Something happened. I can tell. You're... withdrawn." I roll over, leaning my elbow on the bed to prop my head up on a hand.

"Nothing happened. It's just family shit," he says.

"Okay. Vin?"

"Yeah?"

"Why don't you touch me unless I ask you?"

He looks away, his gaze focused on the blankness of the ceiling. "I should go," he says.

"You don't have to."

"I do." He glances at me again, and I can see the indecisiveness on his face.

"Vin, kiss me. Please," I ask him.

He shifts forward and fuses his lips with mine. We lie on the bed, next to each other, kissing. I don't know how much time passes, but when he pulls back, he looks so fucking sad. "Kissing you is the best high I've ever had," he says.

"Then don't stop kissing me." I smile up at him.

He closes his eyes. "I think you might be my personal saint."

"I'm no saint, Vin. I can't work miracles," I tell him.

"But you already have. You just don't know it." He opens his eyes to look at me again. "You make it all go away."

"Make what go away?" I want to reach up and touch him. I want to pull him into me. I don't. Something tells me not to, so I lie here instead. Still. Unmoving. As my heart beats wildly in my chest.

"The nightmares." His words are whispered, almost as if he doesn't intend for me to hear them. Then Vin leans down, kisses my forehead, and climbs off the bed. "I'll see you tomorrow, Cammi," he says and walks out the door.

I don't try to stop him this time. My mind whirls with all the possibilities. Although, when it comes to Vin's nightmares, I have a feeling my imagination couldn't possibly conjure up the sort of demons that live in his head.

I get up, grab the towel from the back of my door, and make my way into the bathroom. Where I stand and stare at the shower for five minutes. I know I need to get in, but I'm hesitant to wash his touch from my skin. Eventually I realise just how insane I'm being and step into the stall. By the time I turn off the water, my fingers are wrinkly and the room is filled with steam. I wrap the towel around myself and walk back into my room, pausing when I find Vin sitting on my bed.

"I thought you left," I tell him.

"What time are your parents coming home?" he asks.

"I don't know. They just said they'd be back late. Why?"

"I need to sleep. For just an hour or two. Can you lie down with me?" He looks so vulnerable right now.

"Give me your shirt." I hold out my hand. Am I literally asking for the shirt off his back? Yes, I am.

Without a second thought, Vin reaches behind his neck, tugs the material over his head, and passes the shirt to me. After I slide my arms through the sleeves and let the fabric fall over my body, I allow my towel to drop to the floor.

I climb onto the bed and get comfortable, waiting for Vin to do the same. Then I slide over and rest my head on his shoulder. "Vin?"

"Yeah?"

"If you ever need to just... sleep, I'll always be available," I tell him.

"Thank you." He sighs, and I swear he's inhaling

the top of my head. Is he sniffing me? Thank god I opted for that shower.

When I wake up, I'm alone and still wearing his shirt. I take a deep breath, check the time, and curse out loud. I'm going to be late. How did I sleep for so long?

I tug a clean uniform down from my closet and quickly get dressed before sliding my feet into my ballet flats. Grabbing a hair scrunchie from my dresser, I throw my hair into a messy bun. I don't have time to apply my makeup. I'll do it in the bathrooms at school during break.

As I'm running down the stairs, I hear my mum call out to me. "Camile, you need to eat."

"I'll get something on the way. I gotta run. Sorry, Mum, I'm late!" I yell back as I open the front door and step out onto the porch. Only to stop dead in my tracks.

Vin is there. In his car. Right out front of my house. I look back at the door. My dad would have already left for work, but my mum is home. I jog over to Vin and lean down into the open window. "What are you doing here?"

"Driving my girlfriend to school. Get in," he says.

"Girlfriend?" I look up and down the street. "Does this girlfriend know you spent last night in my bed?"

"Funny. Get in," he tells me again. Then he reaches across the centre console and pushes open the passenger side door.

I climb into the car, plug in my seat belt, and close the door. "You didn't have to pick me up. But thank you." I smile at Vin. He stares at me, just stares to the point I feel uncomfortable. "What?" I ask him.

"You are fucking gorgeous. You should lose the makeup more often," he says and pulls away from the kerb.

"Thank you." I can feel my cheeks heat up at his compliment.

"Cammi?"

"Yeah?"

"Ask me to hold your hand," Vin says.

"Vin, hold my hand like you don't ever want to let go." I reach across the console, and he entwines our fingers together.

"That's easy, because I'm never going to let go."

Chapter Nine

I had three hours of peaceful sleep in Cammi's bed last night. I crawled out and went home around one in the morning. Sneaking out of her house like a fucking crook while her parents slept. I heard them come home. Neither of them bothered to check on their daughter. I waited for the door to her room to open, to have an angry-as-shit father yelling profanities at me for being in his daughter's bed.

That never happened.

I did lie there for another hour holding Cammi as she slept in my arms. Then I went home and checked on Santo. Gabe and Marcel were still sitting with him in the games room. I really hope Eloise picks out some furniture for this house soon. At the moment, only one room is fully furnished. My big brother has this thing about new furniture, insisting Eloise needs to design the place.

I don't disagree. I know she'll make it feel like a home, unlike the museum we all grew up inside.

I look over to Cammi and wonder what type of house she wants. What kind of future plans she has and how I can implant myself into those plans...

I don't know what she's doing to me. Whatever it is, I like it. I like the quiet she seems to bring. I wasn't lying when I told her she was my own personal saint. Because to be able to do what she's doing to me—putting the demons to rest—it's nothing short of a miracle. I just hope whatever lurks within my soul never reaches out and takes her down with me.

"What classes do you have today?" I ask her on our way to school.

"What? You don't already know my schedule? Vin, you've been watching me for months. Don't pretend you don't have my timetable memorised," she says.

"I might, but I'd still like to hear it from you." I smirk. "I didn't think you noticed me."

Cammi gasps. "Vin, it's impossible not to notice you," she says. "You have this whole..." She waves her free hand up and down my body. "...bad boy thing going on. It's alluring, even though it probably shouldn't be. Plus, you're literally the school's most eligible bachelor. There isn't a girl in our year, or even below us, who isn't after you."

"So what I'm hearing is you find me alluring." My grin widens. "Good to know. Also, you're wrong."

"About what?"

"Me being the school's most eligible bachelor. I'm not a bachelor, and I don't give a fuck what the girls are after because I already belong to someone," I tell her. "That someone is you, just in case you had any doubts."

"Do you think this is happening too fast? I feel like..." Cammi digs her teeth into her bottom lip.

"You feel like what?"

"I feel like you're consuming every fibre of my

being. Like, I don't just want you near me, Vin. I feel like I need you just as much as I need air. It's stupid. I'm sorry. Ignore me." She pulls her hand out of mine.

"Cammi, it's not stupid." I want to reach out and take it back—her hand—but I can't. I can't touch her if she doesn't want me to. I need her to ask me. Fuck, this is fucked up. "It is fast, but you're not alone. I do need you, Cammi. Except it's so much more than I need air. You have no idea how much I need you."

"Really? You feel it too?" She turns in her seat to face me.

I stop at a red light. My hand reaches out, almost touching hers, before I pull it back again. Cammi notices.

"Vin, hold my hand and never let go," she says.

My palm closes around hers. "I feel it too."

A car horn blares behind me, and I look ahead to see that the light is green. Glancing back in the rearview mirror, I mentally tell the impatient fucker behind me to *eat a dick* as I slam a foot down on the accelerator and take off.

That was a little too deep and meaningful for this hour of the morning. Cammi is quiet the rest of the way to school.

I pull into a spot in the car park, and she

unbuckles her belt. "Vin, how dark are these windows?" she asks. "Like, can people see in?"

I had the windows down when I pulled up at her place. I wanted her to see it was me.

"These are blackout. Why?" I tap my knuckles on the glass to my right. The windscreen is a different story. You can see through that.

"So, if I were to ask you to pull me across the seat until I'm straddling you and then ask you to kiss me, no one will see?"

My eyes flick to the windscreen while my dick strains in my pants. "Are you asking me to do that, Cammi?"

"Vin, pull me across the car until I'm straddling you and then kiss me like it's the first and last time you ever will," she says.

I smile, reaching over as I pick her up and position her so her knees rest on each side of my legs. "When are you going to get it? There's never going to be a last time, babe," I remind her before slamming my lips down onto hers.

My tongue pushes out and slinks into her mouth. I fucking love kissing her. I've never been a fan of kissing. But with Cammi, I never want to stop. A knock at my window has Cammi jumping and me ready to kill whoever's on the other side. I turn to see Dash waving, even though he can't see me.

"I thought you said they couldn't see inside," Cammi says while climbing back over to the passenger seat.

"They can't. He's just being an ass," I tell her. Then I consider her words. Does she not want people to see us together? I already publicly announced that she was mine. She *is* mine. I don't give a fuck who sees us together. As long as they don't see any parts of her meant solely for my eyes, then let them watch. "Come on, let's go." I open my door harder than necessary, slamming it into Dash's body before he can move out of the way.

"Ow, fuck. What was that for?" He scowls while clutching his abdomen.

"For interrupting. What the fuck do you want?" I grunt as I round the car. By the time I get to the other side, Cammi is already out of the car. Her bag hoisted on one shoulder. "You okay?" I glance at her flushed face.

"Uh-huh, I'll, um, see you later?" she questions.

I tilt my head to the side. Cammi takes a step closer before she stops. "Want me to walk you in?" I ask her.

She looks from me to Dash. "No, it's okay. I have

to find Elena." She steps around me as she practically runs into school. *What the fuck was that about?*

"So, this is a thing now? You and Cammi?" Dash lifts a curious brow in my direction.

I glare at him. "Why are you here again?"

The fucker smiles. "One, because you love me and I know you missed me last night. And two, I have a new strand you gotta try, bro. It'll blow your mind," he says while waving a rolled-up joint in my face.

I slept without getting off my face last night. It might have only been a few hours, but it was a great fucking few hours. And I haven't needed to smoke as much. Because when I'm with Cammi, all the noise stops.

I swipe the blunt out of Dash's hand. "Get in the car," I tell him before walking back around to the driver's seat. I shut myself inside the car and dig into my pocket for a light. I close my eyes and inhale, enjoying the way the smoke fills my lungs. "What is it?"

"Like I said, it's some new strand. They call it Flight 57." Dash takes the joint from me and sucks it between his lips.

"That's a stupid fucking name," I tell him before snatching it back.

By the time we're finished, the car is filled with smoke, and my body feels fucking light. My head is spinning, though. Whatever this shit is, it's fucking good.

"Let's get in before we're late," I grunt in Dash's direction.

When we walk into school, my mind is set on finding Cammi. I don't know why she doesn't want people to see us together. I should respect it, though, right? Or at least find out if it's something I did.

She doesn't know. She can't know how fucked up I am. I'd get it if she knew. Because what kind of person would want to be with me if they knew? Which is also why she can never know. It's bad enough that Gabe knows, and I have no doubt that Marcel knows too. They went to that house together. I am thankful only one of them brought it up to me. I've seen the looks he gives me, though. I'm not blind.

I never want to see that same pity in Cammi's eyes. The disgust. Hatred. I couldn't bear to see that from her. I just have to do better at trying to act normal. Trying to be like any other teenage guy without a care in the world.

I find Cammi at her friend Elena's locker. Our eyes connect and she smiles briefly before it drops into a frown. She walks over and stops right in front of me. Staring at my eyes before glaring at Dash. "What did you give him?"

"Nothing," he says.

"Bullshit," Cammi fires back at him. "Vin?"

"Yeah, babe?"

"I want to skip class. Take me to the park," she says.

"You can't skip class again, Cammi. You're the good one here, remember?"

"I'm going to the park. You can either come or stay," she says, spinning around to look at her friend. "I'll call you later."

"Wait... Are you sure you're going to be okay?" Elena replies.

"Positive," Cammi says and starts walking towards the entrance of the building without bothering to look back.

"Guess I'm going to the park. Cover for me," I tell Dash, knowing full well the teachers won't give a shit if I'm here or not.

I follow two steps behind her the whole way until she stops under the same tree from that first day I spoke to her. Then Cammi spins around and looks right at me. "Why?"

"Why what?"

"Why would you get so wasted you can barely keep your head straight, right before school?"

"I'm not wasted," I lie. Truth is, right now, I'm seeing two of her. And, honestly, I'm not fucking complaining. Because there is no such thing as too much Cammi.

"You are. You can't go to class like this. Your eyes are bloodshot, Vin." Cammi drops onto the grass and opens her bag. Pulling out a bottle of water before handing it to me. "Drink this."

I smile. "You're really bossy, you know." I laugh, sitting across from her as I take the bottle.

"Why do you do it? Get so high?" she asks me.

"Because I need it," I tell her. "It makes them quiet."

"Makes who quiet?"

"The nightmares, the memories," I say.

"Vin?" She looks at me as she leans forward on her knees.

"Yeah?"

"Hug me. I need you to pull me onto your lap and wrap your arms around me. I need you to hold on to me like I'll vanish if you don't," she says.

I reach out and tug her against me. My arms wrap around her waist and I bury my face in her neck. "How do you know what I need?" I ask her.

"Because I need it too," she says.

Chapter Ten

Cammi

Things with Vin are intense. Not in a bad way. They're just... a lot. We've also hung out *a lot*, all week. He hasn't been as high as I saw him on Tuesday again, which I'm thankful for.

Don't get me wrong. I don't object to his smoking. I just don't want him to get in trouble or be so out of his head he does something stupid. I don't know. I guess I worry. I never asked him to elaborate on what the nightmares or memories were about. They're his, and if he wants me to know, he'll tell me.

When he holds me, though, it feels like completion. I feel complete when I'm with him. It's stupid, but that's the only word I can think of to explain it. Complete. Vin De Bellis completes me.

I smile. My lips still tingle from his kiss when I left school this afternoon. My parents are out of town for the weekend, and I told them I was staying with Elena, so they wouldn't worry. They usually try to drag me with them on their trips. Thankfully, I got out of going this time.

Right now, I'm lying on Elena's bed, dodging her and Devon's questions about Vin. "When did you say Lauren was getting here?" I look between them.

"Don't change the subject. Tell us. How big? Are the rumours really true?" Devon asks.

All they want to talk about is Vin's cock. Like I'm ever going to tell them about it. Some things should stay in the bedroom. And that's one of them. "I'm not talking to you about my boyfriend's cock." I smile. Every time I think of Vin being my boyfriend, I get a swarm of butterflies in my stomach.

"Then don't say. Just tell me when to stop."
Elena slowly starts to widen the gap between her two
palms.

I laugh and shake my head. When my phone
buzzes with a message, I dive for it, thankful for the
distraction. My smile widens when I see Vin's name
on the screen.

VIN:

There's a party tonight. Wanna
come?

ME:

Where is it?

It takes me a moment to realise he's going to a
party whether I go with him or not. I shouldn't care.
He can do whatever he wants. I'm not his keeper.
But a tiny bit of dread, or jealousy, overcomes me
when I imagine him at a party with all those thirsty
girls vying for his attention.

I trust Vin, I remind myself. He's done nothing to
make me question his trustworthiness.

VIN:

Dash's place.

The party is at his friend's house. Well, he's definitely going then.

ME:

Can I bring my friends?

VIN:

I'll come pick you all up at eight.

ME:

I'm at Elena's.

VIN:

I know.

Okay, then. I look up at Elena and Devon, who are both staring at me. Waiting. "Get dressed. We're going to a party. Vin is coming to get us in..." I glance at the clock on my phone. "Shit, one hour!" I squeal before jumping off the bed.

Where did the time go?

I feel like we just got here. I guess I haven't seen my friends as much this week and there was a lot to catch up on. Although mostly we just talked about Vin—the things I could tell them anyway. Like how perfect he is, how sweet, and how he makes me feel. Devon and Elena did not buy for one minute that Vin De Bellis is sweet. But I don't care. I don't need them to believe me. Because I know him. I know the real him and he is the sweetest, most-caring person I've ever met.

"One hour! Someone call Lauren and tell her to

hurry her ass up!" Elena shrieks, pulling her closet open and disappearing inside it.

An hour later, we're all standing out front of Elena's house. I'm nervous. I don't know why. I've spent every night with Vin this week. He's seen me naked. But standing here, in this little black lace dress that... well, doesn't really cover much of anything, I'm nervous. It's too much. I shouldn't have gone to so much effort. It's just a high school party.

An SUV pulls up to a stop, the back door opens, and Vin steps out. His eyes roam up and down the length of my body, twice, before they land on my face. I can't read his thoughts.

"Cammi?"

"Yeah?" I walk over to him. My friends trailing behind me. I lean up on my tiptoes and whisper, "Vin, kiss me."

He smiles, lowering his head to press his lips against mine. His hand lands on my lower back, my bare lower back, and he growls into my mouth. "Did you forget the other half of your dress?"

"No, why? You hate it, don't you? It looks ridiculous." I pull away.

"I love it. You look fucking hot. I'm going to be walking around with a boner all night, staring at you at the same time I want to slash everyone else's eyes out," he says.

"Well, I guess you should probably hold my hand and not let go, then. I'll make sure you don't slash out anyone's eyes." I smile up at him while offering my palm.

Vin takes it. "Let's go." He pushes open the door, cursing when I climb in. I guess he just got a good look at my ass. He waits for Lauren, Devon, and Elena to get into the car after me. Then he eyes Elena, who's sitting next to me. "You need to move," he tells her. "Back there."

She laughs. "All good. I was just messing with you," she says, moving to the third row to sit between Devon and Lauren.

When we walk into Dash's house, the place is empty, bar Dash and Marcus. I look up at Vin, who's standing next to me. So close, but not touching. I've learned he won't touch me unless I ask him to. I just can't bring myself to ask him why he needs my consent so badly. I don't want to push, especially if it's as bad as my imagination thinks it is.

"I thought you said it was a party?" I ask Vin.

"It is. You're here and you happen to be the only person I need to be around." His lips tip up at the corner, that little dimple showing.

Dash and Marcus are on the sofa, playing some kind of video game. Neither pays us any mind. "Help yourself to the kitchen," Dash calls over, never taking his eyes off the screen.

"Don't mind if I do." Elena walks out of the living room.

"Does she know where she's going?" I ask Devon and Lauren.

Lauren shrugs. "She has a nose for sniffing out booze."

A bang forces my attention back to Marcus, who's standing with his controller now on the table in front of him. "Booze? I'm in."

"What the fuck, man?" Dash says before tossing his own controller aside. "Some backup you are."

"You'll survive," Marcus says.

"You want a drink?" Vin asks me.

"Water?" I reply.

He nods. "Come on, I'll show you where the kitchen is." Vin glances down at my hand. I know he wants to hold it, but he won't. Not unless I ask him to.

"Lead the way," I say while offering him my palm. "If you don't hold my hand right now, I might just run away."

"You want me to hold your hand, Cammi?" Vin questions me.

"I always want you to hold my hand," I tell him as his fingers entwine with mine. I follow Vin into the kitchen, Lauren and Devon tagging along behind us.

Marcus walks up next to me. He slings an arm over my shoulder. "So, Cammi, what are your intentions with my boy here?"

My eyes widen. "My intentions?" *He's not serious, is he?*

Vin stops in his tracks before yelling out, "Hey, Dash?"

"Yeah, bro?" Dash pops up from around the corner.

"Call the doc. Marcus is gonna need his fingers reset. Maybe his wrist casted too," Vin tells him.

Dash looks to Marcus. "Dude, really? You're going to poke the bear like that? Come on, my mum's gonna kill me if we get blood everywhere."

I step closer to Vin, forcing Marcus's arm to drop

from my shoulders. "My intentions are to be the best girlfriend I can be, for as long as he wants me to be," I tell Marcus. Everyone goes silent. "What are your intentions with my boyfriend, Marcus?"

"Oh, nice. I like you. But you should know we're a package deal. Me and Him. I'm not going anywhere. Bros before—"

"You finish that sentence and I *will* fucking knock you out," Vin growls.

Marcus snaps his mouth closed. "Sorry, mate. So, who wants booze? I got the best of the best," he says, walking down the hall to where I assume the kitchen is located.

Everyone shuffles past us. I wait until they're all out of earshot. I can feel Vin's hand trembling in mine. His jaw is tight, his eyes drawn down. "Are you okay?" I ask him.

"No." He shakes his head. "Do me a favour? Go into the kitchen with your friends. There're water bottles in the fridge." He lets go of my hand.

"What are you going to do?" I ask him.

"I just need to step outside for a moment," he says.

He's going to go smoke. That's what he wants to do right now. I'm torn. I want to go with him. But I also always want him to be able to have the space he so desperately needs. "Okay, I'll go find the girls, if you're sure."

"Mhmm, I won't be long," he says and turns, walking in the opposite direction of the kitchen.

I stand still. Unmoving. I should give him space, right? It's what he wants. It's what he asked for. Yet there's a huge part of me that wants to go after him. He needs to know that whatever he's going through, whatever he's feeling, he doesn't need to do it alone. My feet are moving before I'm aware that I'm following him. I find Vin sitting on the front step with a joint between his fingers. He brings it to his mouth as I lower myself next to him.

He blows out a billow of smoke, then turns to me. "You shouldn't be out here."

"I should be wherever you are. And you're out here. So here I am," I tell him.

"I'm not..." He shakes his head and puffs on the joint again.

"You don't have to tell me, Vin. You don't need to explain anything. You also don't need to be alone anymore. I'm right here."

"What are your plans this weekend?" he asks.

"Not much. Why?"

"I want you to stay with me," he says.

"For the whole weekend? You'll grow tired of me." I laugh.

"Impossible." He pauses to take another drag of his joint. "So, will you?"

"Okay, I can stay until Monday," I tell him. "My parents think I'm staying at Elena's."

"You wanna go back inside?" Vin puts out the smoke, squashing it under his shoe as he glances back towards the door.

I stand and move down a step so I'm in front of him. "What I want is for you to hug me."

Vin reaches out and grabs my waist, pulling me down onto his lap so I'm straddling him. His arms wrap around me and his face buries into my neck. "I'm sorry I'm so fucked up," he whispers.

I snake my arms over his shoulders and hold on to him as tight as I can. "You're not fucked up to me, Vin. You're perfect just the way you are," I tell him.

Chapter Eleven

I've never brought a girl home before. Our house isn't just where we live; it's also where a lot of business gets done. And outsiders aren't usually welcomed in too easily. There's also the judgement and the questions that'll be asked when someone comes here. The soldiers surrounding the place could be off-putting too, I guess.

I don't know any differently. This is how I grew up. It's how we'll always live. Then there's the fact that I've never wanted to bring anyone home. I want Cammi here, though. I watch for her reaction as I drive through the gates, where two soldiers with not-so-concealed weapons wave me through. I probably should have warned her, told her what to expect. Although, right now, she doesn't seem too fazed.

"This is where you live?" Cammi asks, her eyes wide as she stares up the driveway.

"It's just a house," I tell her.

"That is not just a house, Vin. That's a bloody mansion on steroids," she says.

"Look, I probably should mention that my family... ah... Well, my brothers... shit. We have a lot of security around. Don't be surprised if they want to search you. I won't let anyone touch you, though. But they might ask. Just... don't wander around without me."

"Why do you look stressed? You don't have to bring me here if you don't want to. It's okay. We can go back to my place," Cammi offers.

"I want you here. I just don't want you to freak out or anything," I tell her.

"Okay. Don't worry. I plan to stick by you all weekend. You're going to have to peel me off come Monday morning." Cammi smiles, and my heart literally skips a beat. Emotion clogs my throat. Fuck, I love seeing her smile. "Vin, take me to your bedroom," she says.

I jump out of the car and walk around to the passenger side, getting there before she manages to get out. Holding the door open, I wait for her to step out of the way before closing it.

"You look like you've never taken a girl home before," Cammi hums.

"That's because I haven't," I tell her while glancing down at her hand. "Cammi?"

"Vin, I want you to hold my hand like you never want to let go of me." She smiles.

"Thank you," I say, taking her offered palm. I don't know how she does it, but she just gets me. Sometimes I wonder if she's in my head. But, fuck, that is the last place I'd want her to be. The only good thing up there is her.

I guide Cammi into the house. I take the back stairs that lead to the second story, managing to get her into my bedroom without any of my brothers noticing I'm home. I'm sure it won't be long before Gio's informed of our arrival. If the gate soldiers didn't tell him, one of the three guys we passed while walking through the house will.

I close the bedroom door. Cammi lets go of my hand and steps farther into the room. "This is where you live? Seriously? I'd never want to leave." She laughs.

"It's just a house. We don't even have most of the furniture yet, but it's getting there," I tell her, watching as she takes in my space.

"You have your own living room inside your bedroom, Vin. That's insane," she says, pointing to the black leather sofa in front of her and then to the large flat-screen television that's mounted to the wall. "Also, why is it so clean? Did you forget that you're a teenager or something?"

"We have cleaners." I shrug. I don't tell her that I actually keep my space clean myself. I like having everything in its place. I've always been that way. It makes me feel more in control of my environment.

"Fancy." Cammi laughs. "So, now that you have me here, what are you going to do with me, Vin?" She sits on the edge of my bed, and my cock hardens at the sight.

"What do you want me to do with you?" My buzz is gone, but I know I'm about to get the best fucking high. Just as soon as I get Cammi naked.

I wish I could be the kind of guy who takes what he wants. Who walks up and slams my lips on hers, tears the clothes from her body and sinks into her heat. I'm not that guy, though. I don't think I could ever be that guy. Her consent, knowing she wants this just as much as I do, is a fucking turn-on to me. It also separates me from them.

"We could watch a movie. You do have a pretty big TV," Cammi suggests.

"What do you want to watch?" I try my best to mask the fact that all I really want to do is sink into her. If she wants to watch a fucking movie, then that's what we'll do.

"Or... you could come over here and have your filthy way with me?" she says, raising her eyebrows.

"I'll take option two." I step towards her. "What exactly do you want, Cammi?"

"I want you. Naked," she says. "I want to taste you."

Well, fuck. If my dick wasn't hard before, it sure as shit is now. "You want to taste me?" I ask her.

"I want to suck you into my mouth, Vin. I want to give you pleasure like you've given me." Cammi's eyes bore into mine.

I pull my shirt over the back of my head and toss it to the floor. As I unbutton my jeans, Cammi slides off the bed and drops to her knees right in front of me. I pause. This isn't right. She shouldn't be on her fucking knees for me.

Get on your knees and open your mouth, boy, the Russian voice echoes in my head. No. This isn't happening. They don't invade my mind when I'm with Cammi. Fuck. Squeezing my eyes closed, I take a step backwards.

"Get up," I tell her.

"What?"

"I said get up. Get up off the fucking floor, Cammi." My voice rises and I move back farther.

"Okay." Cammi pushes herself up from the ground. "What's wrong? What happened just now?"

"You don't belong on the fucking floor. You don't belong on your knees," I tell her.

"It's okay."

I shake my head. "No, it's not okay. I don't want you on your knees. Not for me. Not for anyone."

"It's okay. I don't have to be on my knees," she says. "I have an idea. Come and lie on the bed."

"I should take you home," I whisper.

"Do you want me to leave? Because I don't want to." Cammi crawls onto the middle of the mattress and sits.

"No, I don't want you to leave," I tell her. "But, fuck, I can't... There are things... I don't want to fuck this up. I need you." I drop my gaze to my feet. She makes me so fucking vulnerable, and at the same time, I've never felt safer. I've never needed anyone like I need her.

"Come here." Cammi taps the space next to her on the bed. I walk over slowly. I really should send her home. I sit down and Cammi scoots over, closing the distance I left between us. "You aren't going to fuck this up, Vin. Just tell me what you need me to do. This consent thing goes both ways, you know. I don't want to do anything that you don't like or want either."

"I think I should go to church on Sunday," I tell her.

Cammi's brows draw down in confusion. "Okay, why?"

"To thank God for sending you to me. I don't know how many saints he has running around, but I'm sure as fuck glad he let me have you," I tell her. I'm not particularly religious. No one ever answered my prayers when I needed it the most. But I can't think of any other explanation than divine intervention for Cammi.

"If you knew the thoughts in my head right now, you wouldn't think me very saintly." Cammi's lips tip up into a mischievous grin.

"Yeah, what kind of thoughts are they?" I ask her.

"You're sitting here practically naked in front of me, Vin. Trust me. The things I want to do with you are very impure."

"You want to touch me?" I ask her, undoing my belt and then the button on my jeans.

Cammi nods. Her eyes focused on my hands gliding over my zipper.

"You want to taste me? You want to take my cock into that pretty little mouth of yours?" I pull my dick free from the confines of my pants, wrap my hand around my shaft, and tug.

Cammi licks her lips and nods again.

"Ask me, Cammi."

"Vin, can I suck your cock?" she says, her cheeks turning pink.

"It's all yours." I lean against the headboard, and this time when Cammi moves closer to my cock, I don't freak out. She's not on her knees. We're on a bed. Her head lowers. Her tongue runs along the underside of my dick and shivers run up my spine. "Fuck," I hiss.

Cammi shoves my hand aside and takes hold of

my dick, her lips closing over the tip as she gently sucks. "Mmm," she moans, sliding my length farther into her mouth and hollowing out her cheeks before she slides back up again.

My fingers curl into the blanket at my sides. As much as I want to grab her hair and wrap it around my fist, I won't. I need her to have control here. I won't ever take that from her.

Cammi cups my balls with her palm and slides right down my length, the tip of my cock hitting the back of her throat before she gags and moves up. "Fuck, that feels good," I moan.

Her tongue swirls around my tip. Then she swallows me down again, repeating the process over and over. "I'm going to come," I tell her.

"Mhmm. That's the goal here, Vin." She smiles around a mouthful of my cock.

"You don't have to take it in your mouth," I say. "But, fuck. I can't hold back much longer."

Cammi pulls back to respond. "I want to. I want to experience everything with you, Vin," she says before closing her lips around me again. Sucking harder this time. Her head bobs up and down faster, and before I know it, I lose control, coming down her throat. When I'm done, Cammi slides up my body.

"Vin, I want you to kiss me like it's the first and last time you ever will."

I hold her face between my palms and pull her towards me. It's on the tip of my tongue to say those three little words. Now isn't the right time though, so instead, I try to tell her exactly how I feel with a kiss.

Chapter Twelve

Cammi

Being the girlfriend of Vin De Bellis has its benefits. Other than the mind-blowing orgasms he gives me, there are certain advantages I wasn't aware I get because of my relationship with him.

Like right now, for instance, when the lunch lady wouldn't take my cash. She simply said, "Tell Vin it's on the house." I feel strange walking towards my usual lunch table, knowing I didn't pay for the food on my tray.

"What's wrong?" Lauren asks.

"The lunch lady wouldn't take my money today," I say.

"You got a free meal?" Devon asks.

"That's the thing. There is no such thing as a free meal in life," I explain. There's always a price to pay. Isn't that a saying or something? I'm sure it is.

"What'd she say?" Elena asks.

"To tell Vin it's on the house," I repeat right as a body fills the seat next to me. Not just any body. His body. The scent of weed surrounds me.

"What's on the house?" Vin asks me.

"Lunch apparently," I tell him, pointing to my tray.

"Good. It fucking should be."

"Why?"

"Because we're De Bellises, babe. It's how it's done." He lifts one shoulder before nodding at my tray. "Eat."

"*You* are a De Bellis. I'm not. And I'm not even

116

hungry." I push the tray towards him. "But by all means, you eat your free food."

Vin's brows pull down. He stares at me, his mouth clamped shut and his eyes bloodshot. "I fucked up but I don't know what I did. You're going to have to help me out here," he says.

"You're high as a kite. I'd be surprised if you even knew your own name," I fire back at him. I know I'm being bitchy, and I shouldn't take my foul mood out on him. It's not fair.

"I know my name. It's *Cammi's man.*" He smirks, and I fight the smile that wants to spread across my lips.

I don't like it when he gets high. I get why he does it. Sort of. I know he's using it to mask something. Whatever trauma Vin has experienced was bad, and I'm not going to be the one to tell him he can't do something that gives him peace. Although I wish he'd just come and find me. He's told me he doesn't need to smoke as much when I'm with him, because I quiet his nightmares. I also don't want to be that girlfriend who's super needy and annoying.

Argh, why are relationships so hard?

I've had flings before. Steady boyfriends, in a way. But nothing compares to what I have with Vin.

It's as if he's a part of me. I can't imagine living my life without him now that I've got him, and I know he's afraid of fucking this relationship up. But so am I.

"You're really mad, huh? I'm sorry. Whatever I did, I won't do it again," he says.

"I'm not mad at you," I tell him. Everyone at the table—Lauren, Devon, Elena, Dash, and Marcus—is watching us. I glare in their direction. "Don't you all have a better form of entertainment than me and Vin?"

"Nope," Dash answers.

"It's like watching an episode of some bad reality show, except I'm rooting for you both. I think you'll go the distance," Elena says.

"Gee, thanks." I scowl at my friend.

"If any of you piss her off or upset her, I will shoot you." Vin points to everyone at the table.

"No, he won't," I say.

"Yes, I will," he repeats, his tone deadly serious.

I roll my eyes. "Stop being dramatic. Did you ever think that perhaps I'm just moody? I am a seventeen-year-old girl, Vin. We have weeks where we get moody and emotional."

"You on your period? That explains a lot," Marcus grunts.

Vin looks at me with a raised brow. He knows damn well I'm not on my period, considering he had his fingers inside me before school today. Then he turns to Marcus. "Don't talk about my girlfriend's vagina." He scowls. Then he leans in and whispers against my ear. "Tell me what to do. I don't want you angry at me."

"Hug me. Hold on to me like the apocalypse is upon us and we don't have a tomorrow," I tell him.

Vin wraps his arms around me. This hug is just as much for him as it is for me. We need this. I can't explain it, but when I touch him, it's like a weight is lifted off my shoulders. I feel lighter. Freer. I can only hope that he feels half of what I do.

"Fuck, I'm going to miss you," Vin says against my neck.

My body tightens. "Why? Where are you going?"

"Gio's getting married this weekend. I have to go to Queensland with the family." He sighs.

"You're going to be gone the whole weekend?" I pull back. My teeth dig into my bottom lip. I don't want to spend the whole weekend without him. He's crept into my room every night this week. He's stayed a few hours and then left sometime after I fell asleep.

119

How am I supposed to go a whole weekend without him?

"I have to. I'm sorry." Vin looks torn, like he doesn't actually want to go. But I know how close he is to his brothers, and he'd hate to miss one of them getting married.

"Are you going to be okay?" I whisper to him.

"It's only a weekend, and I'll come find you as soon as the jet lands back in Melbourne on Sunday."

"Okay. I just... I'm going to miss you," I admit. "Vin, kiss me. Kiss me like you're not going to see me all weekend, because you're actually not."

His lips press against mine. The noise of the cafeteria drowns out. The only thing that surrounds me is Vin. His scent, his taste, his touch. It's all him and I love it. I love him.

Holy shit, I love him.

Should I tell him? Or should I wait for him to tell me first? I need a *how to do relationships* guide for dummies at this point.

Vin's tongue pushes into my mouth, swirling around mine. I can't get close enough. I need to remember we're in the cafeteria and not in the privacy of a bedroom or a car.

"Okay, get a room," Lauren says right before a fry hits the side of my face.

I pull back from Vin and glare at Lauren. "Did you seriously just throw a fry at me?"

"Yep. It was either that or pour a bottle of water over the two of you. You're making a scene," she says.

I look around and notice everyone in the cafeteria staring. One guy has his phone up. "Is he recording us?" I ask Vin.

Before I know what's happening, his chair scrapes across the floor and he's on his feet and storming towards the guy.

"Oh shit." Marcus jumps up to follow him.

"Some people really do have no sense of self preservation," Dash says, rising to his feet before creeping up behind his friends at a much slower pace.

Vin grabs hold of the guy's phone, smashing it to the ground before his booted foot stomps on the screen. I don't hear what he says before his fist slams into the kid's face. I'm frozen. I know I should get up and do something. Pull Vin back. Something. I don't want him to get hurt. But all I can do is sit here and watch as Vin and the other guy end up on the ground.

It's a blur as an all-out brawl breaks out in the cafeteria. Marcus and Dash are both in the throes of fighting. I'm not concerned about them, though.

Finally getting to my feet, I push my way through the crowd to find Vin.

He's on the ground, on top of the same kid. I'm just about to reach out for him when someone knocks into me and I fall onto my ass. "Ow, fuck!" I yell out.

Vin's head snaps in my direction. His eyes go wide and a feral growl escapes his throat. He pushes off the guy and takes two steps before reaching me. He tugs me to my feet. "Who the fuck just knocked her to the ground?" Vin shouts over all the noise.

Suddenly, everyone stops moving. It's as if the king has spoken and all the humble servants are waiting for his next decree.

Vin turns to me. "Who pushed you?"

"I don't know," I tell him. I honestly didn't see who ran into me.

"Whoever it was, I'm going to find you. So might as well come forward now," Vin says while his eyes flick around the crowd.

Before anyone can say anything, a heap of teachers rushes into the cafeteria, ushering our class-mates out of the room. "De Bellis, the office now," one of them says. "You two as well." He points to Dash and Marcus.

Ignoring the teacher, Vin looks me up and down. "Are you okay?" he asks.

"I'm fine. Do you think you're going to get into much trouble?" I ask him.

"Nah, it'll be fine. Go to class. I'll catch up with you later." He leans forward and kisses my cheek. We stare at each other for a moment. This is the first time he's kissed me without me asking him to. Granted, it was only my cheek.

I smile, and Vin takes an audible breath. "Will you find me before you leave? Please?" I ask him.

"I will," he says.

I walk out of the cafeteria, doing my best to ignore the stares and whispers being directed my way.

"That was... intense," Devon says while linking her arm with mine. "Don't you think he's a little much?"

"Who?" I ask her.

"Vin? It's like he's all caveman or something. Someone just has to look at you the wrong way and he freaks out." She keeps her voice low, but her words sting.

"I think he's perfect."

"I think he's obsessed with you. I'm just not sure if it's a good thing or a bad thing yet. But if you ever disappear, the De Bellis family basement is the first place I'll send the cops." Elena laughs.

"Leave her alone. She's happy." Lauren comes to my defence. "Besides, I think whatever they have is special."

I want to tell them that I love him, but I don't think it's fair to Vin for me to tell my friends before I tell *him*. I just need to find the right moment...

Chapter Thirteen

I love my brothers. But, fuck, I wish Gio could have just had a local wedding. Besides the gruelling heat up here, I fucking miss Cammi. My head has been more fucked up over the last twenty-four hours than it has been in weeks.

I credit Cammi for that. The peace she gives me

is unlike anything else. Right now, though, the night-mares are wreaking havoc. I can't seem to smoke enough to fog out the voices. And then there's my brother Santo.

I thought I was fucking crazy. Seeing him talk to a blank wall, thinking it's his dead fiancée, though? That's the height of crazy, if you ask me. And there's fuck all I can do to help him.

We've been watching him all night. Marcel and I. He just went to get Gabe to come and take over. We haven't been able to get through to Santo. And although I know it's all in his head, he's happy talking to Shelli. Even if she doesn't exist. It's fucking hard. Santo and Shelli had been together since they were teenagers. Her death rocked the whole family but obviously it's hit him hard.

I'm standing outside of Santo's room lighting up a blunt, trying to ease my mind while I have two minutes alone. I don't doubt that my brothers know I smoke, but it's an *if you don't see it, it doesn't exist* kind of thing.

I'm puffing on my little happy stick when Gabe and Marcel appear. I flick the blunt to the ground and quickly stomp it out.

"Don't let Gio see you doing that." Gabe juts his chin towards my foot.

"Good thing he's too busy playing house then." I chuckle. I follow my brother into the room and watch as Gabe works fucking wonders on Santo, who finally lies down and goes the fuck to sleep.

By the time I get to my own room, I have a few hours before we jump back onto the jet. I pick up my phone and message Cammi.

ME:

I think we should move in together. I can buy us a house or an apartment.

CAMMI:

That's... a lot. Are you okay?

ME:

I'm not with you. So, no, I'm not okay.

CAMMI:

When do you get back?

ME:

We should land around lunchtime.

CAMMI:

I can't wait. How was the wedding?

ME:

It was good. Until Santo got wasted and started talking to a ghost.

CAMMI:

Really? A ghost? What ghost?

ME:

It's a long story.

My phone starts ringing in my hand and Cammi's picture lights up the screen. "Hey."

"How are you really?" she asks.

"Tired," I admit.

"Have you slept at all?"

I can hear the concern in her voice. I hate that she's worried about me. She might not know why I don't sleep well, or what my nightmares are about, but she realises that I sleep better when I'm next to her. "A couple of hours. I'm fine though. I don't want you to worry."

"I'm allowed to worry about you. It's what girl-friends do," she says, then adds, "I have an idea!"

"I don't like being the thing that makes you worry. But what's your idea?" I ask her.

"You'll see when you get back. I'm going to send you an address. That's if you still want to see me this afternoon?"

I laugh. "There is nothing I want to do more than see you, Cammi."

"Okay. I'm going to text you a place before you land. Meet me there."

"I'll be there. What did you end up getting up to last night?" I question her.

"I stayed home and wallowed over the fact my boyfriend's out of town," she says. "And I watched *The Princess Diaries* with my mum."

"I'm sorry." I hate that she spent the weekend missing me. At the same time, it's fucking good to know I'm not in this thing alone.

"It's not your fault, and I'll get over it. How was the ceremony? Was it romantic? What about the reception? Did you dance with anyone?" There's a hint of uncertainty in her voice. Jealousy too.

"It was a wedding. I danced with El once. We all had to," I explain.

"Are you really okay?"

She can tell I'm barely holding on. I'm out of weed and, honestly, I just want to get back to Melbourne and back to her. I need a few minutes of quiet. "I am. I gotta go. Gio's calling, but send me the address of where you want to meet. I'll see you soon."

"I'll see you soon." She cuts the call.

I want so badly to be able to tell her how I feel. It's

not fair to put that on her, though. I know she's here now, but if she ever finds out about me, she's not going to stick around. I wouldn't blame her for it. I'm not a lovable person. I'm not someone who can love her wholly the way she deserves to be loved, because there's always a chance the monsters will creep in and mess up my head.

They won't let me keep her forever. And there's nothing I can do to shut them up for good. I will, however, take advantage of whatever time I have with her and hope like fuck that it doesn't completely destroy me when I lose her.

I step off the plane and look at Cammi's message for the tenth time.

CAMMI:

Meet me at the Sheridan. The girl at reception has a key for you. Room 1012.

ME:

Just landed. Be there soon.

I have no idea why she wants me to meet her at a

hotel. It's also not something I'm going to question. Honestly, she could have told me to meet her at the landfill and I'd be there in a heartbeat.

"Where are you going?" Gabe asks when I walk in the direction of the small office at the private airfield.

"I got plans. Catch you all later." I wave a hand over the back of my head as I keep walking.

Thankfully, he's too preoccupied by his girlfriend to question me. I don't think they've technically put a label on it, and the fact they are trying to hide that they're fucking every chance they get tells me Daisy doesn't want people to know.

She's one of El's friends, and not a bad chick. A bit too intuitive for my liking. She took one look at me and could tell I was masking my anxiety. Given she's a social worker, I guess she should be good at it. It's what she does for a living. I don't need anyone trying to work out the mess that is in my head, though, so I plan to steer clear of her.

I pull out my phone and call for an Uber. The hotel is only fifteen minutes from here. I wonder if this is what junkies feel like? Itching for their next hit. My body's hyperalert. It's like every fibre of my being knows we're going to get to touch her again soon.

The moment I push through the doors of the hotel, I make a beeline for reception and give my name. I'm handed a card and directed to a bank of lifts. When I finally reach the tenth floor, I find the door and raise my hand to knock, but it swings open before I can bring my fist down.

"Get in here." Cammi reaches out, taking my hand and pulling me into the room. Before the door can shut, she wraps her arms around my neck and her body presses up against mine.

I go still. It's not that I don't want her to touch me. It's just that I'm not used to people just doing it. I need a bit of warning.

"Vin, I want you to hug me and I want you to never let go. Don't ever leave me again. I missed you so much," she says.

I feel it too. It wasn't even forty-eight full hours. But, fuck, I hated every second I was away from her. My arms wrap around her waist and I hold her tight. My body relaxes, and I feel like I can breathe properly.

I sink my face into the crook of her neck and sigh. "I fucking missed you too."

Cammi drops her arms way too fucking soon. "Come over here. Lie down with me." She drops her robe, and now she's only wearing a pair of pink lace panties. "Give me your shirt." She holds out a hand.

Reaching behind my back, I pull the shirt over my head and hand it to her. As painful as it is to cover those fucking tits up, if she literally wants the shirt off my back, I'll always give it to her.

Cammi covers herself and then slides under the blankets. I slip out of my shoes, standing in just my jeans before hopping on next to her.

"I want you to hold me and I want you to sleep," she says.

"You want to sleep?" I ask, pulling her against me.

Cammi rests her head on my shoulder. "I want you to sleep, so that's what we're doing. Sleeping." She tilts her head up so that her eyes connect with mine.

My fingers brush the stray strands of hair away from her face. I'm overwhelmed with emotion. She knows that I sleep better when she's next to me. And here she is, offering to just stay and bed so I can sleep.

"I love you." My words are whispered and I think they shock both of us.

Cammi blinks her eyes a few times and then she smiles. "Oh, thank god. I love you too. I wanted to tell you before, but I didn't want to seem crazy," she says.

"Why the fuck would you think you'd come across as crazy to me?" I ask her.

"Because of this. You and me. It's a lot and it's fast. But I just... I don't know. I feel it, though, so deep. It's like you're in my blood. Your soul and mine are linked," she tells me.

"You don't want to be linked to my soul, babe. It's not going anywhere good. And you? You're a saint. You belong up, not down."

"I belong wherever you are, Vin. I don't care where that is." She snuggles into my chest.

I close my eyes and inhale her scent. I can feel sleep wanting to take hold already.

Chapter Fourteen

Cammi

I t's almost spring break, our last lot of school holidays before we're done with high school. I got a letter yesterday afternoon with my early acceptance into the University of Sydney. Over the past few weeks, I haven't thought much about uni.

I've been so caught up in Vin and spending as much time as possible with him that everything else has taken a back seat.

Getting that envelope yesterday was like having a cold bucket of water tipped over my head. My parents were thrilled, of course they were, and I did my best to fake my excitement. When Vin snuck into my bedroom last night, I didn't tell him about the acceptance letter.

We haven't really talked about next year. I have no idea what his plans are for university. I know his brother goes to Melbourne Uni. I assume Vin will go there too. I had my heart set on moving to Sydney, attending university there. They have a great architecture program. I've been planning to study architecture for as long as I can remember. I can't see myself leaving Vin, which I know is stupid. I can't make life-altering decisions based around a guy.

I shouldn't...

It's not too late, though. I could apply to Melbourne. I could stay here. I wouldn't have to leave Vin. I would still graduate with the degree I want. Sometimes I wish I could press fast-forward on this part of my life, get to the part where I'm done with school, where I'm an adult, living with a husband who I'm madly in love with. We'd have a puppy. I want to start that part of my life.

All of this lead-up to getting there seems pointless at times, especially when I already know the future I want. Who I want that future to be with. I need to talk to Vin about this. I feel like we should make this decision together. What if he's not even planning on going to university? He could come to Sydney with me.

"There you are. I've been looking everywhere for you." Vin appears at my locker right as I close it.

"You just left my side five minutes ago." I laugh.

"Five minutes too long, if you ask me." He smirks.

"What are your thoughts on ditching school today?"

"Are you feeling okay? What's wrong?" He scans my body, not once but twice, looking for only God knows what.

"I'm just not feeling it today. That's all. But it's fine. Let's go to class." I hoist my bag up onto my shoulder.

Vin reaches out and takes it. "I know where we can go. Come on, let's be rebellious."

I offer him my palm. "Vin, hold my hand," I tell

him, and he does. "Now get me out of this place, please."

Once we're enclosed in his car, Vin's fingers tap the steering wheel. I have no idea where he's taking me. And, honestly, I don't think I care. I just needed to get away. My mind is whirling with how to bring up the acceptance letter.

"Okay, spit it out." Vin says.

"Spit what out?"

"Whatever it is that's dimming your smile. What's on your mind, Cammi?" he asks.

"I, uh... I got an acceptance letter for university." I turn and look at his profile, watching his reaction.

"Babe, that's great. Usually people are happy when they get those letters. Why aren't you happy?"

"It's for the University of Sydney," I explain.

"Sydney?"

"Uh-huh. I applied before I met you. They have a really great program there."

"You're moving to Sydney?" he questions.

"I don't know." I sink down into my seat. "It was always my plan before..."

"Before what?"

"Before you."

"Cammi, you're not changing your life plans for me. If Sydney is your dream, then do it," he says. "I won't be the reason you're not living out your dreams."

"I won't be living any kind of dream if you're not part of it, Vin." I sigh.

"We still have time to figure out the logistics," he says. It's not what I wanted to hear. I want him to tell me that he can't bear the thought of living without me. I want him to tell me not to go.

When Vin stops the car, I look up and see we're at the beach. I haven't been here for ages. I love the beach. The sand? Not so much. But I love everything else about the ocean. The sound of the waves crashing. The smell of the sea air. The cool breeze...

Vin steps out of the car and walks around to the passenger side, opening my door. I jump and inhale the salty air. "I haven't been here in so long."

"Let's go for a walk." Vin picks up my hand without me having to ask him. We both look down at our joined palms, and then I take a step towards the beach. Vin follows.

It's a huge moment. We both know it. I just don't think I want to make a big deal out of it. I want him to be comfortable touching me whenever he wants to touch me. Without needing my permission.

We silently walk along the sandbank, stopping just before the water's edge. Vin sits on the ground, pulling me down with him. Hand in hand, we sit and stare out over the ocean. "I want to be selfish and tell you not to go. I want to tell you that I need you. That I can't possibly fathom going back to a life without you," Vin whispers.

"Then tell me," I say. "Tell me that, and I'll stay."

"I can't." He shakes his head. "I can't be selfish with you."

"Then come with me. Come to Sydney." I'm practically begging him.

"You want me to come with you?"

"I want to be with you. I don't care where it is, Vin," I admit.

"Okay," he says.

"Okay? You'll come? Or... okay, you'll think about it?" I really need him to clarify this.

"I'll come with you." He smiles. "You know I would have followed you anyway."

"You would?"

"There's nothing that could possibly keep me away from you, Cammi." Vin's face drops closer to mine.

"Kiss me," I tell him. "I want you to kiss me like the world is burning around us, and we only have minutes left to live." I smile up at him.

"Just so you know, I'd find a way to save you even

from a burning world," Vin says before his lips press against mine. His tongue pushes past the seam of my mouth, twirling around.

I rise to my knees as I straddle Vin's lap. "I love you," I tell him, barely pulling away to speak.

"I love you. So damn much," he says as his fingers brush through my hair. "My little Saint Cammi. I will worship at your altar every day for as long as you want me, whether that be here in Melbourne, Sydney, or fucking Timbuctoo."

"I have no plans of going to Timbuctoo, but I will follow you there if you ever go."

Vin's phone vibrates in his pocket, pulling us out of our bubble. Shuffling off his legs, I plop onto the sand as he pulls the device out of his pocket. "It's my brother," he says, tapping on the screen.

"Marcel, what's up?"

"Santo's missing." I hear his brother's words come out of the speaker of the phone.

"Whoa, slow down. What do you mean *he's missing?*" Vin asks.

"As in, no one can fucking find him, Vin!"

"Okay, I'm coming home." Vin pushes to his feet and holds out a hand to me. I place my palm on his and let him pull me up. He drops my hand as soon as I'm standing. "There's no point. He's not there," he says into the phone. "Look around the city. And call me if you find him." Vin shoves the device into his pocket before turning to me. "I can drop you back at school."

"Or I could come along with you? Help you look?" I suggest. I have no idea how I'd help with anything. I just want to be with him in case he needs me.

"Okay, I think I know where he might be," Vin says.

We end up parked next to a cemetery. I can tell Vin is worried about his brother. He's told me a few things about Santo and how the guy's struggling with his grief. I have no idea what the right thing to say is, though.

"Just wait here. I won't be long. I'm going to check Shelli's grave and see if he's there," Vin tells me.

"Are you sure? I don't mind coming with you?" I offer.

"I'm sure. I'll be back." He gets out of the car and jogs off.

After five minutes passes with no sign of Vin or his brother, I climb out and go looking for them. It doesn't take long to find them, and as soon as I do, I wish I hadn't. I've never seen a more disturbing sight in my life.

Vin is sitting next to his brother, their legs dangling in front of them. But that's not the disturbing part. The disturbing part is the giant hole in the ground. The open casket. And the corpse staring back at me from inside it.

Chapter Fifteen

I thought I'd seen my brother's grief hit rock bottom. I was fucking wrong. I had a feeling he'd be at her gravesite. He comes here a lot. I was not expecting to find him sitting on the edge of a six-foot hole. A hole that was filled with a casket and dirt last week.

It's not the hole that's the real problem, though. It's the open casket with the rotting corpse sitting inside it. It's a good thing I don't have a weak stomach.

Standing back a little, I watch and listen as my brother pours his heart out to Shelli's dead body. I should tell him I'm here. I shouldn't be listening in on this conversation.

"Why? Shelli? Why the fuck are you doing this to me?" Santo says, his words broken. "We were meant to have forever. Now I'm left with a forever of you haunting me. A forever of not fucking knowing." His voice gets louder. "I just want to know why!"

I walk over and drop down next to him, my legs hanging over the edge of the hole. "What's up?"

Santo looks up at me, obviously shocked. He didn't even hear me approach. He's a sitting fucking duck out here, an open target for any one of our enemies. "She's really dead," he says.

"Yeah, bro, she is." I glance at the casket. It's funny how quickly a body decomposes—although I would have expected worse. Shelli was a beautiful girl, on the outside anyway. I've since learned things about her that I hope my brother never finds out.

"I see her though, Vin. She's standing right there." Santo points to the end of the grave. Right fucking next to me. "How is she standing there if she's in... *there?*" He shifts his focus to the casket again.

"I think that maybe you want her to be here so badly that your mind is playing tricks on you, Santo. She's not here. I wish more than anything that she were. I wish I could bring her back for you, but I can't. We can't," I tell him gently.

"What if I don't want her back? What if I just want answers?" he asks me.

"Answers to what?" I have no idea what he knows. I really fucking hope it's not much...

"Too fucking many questions. What if that's not her?"

"Santo, you found her, remember? You held her body in your arms. You know it's her." I remind him of what I'm sure was the worst night of his life. The night he found his fiancée beaten to death.

"We were going to be parents. I was going to be a father." Santo glances beside me. I don't think he's talking to me. He's talking to her, the ghost that haunts him.

"Yeah." I don't know what to say. I have no fucking idea how to help my brother through this.

Then Santo suddenly slips down into the hole.

"You should leave, Vin. This isn't your problem," he says.

"Get the fuck out of the hole. And you are my brother. Your problems are my problems."

"I can't, Vin. I can't keep doing this. I'm losing my fucking mind. I died with her. He won. The old man fucking won!" he yells out while tugging at the ends of his hair.

"No, he didn't. That fucking bastard will not win. I won't let him," I grunt before jumping down into the hole with my brother. I press a hand on his shoulder and lean my forehead against his. "I didn't let him win when he put me in a room, month after month. Nor when he let a bunch of sick fucking assholes use and abuse me time and time again. I'm not going to let him win now either. He will not beat you, Santo. You're stronger than this." My words are clogged with emotion.

Santo's entire body goes rigid before he pulls back to look me dead in the eyes. "What?"

"I won't let him beat you," I repeat.

"Not that. What do you mean you were abused?" he asks.

"It doesn't matter. What matters right now is you and the fact that you are going to get through this," I tell him.

"It matters to me. What the fuck happened, Vin?" Santo is vibrating with rage. Maybe that's a good thing. Gives him something else to focus on than his grief.

Gabe knows what happened. Marcel knows what happened too, but I've never voiced any of it to a single soul. Even dead, my father scares the shit out of me. "It started when I was eleven. Stopped when I was fourteen," I explain simply.

I can see the wheels in Santo's head turning. "Three years? Three fucking years, Vin?"

"He had a house. I wasn't the only kid to get locked up in those rooms. But I was the only one related to *him*. Once a month, the old man took me there. Sometimes I'd be there for an hour. Other times... with other men... Well, they wouldn't leave until I broke." I swallow. My throat is dry. I can hear their voices in my head. I can feel the monsters taking over my mind.

"Why didn't you tell me? Or Gio? Or any of us? We would have never let that fucking happen, Vin," Santo says.

"I couldn't... He said if I told any of you, then he'd take you there too. Better me than any of my brothers." I shrug.

"That wouldn't have happened. You should have

come to us. Fuck!" Santo yells out as he kicks the dirt wall beside us, causing clunks of soil to topple down.

"It's in the past, Santo. I've dealt with it," I tell him. Movement catches my attention. I quickly turn and find Cammi standing near the tree. She's within hearing distance, close enough that I can see the horror on her face and the tears wetting her cheeks. "Fuck."

I reach up and pull myself out of the hole before rushing around to slam the casket closed. "RIP, Shelli," I whisper to the lid. I shouldn't hate her. I loved her like a big sister for so long, but knowing what I know now? Seeing my brother's heart not just break but shatter beyond repair? Well, now I fucking hate her.

I need to talk to Cammi. I don't know how much of that conversation she overheard. I'm hoping none of it. But my brother needs me. I can't just leave him here either.

"You know her?" Santo asks while staring in Cammi's direction.

"Yeah, she's my girlfriend," I tell him, not taking my eyes off Cammi. *Was* my girlfriend is probably a better description. If she overheard even a portion of that exchange, no way is she going to stay with me.

"Go home, Vin. I need to clean up here." Santo sighs.

I shake my head and pull my phone out of my pocket before quickly sending Marcel a message.

ME:

Found him. Shelli's grave. Get here ASAP. It's bad.

MARCEL:

On my way.

"I'm not leaving you alone," I tell my brother while pocketing my phone again.

"I'm not alone. I've got Shelli right here." Santo points to the wooden box.

"That's fucking morbid, even for you."

He pulls himself out of the hole. "I wanted the casket to be empty," he says, keeping his voice low as we both watch Cammi turn and walk away.

Every fibre of my being wants to chase after her. Explain everything to her. But how the fuck do I explain all of... this? Instead, I let her go and turn my focus back on my brother.

It took almost fifty minutes for Marcel to turn up. And as soon as he did, I made an excuse to leave. I'm shocked when I find Cammi sitting in the passenger seat of my car. I stand still while our eyes connect through the windscreen. I can see so much emotion on her face. I don't see pity, though. There's anger and sadness swirling around in her gaze. But no disgust.

I continue to the driver's side and climb in. Neither of us says a single word. I think ten minutes pass before I can turn and look at her. "I'm sorry you had to see that," I say, my voice hoarse.

"Vin?"

"Yeah?" I don't think I want to hear what's coming. I can't hear that she's done with me. I don't blame her, but I'm not ready to lose her yet either.

"I want you to pick me up, pull me over to your seat, and hold me. I want you to hold me so tight, as if I'm going to float away if you don't," she says.

"Why would you want me to touch you?" I ask her, my brows drawn down.

"Because I'm scared. I'm petrified and I need you to hold me."

"I'm sorry. You really shouldn't have seen that. My brother... he's not himself right now." I try to find words to explain why someone would dig up the body of their dead fiancée. But there're just no words for that.

"That's not what I'm afraid of," she says.

"Then what are you afraid of?" I ask her even when I know the answer.

Me. She's afraid of me. Fuck.

"I think I'm losing you, and I'm terrified of that happening. I can't lose you, Vin. I won't lose you. So, will you please hold me?" Her voice rises in volume with each word that leaves her beautiful mouth.

I reach over, take hold of her hips, and drag her across the car until she's straddling my lap. My arms wrap around her as tight as they can without hurting her. "You are not losing me. I'm right here. I'm not going anywhere," I whisper into her hairline.

I feel her body shake. She's crying. Her arms are closed around my neck and her face is buried in my chest. "If your father wasn't already dead, I'd kill him myself," she says through her tears.

"I would never let you anywhere near a demon like my father, babe," I tell her.

"I'm sorry, Vin. I'm sorry that happened to you. I'm sorry I eavesdropped on a conversation that wasn't meant for me to hear. I'm just so freaking sorry."

"I'm sorry I'm not the guy you thought I was," I

counter. "I'm broken beyond repair. I told my brother that I didn't let my father win, but I lied. He wins every fucking time I close my eyes and I see their faces."

"You're not broken, and you don't need repairing. You are exactly the guy I thought you were. The guy I *know* you are. You are kind, loyal... and when you love, you love hard. You're a fighter, a survivor, and you are my anchor." Cammi lifts her head to meet my glare. "I love you. Nothing will ever change that."

God made a mistake when he assigned this woman to me. Because no way in fucking high heaven or hell am I deserving of her. I will take her for as long as I can have her, though. After all, it's not like there's a return hotline for misdelivered saints.

Chapter Sixteen

Cammi

I knew that whatever caused Vin's nightmares... it was bad. I'd thought up all sorts of possibilities for why he had an aversion to touch, why he was so insistent on getting my verbal consent every time he kissed me. Every time he held my hand.

Despite all the scenarios I conjured up, nothing compared to the truth. A truth I wasn't supposed to overhear. And now, because I stuck around to listen to a private conversation, I know. I know something I'm not meant to know. Something Vin doesn't want me to know. He's ashamed. I can tell. But what happened to him was not his fault. It doesn't change how I feel for him either. It doesn't change the fact that he's perfect to me. I will do whatever I can to help him through this.

I know that being abused for years isn't something someone just *gets over*. But we can learn to live with this nightmare together. We can learn to navigate the monsters that taunt him. I will willingly jump into that black hole with Vin. I'll hold his hand and face-off with them right by his side.

What I won't do is lose him. I won't let this affect us. Knowing his truth only strengthens our bond. I meant what I said to him. If his father were still alive, I'd find a way to kill him for what he did to Vin. What kind of man willingly offers his child up to be sexually abused? Tortured?

Vin likes to call me a saint, but I'm not. Right now, I have a thirst for blood... the blood of every single person to ever lay a hand on him. I want vengeance for him. If his brothers don't make that happen, I'll figure out a way to do it myself.

I check the time on the little clock on my bedside table. He's late. It's almost midnight. He's always here by now. *Where is he?*

I pick up my phone and dial Vin's number. It rings out and goes through to his voicemail. After leaving a message for him to call me back, I send him a text.

ME:

Is everything okay? Are you coming?

The little bubbles pop up to indicate he's replying.

VIN:

I can't tonight. I'll see you tomorrow.

ME:

Why? Where are you?

VIN:

At home. I'm just going to stay here tonight.

I should give him space, right? The second the

question pops into my head, I know the answer. *Hell no.*

He does not need space. He's distancing himself. I could feel him pulling away in the car before he dropped me off. I knew something wasn't right.

I jump out of bed and quickly throw on a pair of shorts and a hoodie. Slipping my feet into a pair of slides before I pick up my phone and wallet. And make it all the way to the front door before my mum sees me.

"Where do you think you're going at this hour?" Her voice has me spinning around.

"A friend needs me, Mum. I have to go and help them," I tell her honestly, leaving out the part that that friend is a boy and a De Bellis boy at that.

"Take my car, and text me when you get there and when you're leaving," she says.

My mum is a loyal friend. She's always drilled into me that friendships take work, but they're worth everything if both parties are invested. She's still best friends with the same group of girls from high school. So, when I tell her a friend is in need, she's more than willing to let me go and help that friend. Because that's what a decent person would do.

And right now, Vin is in need.

I know he doesn't sleep if I'm not in the bed. He

gets a couple of hours of rest at most every night when he climbs through my window.

"Thanks, Mum. I'll text you. Love you." I kiss my mother's cheek as I take the keys from her hand.

I park on the side of the street and look over at Vin's house. Then I take a deep breath, jump out of my car, and walk up to the gate. I'm not stupid. I know there is no way of sneaking into this place. Well, not for me anyway. Maybe a skilled ninja or assassin could do it.

Huh, if architecture doesn't pan out for me, maybe I could go to ninja school. Is that a thing?

Two big, burly men in dark suits step out from nowhere, appearing in front of me. "Are you lost?"

"No, I'm here to see Vin." I smile, thinking maybe politeness will help my chances.

The men give each other a knowing look and then turn their glares back to me. "Is he expecting you?" one of them asks.

"Are you guys twins?" I blurt out randomly, because the question is seriously on my mind right now. They look the same, dress the same. They have the same mannerisms too.

"Is Vin expecting you?" The second man repeats the question I failed to answer.

"No, but if you tell him Cammi is here, he'll want to see me," I attempt to explain.

"Yeah, they all think that." The first guy laughs.

"Let her in." This comes from a deep, gravelly voice behind the gate.

"Sure thing, Santo. Girl says she's here for Vin." The second man presses a button that makes the gates open.

"She's his girlfriend. Put her on the list," Santo says. I recognise him from the cemetery. He was the one who was digging up the grave earlier today.

I walk through the gates, stopping in front of Vin's brother. "Thank you," I tell him.

"He really not expecting you?"

I shake my head. "He... uh... usually comes to my place. But he's not... I don't think he should be alone right now."

Santo nods his head. "What you saw today... I..."

"I didn't see anything," I quickly cut him off. "Other than someone drowning in his grief. I'm really sorry."

Santo's features soften ever so slightly. "Thank

you," he says, pausing before adding, "Vin... How is he really?"

How is Vin? If I'm honest, he's struggling. But I'm not about to tell a single soul that. Not unless I thought it would help him. And right now, I don't.

"I think that's something you need to ask Vin yourself."

"I'm asking you. You're close with him. I thought I was, but I missed something I never should have fucking missed. So, again, how is he doing?" Santo repeats, his tone hardened.

"Honestly, he has good days and bad. But I can't tell you anything. I won't betray his trust. If he wants people to know something, he'll tell them. I'm sorry."

The surprised look on Santo's face tells me the guy's not used to hearing no. "Okay then. Just... whatever you're doing, keep doing it."

I nod my head and continue up the front steps of the house. Before I reach for the knob, the large wooden door swings open. And another man in a matching black suit stands on the other side. "Come on in," he says.

I've heard the stories about Vin's family. I've been here before, seen how tight security is firsthand. But showing up alone? Being in this house? With all the men in black suits standing guard...

Well, you'd have to be stupid to not believe all the rumours. I haven't really thought too much about them. I don't know if I care about what his family does, or if I should. It doesn't involve me, and I know that Vin loves all of his brothers. And judging by the brief interaction I just had with Santo, they are fiercely protective of Vin too.

After thanking the suited-up hulk, I make my way upstairs and stop outside of Vin's bedroom door. Suddenly feeling full of nerves. What if he really just wants to be alone and doesn't want me here? He could send me away.

Shit. Maybe I should have called first.

The door opens and a shirtless, restless-looking Vin stands in front of me. "Cammi? You okay?" he asks, running his eyes all over me.

"Can I come in?"

Vin steps to the side, giving me space to walk into his room.

"Close the door," I tell him as I make my way over to his bed. I slide my feet out of my shoes and crawl up on the mattress, laying my head on his pillow.

"What are you doing here, Cammi?" he questions from where he's now standing on the other side of the bed.

"You didn't come to my place," I explain simply.

"I'm really not good company right now." Vin turns around and walks over to his dresser. He picks up that little tin. I know what's in it, and I also know that he thinks he needs it.

"Vin, I need you to come and lie down with me. I need you to hold me." As much as I try to keep the desperation out of my voice, I know it's there. I can hear it.

Vin sets the tin back down on the dresser and comes over to the bed. Then he climbs on and curls up next to me while his fingers brush along the side of my face. "What's wrong?"

"I feel like you're slipping away from me. I can't lose you, Vin." I move over so my body is pressed right up against his.

"You are never going to lose me, Cammi. I'm just... I don't want you to see me when I'm at my worst."

"That's exactly when I should see you, Vin. That's what girlfriends are for, you know. To be there for their boyfriends when they need them."

"Yeah, but I need you all the fucking time. I'm a selfish asshole, Cammi, but I will not be a burden on you."

He thinks he's a burden? Well, that's just stupid. I've never heard anything more ridiculous.

"Wait... Do you think I'm a burden on you?" I sputter.

"Fuck no. You are a lot of things, Cammi. A burden is not one of them," he says.

"I love you," I tell him.

"And I love you. Which is why I don't want my issues to become yours."

"I've already jumped in, Vin. There's no climbing back out of that hole for me. I will sell my soul if it means being with you."

"That's what I'm afraid of. You can't do that. Your soul is pure. Let's keep it that way."

"My soul will be just fine as long as I have you. Now, can you please wrap your arms around me and close your eyes? Let's sleep."

"Cammi? Ask me," he says.

"Vin, can you kiss me?" I smile, and Vin gently presses his lips onto mine.

"Thank you for coming over," he says against my mouth.

"I will always be here when you need me," I tell him.

Chapter Seventeen

There's a saying about how bad shit always seems to happen in threes. Over the last couple of weeks, my family has had two. First, my sister-in-law was attacked. And then, one of my brothers got fucking locked up.

Gio is still in Sydney. Dealing with everything.

Trying to get Gabe out. My big brother is confident that this shit is only temporary, insisting that Gabe will be freed in no time. I hope he's right. But until that happens, it's me, Santo, Marcel, and Eloise at the house. Oh, and Daisy—Gabe's girlfriend. She's a mess and I'm doing my best to split myself between everyone who needs me. Cammi included. It's fucking hard. But family is family, and I'll find a way to manage.

Cammi has been my rock over the last few weeks. If God designed the perfect girlfriend, it was her. I don't have to explain shit. She just gets it. Considering she's an only child and comes from a small family, I appreciate how tolerant she is of mine. I want to show her just how grateful I am. I've planned a date night. It's out of my comfort zone. I'm not romantic like Gio. He's got the romance shit down to a T. He's always making grand gestures for El.

And I want to try to be like that too. For Cammi. I don't want her to miss out on anything, which is why I'm standing at her front door, about to knock and meet her parents for the first time. I'm fucking nervous. I get that no father in their right mind would want their daughter to be dating a De Bellis. We're known around town as not exactly being on the up-and-up. And now, with the news of Gabe's arrest and pending charges hitting the papers, it's probably the worst time to do any of this.

The door opens, and Cammi stands there in a white sundress that reaches her ankles. She has strappy little gold sandals on her feet. "Hey," she breathes.

"Hey yourself. You look beautiful." I hand her the flowers I picked up on the way. Rainbow roses, because no matter how dark my days are, Cammi is the rainbow after the storm.

"Thank you. Come in. I'll put these in a vase. Then we can go," she says.

"Are your parents home?" I ask her.

"My mum is around here somewhere. My dad's at work."

And just like that, a huge weight is lifted off my shoulders. I don't have to meet my girlfriend's father today.

"You want to meet my mum?" Cammi questions as I follow her into the kitchen.

"Do you want me to meet your mum?" I throw back.

"It doesn't bother me. She's out there." Cammi points to the window that overlooks the backyard. A woman in her forties is bent over, digging weeds out of a garden.

I glance back in Cammi's direction. "Did your parents have you when they were ten?"

"What? No." She laughs.

"Your mum looks really young." I don't know what I was expecting, but it wasn't... this.

"Yeah, they were teen parents. Not ten, though," Cammi explains. "Let's get out of here. We can do the *meet the parents* thing another time."

Sounds like a fucking fantastic idea to me. "Lead the way." I follow Cammi through the house and out to my car before opening the passenger side door for her.

"Where are we going?" she asks as I slide behind the wheel.

"Dinner," I tell her.

"But where?" She tries again.

"Cammi, it's not a surprise if I tell you."

"I can act surprised when we get there," she deadpans.

I shake my head and laugh as I reach over. I'm about to pick up her hand when I stop. I've done it once before without asking her, without getting her permission. And although she doesn't need it, I still do. I still need to hear that she wants me to touch her. That I'm not like *them*. That I'm not touching her against her will.

"Vin, can you hold my hand? Please," Cammi asks with a smile.

I hate that I need this from her, but I love that she somehow knows. She doesn't complain or try to push me past it. She just accepts me... and my quirks. I really do believe she's a saint, and no one will ever be able to convince me otherwise.

I entwine my fingers with hers and instantly get that sense of peace that washes over me every time we touch.

I made a booking at one of the nicest restaurants in town. It's not somewhere I've been before but I do know Gio has taken Eloise here a few times. I pull to a stop out front, get out of the car, and hand the keys to the valet. By the time I reach Cammi's door, she's already standing on the kerb looking towards the restaurant.

"Vin, I'm not really dressed for a place like this," she whispers.

"You look gorgeous," I tell her.

She glances over at me with slightly pinkened cheeks. "Thank you, but still... this looks... fancy."

"You hate it." I sigh. I really thought this was

what I needed to do to step up my game in the romance department.

"No, I love it. I just feel like I don't really belong here," she says.

"You belong anywhere you want to be, Cammi. You're a De Bellis now." I hold out my hand and wait for her to reach out and grab it.

"Did we get married and I forgot?" She raises a questioning brow.

"Not yet, but we will one day. Might as well get used to it now," I say.

"Mr De Bellis, welcome. Your table is ready." The host leads us to a private area towards the back of the room. There are three other tables in this little corner with other couples already filling the seats.

I pull Cammi's chair out for her. Everyone is looking at us. It's because they know who I am, and within minutes, the streets will know who Cammi is too.

"Do me a favour? Don't go anywhere alone for a while," I tell her.

"Where would I go? I'm always with you or the girls?" she says.

"I know. It's just... some people don't like my family and I didn't think... I should have considered what it meant to come here. I don't want to scare you, but when word gets out on the streets that we're together... well, I don't want anyone thinking they can target you. That's all." I try to explain it, downplay it. But after what happened to Eloise, I'm not taking any chances. Cammi should know the dangers of this world.

"I get it," she says. But I don't think she really does.

"Compliments of the chef, sir." A waiter comes over with a bottle of Dom. He picks up a champagne flute, fills it, and sets it down in front of Cammi before doing the same for me.

"Thank you." I vaguely pay him attention as he places the bottle in the ice bucket and walks off.

"Do they know we're underage?" Cammi whispers across the table.

I laugh. "They don't care. Perks of being a De Bellis." I lift my glass and wait for her to do the same. "I love you, Cammi. More than I've ever loved anything in my life."

"I feel it too," she replies while tapping her glass with mine.

"Get me another, boy," a familiar voice calls out from behind me, and my entire body goes rigid. Sweat forms on my forehead.

No, this cannot be happening here. Not right now.

I want to give Cammi romance. She deserves fucking romance with a normal boyfriend. Not with someone who's so fucked up they can't go out to dinner without hearing voices in their head.

And then I hear it again. "Just leave the whole bottle."

I never saw their faces. But I did hear the voices —all of their voices—and I'll never forget that accent. That thick, Russian accent.

"Vin, what's wrong?" Cammi asks, drawing me from my thoughts.

"I can't..." I shake my head. "We need to go." I cannot sit here. I cannot be in the same room as this man. I will not. My hand clenches around the steak knife on the table. I have a better idea. "I'll be right back."

I push up from my seat, with the knife still clutched in my hand, and quickly turn around. The fucker is talking, which makes him easy to identify. I walk up behind him, pressing the serrated edge to his throat.

"You are going to stand up and walk through that kitchen to the back alley without saying a fucking word," I hiss into his ear.

The second man at the table looks at me, jumps

up from his seat, and leaves. Good. No one is coming to save this asshole.

"Get the fuck up now," I grunt in his ear. My stomach churns, bile threatening to come up, and my hands are shaking. Being near him makes me physically ill. I have to fight to stay in the present, to not get dragged back into the past. He can't fucking hurt me now.

Without a word, the fucker pushes his chair back and stands. "Through the kitchen and out the fucking back door," I growl. I've felt a thirst for blood before. But what I feel right now is more than that. I want his blood, but I also want to rip his depraved fucking soul from his body and return it to the devil himself.

The Russian starts walking and I follow close behind him, adrenaline pumping through my veins and increasing with each step I take. I've thought about this moment often, what I'd do if I ever found any of them. I guess I'm about to find out.

The fat fucker slams the back door open so the heavy metal hits the brick wall. Then he spins around, his hands raised like he's ready to take me on. I close the distance with a laugh. It's fucking funny that he thinks he's any match for me now. My booted foot lifts off the ground, landing in the middle of his chest. He stumbles backwards three steps before he regains his balance.

"You know who I am, and you know why you're about to die by my hands," I tell him.

"Fuck you, boy," he sneers.

The little composure I had snaps, and I find myself slamming my boot against his gut before landing it on the backs of his ankles. This time, he can't stay upright and hits the ground. I jump on top of his body, bringing the steak knife to his throat. I make a swift slice, right across the front. Blood sprays out everywhere as the fucker struggles to grab at the wound. It's pointless, though. There's no stopping the blood flow.

None of it is as satisfying as I imagined it would be. It's too quick. Too merciful a death. So I grasp the knife in my fist and bring it down, slamming the tip into his chest before pulling it back up again. I repeat the process over and over. It's still not enough.

"Vin?" I look up and see Cammi standing right in front of me. Watching me. Her eyes wide and her face pale.

I open my mouth to say something but I can't get any words out. I stand and kick at the now lifeless body before taking a step forward. Towards Cammi.

The knife drops to the ground. I hear it clank. But I don't remember letting it go.

Cammi closes the gap between us. "I'm going to hug you. Is that okay?" she asks. I nod my head. She wraps her arms around my waist and presses her face against my chest. "It's going to be okay."

I hold her tight, even though I know it's not going to be okay. She just saw me kill a man.

Cammi lifts her face to look up at me. "It's going to be okay," she repeats.

My arms drop from around her waist, and I take two steps backwards while shaking my head. "No, fuck. Cammi, I'm so sorry," I tell her.

She's covered in gore, her white dress now stained with the blood of a monster. I did that to her. I did *this* to her. It's all my fault.

Chapter Eighteen

Cammi

"Vin, I think you should call one of your brothers." I can see him unravelling. I don't know what happened, why he did what he just did.

When I saw Vin disappear into the kitchen with that man, I got up and followed them. I knew something was wrong at the table. He was sweating and his hands were shaking. I've watched it happen before, and it's always been when his mind gets taken back to that time...

"You need to leave, Cammi," Vin says. "You can't be here. You can't..." He shakes his head.

"Yeah, too bad. I'm not leaving. Give me your phone." I hold out my hand and have to admit I'm surprised when Vin pulls his phone from his pocket and passes it to me.

I wipe the screen down the fabric of my dress, attempting to clean off some of the blood—although it doesn't do much—and quickly push past it. At this point, both Vin and I are covered from head to toe. And right now, I need to help him. He's not going to let me touch him. I can tell. I scroll through his contacts until I find Santo's name and hit the *call* button.

"Hey," Santo answers.

"Hey, it's Cammi. I need help. Vin needs help," I say, my words rushed.

"Where are you?" Santo asks.

"We're in the alley behind Hall's restaurant," I tell him.

"I'll be right there. Where's Vin?"

"He's here. He just... He needs help right now."

"Okay." The line cuts out. I return Vin's phone and he tucks it into his pocket without looking at me. "Your brother's coming. It's going to be okay, Vin. We are going to be okay." I take a step closer to him, and he steps back again.

"Don't come near me, Cammi. I did this to you." He's staring at my dress. It's covered in blood.

"Vin, I'm fine. You didn't do anything to me. I'm right here," I tell him. My words have no impact. He's staring at me with so much remorse now.

"You can't be here, Cammi. This wasn't supposed to touch you. I don't want the monsters to touch you," he whispers as he takes another step away from me.

I sit down, right in the middle of the alleyway, in the dark, next to the body of the man my boyfriend just killed. "I'm not going anywhere," I say more firmly. If he wants me to leave, then he'll have to move me himself. Something we both know he won't do. Not unless I ask him to.

We stay staring at each other in silence until two of Vin's brothers come running towards us.

"Vin?" The one I recognise to be Marcel is the first to speak. "What happened?" he asks, looking around. His glare lands on the dead guy before flicking back in my direction.

Santo squats down so he's eye level with me. "Are you okay?"

"I'm fine. I called you here to help Vin. Not me." I push to my feet and Santo follows me up.

"Take her home," Vin says. "I don't want her here." His voice has gone cold. Hard. I've never heard him sound like this before.

"I'm not going..." I start to argue, only to slam my mouth shut when Vin looks at me.

"I don't fucking want you here, Cammi. You need to leave," he growls.

"Too bloody bad." My hands land on my hips. I'm stubborn at the best of times. But when it comes to Vin, I might just be finding new heights of obstinance I'm willing to go.

"What happened here?" Marcel asks again.

"I heard his voice. In the restaurant. He was... He..." Vin can't get the words out, but he doesn't need to. We all know what he's trying to say. I want to go over and wrap my arms around him. He needs to know that I'm still one hundred percent in this. I don't care about what happened. I care about him. That's all.

"Okay. We need to get this cleaned up. I have to make a call." Marcel reaches into his pocket. "I might need your help," Marcel says into his phone seconds after he dials.

"Why?" Vin's oldest brother's voice shouts through the speaker.

"I just killed a Russian..." Marcel sighs, and my brows draw down. *Why is he taking the blame?*

"I'll be right there. Drop me a pin," the voice replies, and Marcel cuts the call.

"Get out of here. Both of you. You were never here, got me?" he stresses, and I nod my head.

"Marcel, you can't take the fall for this. It's on me, not you," Vin argues.

"Yeah? Well, either I tell Gio it was me, or you explain to him why his kid brother killed a Russian made man?" Marcel grunts. "And I promise you don't want to do that, Vin. Now, get out of here. I'll sort it."

A Russian made man? Vin killed a Russian mafia member. Is this going to come back on him? There were a lot of people in the restaurant, a lot of people who saw them walk out here together. "Witnesses." The word slips out of my mouth before I realise I'm speaking.

"What?" Santo asks. He's the only one close enough to hear me.

"In the restaurant, there were a lot of people..." I explain. "A lot of witnesses."

"It's okay. No one is stupid enough to say anything," Santo tells me.

"Take her the fuck home. Get her out of here." Vin throws an arm in my direction. He's pacing up and down the alleyway while tugging on the ends of his hair.

"Let's go. You being here right now isn't helping him," Santo whispers.

"I'm not leaving him." I readjust my arms, crossing them tighter over my chest. I take a step towards Vin.

Marcel steps in front of me. "He wants you to leave. Santo will take you home. I've got this."

"I... Vin? Don't make me leave you right now," I plead with him.

"You should never have been with me, Cammi," Vin says, his eyes devoid of emotion before he turns his back to me.

I might not have been the one he stabbed, but I sure as hell feel like I have a huge gaping wound in my chest right now. I can also feel the tears building. I will not cry. This isn't about me. I won't put that added pressure on him.

I pivot on my shoe to look up at Santo. "Can you take me home? Please?"

"Let's go." He nods, and without looking back, I follow him over to the blacked-out SUV idling in the distance.

Santo didn't take me home, though. He brought me to the De Bellis estate. Told me to get cleaned up, explaining he'd drop me off after. Which is why I'm now standing in Vin's bedroom. Alone. I take a deep breath, make my way into his attached bathroom, reach a hand into the stall, and turn on the shower.

It's strange being in here without him.

I didn't want to leave. I wanted to be the one he sought out, the one he took comfort in. When he looked at me like he was disgusted by me, my heart shuttered. I've done my best to keep the tears at bay. Until now.

Stripping off my ruined dress, I slide my panties down my legs and step into the shower. Immediately falling to the tiled floor as I let everything pour out. My own heartbreak. The ache I feel for Vin. The frustration that I can't get rid of his nightmares for him. The anger I have towards his father for doing what he did, and the men who did those horrible things to him. I want to be able to wave a magic wand and make it all go away. Seeing him hurting *hurts* me. I can't pretend to understand or feel even a tenth of his pain, his trauma. But I physically ache when I see him so broken.

I bring my knees up and rest my forehead on them. The hot water washes over me while the red stains the water before disappearing down the drain. I need someone to tell me how to help him. I can't figure it out on my own. I'm in over my head. I can admit that. I also can't ask anyone. If I did, I'd be betraying him and that's something I will never do.

I'm not sure how long I've been sitting in this shower. But, eventually, I manage to pull myself together. I stand and wash myself off with Vin's soap. His scent surrounds me, and a fresh set of tears falls. I swipe at my face before turning off the faucet and grabbing a towel. Drying off quickly then wrapping the plush material around my body.

I probably shouldn't, but I help myself to Vin's wardrobe. I pull one of his hoodies over my head. It reaches my knees. It's basically a dress. And when I walk out again, something shiny on his dresser table catches my eye. The little tin that he carries around with him. I've never smoked a day in my life, but right now seems like a good time to give it a go. It works for Vin, helps him numb the pain. Which is something I need. I need to not feel.

So I open the tin and take out a joint. I search for a light but there isn't one. I move over to the bedside drawer. Open it and find a few lighters, snagging one before I walk out onto the balcony and shut the door behind me.

Sitting on the small outdoor sofa, I put the joint in my mouth and light it up, inhaling as much of the smoke as I can. My chest burns and I cough up a lung while exhaling. But I am not deterred as I puff on it again. A little slower this time. I still cough but nowhere near as much. By the time I get near the end of the joint, I'm starting to feel lighter. And I finally understand the appeal.

The door to the balcony opens, and I look up to see a very pissed-off Vin. He appears freshly showered. *How long has he been here?*

"What the fuck are you doing?" he snaps, reaching out to snatch the joint out of my hand.

Chapter Nineteen

I wasn't expecting Cammi to be here. Why the fuck my brother brought her back to our place, I have no idea. He should have taken her home. To her house. I certainly wasn't expecting to find her out on my balcony smoking fucking weed.

I rip the joint out of her hand and put it out in

the ashtray I have on the table. Although she's already smoked just about the whole thing by the looks of it.

"I was enjoying that," Cammi says, blinking up at me. Her eyes are fucking bloodshot. And I can't tell if it's because she's stoned or because she's been crying...

"Yeah, not anymore. Get up. I'm taking you home," I tell her.

"You're taking me home?" she questions and then laughs. "I am home, Vin. Home is wherever you are. And you're here. So really, you don't need to take me anywhere."

"Cammi, I can't do this to you. I won't do this to you. Let me take you home." I'm practically pleading with her. I need to get her as far away from me as possible. I knew I'd eventually take her down with me. And now that I have, the only way I can fix this is to let her go.

"Do what?" she asks.

"Ruin you," I tell her.

"You haven't ruined me, Vin," she says, her ass firmly planted in the seat. It's clear she has no intention of moving.

"Haven't I? Look at yourself, Cammi. You're stoned. And you've been crying. Just an hour ago, you were covered in blood. The blood of the man you watched me kill. So, yes, I have ruined you, and I won't keep doing it. We can't do this anymore, Cammi. It's not right." My heart feels like it's tearing apart as the words leave my mouth. But I need to put her first.

"I'm fine. In fact, I've never felt better in my life. I want you to come over here and kiss me, Vin. Kiss me like it really is the last time you will," she says.

"I can't..." I shake my head. It goes against every-thing I feel to deny her that request. But I know if I kiss her, I won't want to stop. "Get up, Cammi. I need to take you home."

"If you want me to get up, you're going to have to make me. You're going to have to come over here and move me yourself, because I'm not leaving, Vin. I don't know what's going on in that head of yours, but this is not the end of us." Cammi folds her arms over her chest. She fucking knows I can't just pick her up and drag her out of here.

"Fine, *I'll* leave." I turn and walk through the door. If she won't let me take her home, she can stay here as long as she wants. She'll have to go eventually.

"What? No." Cammi comes rushing through the door behind me. "Don't do this, Vin."

"I have to," I tell her.

"No, you don't. I'm begging you not to do this. You promised me. You said you'd love me forever, remember? I'm not dead yet. This isn't forever yet." Cammi wipes the wetness from her cheeks. She's fucking crying. All I want to do is wrap her in my arms and tell her everything is going to be okay.

I can't do that, because it's not okay. None of this is okay. I'm not okay.

"I will love you forever, Cammi. I just can't be with you," I tell her honestly. There won't be a single day I won't love this girl. She's part of me. The good part. And I want to keep her that way. If I stay with her, if I continue this relationship with her, I'm going to destroy her.

"Telling me we can't be together isn't loving me, Vin," she says. "If you loved me, you wouldn't be trying to get rid of me."

"It's because I love you that I'm breaking up with you," I attempt to explain. I don't want to hurt her, but I can't let her become like me.

"You're b... b... breaking up with me." She stutters out the words, her voice clogged with emotion. And then she falls to the floor.

Her entire frame heaves with her sobs, and my heart explodes, my body taking the force of the shrapnel tearing out of my chest. Everything I've experienced, the pain, the torture, all of it pales in comparison to what I'm feeling right now. Seeing what I've done to her.

I drop to my knees in front of her, reaching out to touch her, comfort her, only to quickly pull my hands back. I can't. I want to, and I fucking can't. Cammi deserves so much more than to be stuck in a relationship with someone who can't even bring themselves to touch her without her having to ask.

"Cammi, can I pick you up and take you to bed?"

She looks up at me, her face showing all the emotion she's feeling. "Yes."

I push to my feet, bend down, and pick her up. Her arms wrap around my neck, and she holds on tight, tighter than I've ever felt her hold on to me before. I look at my bed and then decide I can't put her there. I walk out of my room instead, right into one of the guest rooms, and lay her down on the bed. Her arms stay wrapped around my neck when I go to stand up.

"Cammi, I need you to let go," I tell her.

"I can't. How can I let you go, Vin? How can you let us go so easily?" she asks through her sobs.

Reaching behind my neck, I take hold of her hands and pry them off me. Against my better judgement, I lie down next to her and she shuffles over until her head is resting on my shoulder. My arm closes around her back. "This is the hardest fucking thing I've ever had to do, Cammi. There is nothing easy about it."

"What did I do wrong? Just tell me what I did, and I'll fix it," she says.

"You are perfect, fucking amazing, Cammi. You didn't do anything wrong."

"I love you, Vin. I don't care about any of it. I love you. *Please*, I'm begging you not to do this."

"I love you." I can't give her what she's asking for, and I won't make any false promises. What I can guarantee is that I will never love anyone else the way I love this girl.

I don't know how long it takes. But eventually Cammi falls asleep. Her body stills and her breathing evens out. I don't want to get out of this bed. But I can't stay here either.

I slowly slide out from underneath her and fall off the edge of the mattress. Then I stand up, walk out of the room, and close the door. I can't bring myself to step away though. I slide to the floor, lean my back against the wall, and close my eyes. Only to open them again when the image of Cammi in a white dress covered in blood fills my mind.

"What are you doing sitting in the hallway?" This comes from Gio.

I look up at my oldest brother. I know what I have to do. I have to tell him. I can't let Marcel take the fall for what I did. I'm not an asshole. I am thankful to my brothers for keeping my secret. But this is on me. Not them. "Can we talk?"

Gio's brows draw down. "Always. Here?" he asks while gesturing to the hallway.

"Your office?" I suggest.

"Let's go." He spins around and walks back in the direction he was going.

Pushing myself up to my feet, I stand and follow him. This is shitty timing. My big brother is dealing with a lot right now. His wife is recovering from her assault. Gabe is still locked up. And now I'm going to drop this bomb on him. Out of all my brothers, I know Gio is going to take it the hardest, blame himself the most. I don't have any resentment towards them. They had no idea what was happening. The old man hid it well.

Gio closes the door, and I peer up to see Santo and Marcel already inside. "What's going on?" Marcel looks directly at me.

"I have to tell him," I say.

"You sure?" Marcel asks. "I don't give a shit, Vin. I can handle this."

"Someone want to fill me in on what the fuck is going on with all the side-bar conversation?" Gio's tone is demanding. He leans against the front of his desk, his hands in his pockets. He looks calm and relaxed, but it's a mask.

I square my shoulders and meet his eye. "Marcel didn't kill that Russian tonight. I did."

"You what? Why the fuck would you kill a member of the Bratva?" Gio shouts.

"I... ah... Dad." The moment I say the words, my brother's body stiffens while Marcel and Santo stare at me with fucking pity, anger, remorse. "When I was twelve, the old man took me to that house. That's how I knew the address..."

"They were running a child sex ring out of there. Why the fuck would that stupid son of a bitch take his twelve-year-old son to a place like that?"

"He sold me. To them. Once a month, he'd lock me in a room and men would..." I squeeze my eyes shut and shake my head. The only thing worse than what happened to me there is seeing the realisation spread across my brother's face like an infectious disease. And there ain't no cure for this. When I open my eyes again, Gio appears two shades paler. I don't think I've ever seen it so fucking white before.

"He what?" His voice is low, broken. Almost as broken as I am *watching* him break. "How long?"

"Three years," I tell them.

Gio doesn't say a word. What he does do is swipe out an arm, shoving the contents of his desk onto the floor. Then he turns around. "Three fucking years. What the fuck, Vin? Why wouldn't you tell me? Us?"

"I couldn't. I didn't want it to happen to any of you," I explain.

"Fuck!" Gio picks up a bottle of whiskey and tosses it against the wall. "I'm going to kill them. Every fucking single one of them. I want their fucking heads on a spike!"

"The Russian, tonight... I heard his voice in the restaurant. I never saw their faces, just heard voices. And I snapped. I wasn't thinking, Gio. I just..."

"No!" he barks out. "Don't you fucking dare apologise. You did the right thing. And I'll make sure none of this comes back on you." Gio walks over and wraps his arms around me. "I'm sorry," he whispers. "So fucking sorry. I should have known. If I did, I would have killed the fucker sooner."

I don't know which part sets the tidal wave free,

but suddenly I'm crying for the first time in years. In my big brother's arms. A weight I've been carrying around lifts from my shoulders. I pull back and wipe at my face. I don't know what to say. A silence fills the room. All four of us just standing here, not knowing what to fucking say.

"Fuck," Santo curses under his breath. He walks over to the wet bar and picks up a bottle of Cinque. Pouring four glasses before handing one to each of us. "We will have their heads, no matter how long it takes."

I'd settle for just fucking forgetting those fucking three years of my life. But I'll also help in any way I can. "Thank you."

"You need to talk to someone," Santo grunts, and I laugh.

"I just found you talking to your fiancée's corpse. I don't think you're one to advise *me* on *my* mental health."

Santo shrugs. "Had to be sure she was dead."

"What about Daisy?" Gio suggests.

"What about her?" I ask. I've built a pretty decent rapport with Gabe's girlfriend, especially since he's been gone. She's a mess without him. I see so clearly how much she loves my brother, which means I'll do whatever I can to help her.

"I'm fine. I don't need to fucking talk to anyone," I grunt back.

"The girl in the guest room?" Gio questions. "The one you've been sneaking in and out of here. Who is she?"

"Cammi. Don't worry about her. She's not coming back after tonight," I tell him.

"I wouldn't be so sure of that," Santo says. "That girl is your ride or die, Vin."

"I know, which is exactly why she won't be back." I swallow down the contents of the glass and walk out of the office.

I've done what I had to do, so Marcel won't have to take the fall for me. Now, I need to make myself scarce. I can't be here when Cammi wakes up and starts looking for me.

Chapter Twenty

Cammi

I know I'm alone even before I pry my lashes apart and look around the room. He's gone. I've really lost him, and I don't think I can get him back.

My eyes burn with unshed tears. I'm not going to fall apart right now. I'm going to drag myself out of this bed, try to find Vin, and see if by some miracle he's had a change of heart about this *break up* thing. He calls me a saint, but if I truly were one, I'd perform that miracle myself.

I glance around the room again, the room he put me in. The fact he didn't want me in his own bed speaks volumes. Maybe I should just save face and leave. I shouldn't have to beg my boyfriend not to break up with me. Then again, if I thought it'd work, I'd get down on my hands and knees and beg him. I'd do whatever it took to get him back. I can't fathom not being with him. I also can't force him to do something he really doesn't want to do.

I'm so confused. Again, I need a *relationship for dummies* book or at the very least some kind of guide. I can't even talk to my friends about this, because I can't tell them anything about Vin. The only person I can talk to is the one person who doesn't want to talk to me right now.

Maybe we can still hang out as friends. Over the last couple of weeks, Vin's become my best friend. I can't talk to my girlfriends the way I can talk to him. And I get the feeling he doesn't talk to his friends about anything deep and personal either.

He'll agree to being friends, right? He has to.

With renewed faith and determination, I open

the door and walk out of the bedroom. I raise my hand to knock on Vin's door before I decide to reach for the knob and let myself in.

I know right away that he's not in here. But I peek into his closet and bathroom anyway. He's not on the balcony either. I do notice that the clothes I left on the bathroom floor last night are gone. So is his little silver tin. I'm not going to lie. I felt good when I smoked that joint. Right up until Vin came in and stomped all over my heart.

I can feel the tears starting to form again. I take a huge breath and straighten my shoulders. I will not crumble. He needs me. He might not want to acknowledge it, or want me around *full stop*, but he needs me.

And I need him.

I find my way downstairs and start walking through the house. No one says anything to me. I step past a few of those bulky men in suits, who all give me curious glances but don't say a single word. It's not until I walk into the kitchen that I'm stopped.

"Are you lost?" This comes from Vin's oldest brother. Gio. I haven't officially met him yet. But I know who he is. And, honestly, he's outright scary as hell.

"Ah, I was looking for Vin," I say.

"He's not here."

"What do you mean he's not here? He was here. Where is he?" My questions come out before I can think better of them.

Gio raises a single brow at me. "If Vin wants you to know where he is, you'd know," he says, bringing his cup of coffee to his lips.

"Don't be an ass," a female voice cuts in. I turn to see a beautiful brunette. Eloise, Gio's wife. Vin showed me pictures from their wedding. "He just left. But I'm sure if you call him, you can catch up with him later. You want anything to eat? Coffee?"

"Ellie, we are not turning this kitchen into a morning-after diner for all of Vin's sleepovers," Gio grunts.

My eyes close. I know Vin said he hasn't brought any girls home before. But now that he has, will he?

I can't think about that right now, or the tears really will fall.

"Ignore my brother. He lost his manners somewhere between puberty and adulthood. I'll give you a ride home," Santo says, walking in behind me.

I want to tell him that I don't need a ride home. That what I need is to find Vin. Bring up my idea of being friends. I can't fully lose him. I don't do that though. Instead, I find myself nodding. "Thank you, but I should get home," I tell Eloise.

"Anytime. Despite what my husband says, Vin doesn't have sleepovers. You're the only girl I've ever seen him bring home," she stresses to me while sending an icy glare in her husband's direction.

"I know." I try and fail to give her a smile. I know it's not her fault, but right now, I feel worse than I've ever felt in my entire life.

Thankfully, Santo doesn't try to make small talk when he drives me home. I should ask how he knew where I lived. I don't bother. It's pointless and really doesn't matter.

He stops me when I go to open the door. "Don't give up on him," he says.

"He gave up on me." My voice is quiet, and I'm struggling to keep the tears from falling.

"He's going through a lot right now. He thinks he's doing the right thing by you. Trust me, he cares about you."

"I tried to be what he needed and I'm not it," I say. "Just... if something happens, can you let me know? Call me."

Santo nods in agreement, and I climb out of the car. My mum appears in the doorway. She takes one look at me as I shuffle by her and asks, "What happened?"

I burst out in tears. She quickly rushes over and wraps her arms around me. "Oh, baby, what on earth happened?"

"I... I... love him," I cry.

"Okay. It's going to be okay. Who is *him*?" Mum guides me into the living room and sits me down on the sofa. I don't give her a name. I can't get the words out. "It might help if you talk about it."

I shake my head. "I don't want to. I just don't want to feel. I want it to stop hurting," I tell her.

"It will. I promise, baby, it will." Mum strokes my hair. I've always been able to seek comfort in my mum. But right now, it's not working. Nothing is taking the pain away.

Well, almost nothing. I just don't know how to go about getting it. Vin certainly isn't going to give it to me. I can find someone at school tomorrow to sell me some, though. I just have to get through tonight.

I can do that...

As soon as I walk on to the school grounds, I bypass my locker and head straight for the field. It's common knowledge that the stoners like to hang out under the bleachers. So that's where I'm headed.

My entire body aches. Vin didn't just break my heart; he broke *me*. Body, mind, and soul. I let myself fall so damn hard. I didn't ever stop to think about the consequences of what would happen if things ended.

Straightening my shoulders, I walk under the bleachers like I'm still the girlfriend of Vin De Bellis. Nobody says no to Vin at this school, and when he made it public I was his, I was given that same privilege. Not that I've ever used it.

"One of you is going to sell me some weed, and make sure it's decent shit," I tell the group of guys now staring back at me like I've lost my head. "Is there a problem?"

"Ah, no. Cammi. Here, on the house. Tell Vin we looked after you," one guy says before handing me a bag of green buds.

What the hell am I going to do with all this?

"Yeah, I don't want this. Just a joint. Something ready to go." I shove the bag back into his open palm.

"Here." Another guy hands me not one, but two joints.

"Thank you. Don't suppose you have a lighter?" I ask them.

The third guy passes me a lighter. After thanking him, I walk out and around the building. I don't need an audience. I'm not ashamed of smoking. I just don't want company right now.

I place the joint between my lips, light it up, and inhale. Coughing as the smoke fills my lungs. I don't like it, but I do like the effects. I want to be numb. If I have to see Vin around school and have him ignore me, then I need to just not feel.

I smoke the entire joint before shoving the second one into my bag for later. I probably should learn how to roll these things myself.

I giggle. *Damn, I do feel better.*

I slide on my sunnies as I walk back inside and head for my locker. Lauren, Devon, and Elena are all there waiting for me. "You're late. Where you been?" Devon asks.

"I was busy," I tell her.

"Busy doing what? And where's your shadow?" Lauren peers down the hall. She's looking for Vin. I can't help but follow her gaze. I don't know if I want to see him or if I'd be better off not knowing. Not that it matters. He's not there.

"I don't know where he is. We broke up," I tell

them, and all three girls stare at me. "What? It happens. I need to get to class." I pull my English books out of my locker.

"Are you okay? What happened? What did he do? I'll cut off his balls," Elena says.

"Don't do anything to him. It's fine. I'm fine. I'll talk to you all later." I turn and walk off, leaving my friends behind. I can't talk about it. I don't want to talk about it. I just need to get through today, and then tomorrow, and then the rest of my life without him.

I make my way into my English class and sit in the back row. I don't want to interact with anyone. I just want to be alone. Well, I want to be with Vin, but that's not an option. And then, as if I've conjured him up, he saunters into class and sits right bloody next to me.

My sunglasses are dark, which gives me the opportunity to steal a glance at him without him noticing. He looks as bad as I feel, which only makes me feel worse. I hate seeing him like this. More than that, I hate that he's doing this to *us*.

Chapter Twenty-One

I shouldn't be here. I should have fucking skipped today. Seeing her is both a blessing and a curse. I was desperate to see her, to check on her. But now that I have, I hate myself even more.

I fall into the seat next to hers, because fuck if

I'm going to let any other fucker get close to her. *I know.* I'm an asshole. Cammi's hiding her face behind big dark sunglasses. I don't need to see her eyes to know she's been crying, though. I can feel the pain radiating off her.

I have no one to blame except myself. I caused this. I broke her, and I'll never be able to put her back together because I can't give her what she wants. What we both want.

I need her safe. I need to not drag her any farther down into my darkness. She will get over this. She will be happy again... I hope. I know I'll never be able to move on from her, but maybe she can move on from me. She'll learn to hate me. I broke her heart. How could she not hate me?

I hate myself. I tried. I fucking wanted to be someone else for her, but I should have known. They always win.

The monsters, the nightmares. They will never let me go. Just when I think I'm breaking free, I'm pulled right back into the darkness again. And now, I've managed to get my brothers mixed up in my mess. Something I never wanted to fucking do.

I saw the way Gio looked at me this morning. I could also tell he didn't sleep last night. Thankfully, I don't think he told Eloise. She acted like nothing's changed. If she does know, she's good at hiding it. While Gio is barely controlling his rage.

I get it. If it happened to any of them, I'd be out for blood too. As it is, I want to bring Shelli back to life just to strangle her myself for what she's done to Santo. I'm not talking about the grief. That shit isn't her fault. It's our father's. I'm talking about the journal Gio and Gabe found that suggests she wasn't who any of us thought she was.

I take the chance to look across to Cammi. My mouth opens to say something before I think better of it and snap it closed.

"Ms Taylor, the glasses, lose them," the teacher calls out.

"I have a headache," Cammi says.

"Then go to the nurse."

I watch as Cammi packs up her stuff and walks out of the classroom. I'm calling bullshit on the headache. And before I can talk myself out of it, I'm on my feet following her.

I catch up to Cammi in the hall, jogging to get in front of her. She stops and stares at me from behind those fucking glasses. I reach out and snatch them off her face.

"What's wrong?" If she really is sick, I'll get the doc to check her out.

Cammi laughs. "You have to be fucking kidding me right now, Vin. What's wrong? Seriously? You're really going to stand here and ask me what's wrong?" she yells. "How about the fact that my boyfriend who I thought loved me more than life itself—*his words, not mine*—dumped me last night? Or the fact that my heart has been torn to shreds to the point I'm surprised there's even enough of it left to keep beating. To keep me alive, when right now I'd rather not be. Maybe death will be less painful than this." Her arms wave around her face. She's looking everywhere but at me. Until she does and I wish she hadn't. There is so much despair staring back at me.

She can't be serious, can she? My entire body goes cold at the thought of her doing something to end her life. I won't let that happen. I'm completely speechless. I don't know what to say to her right now.

"Why are you even here, Vin? To torture me? To remind me of what I can't have? To make me look like an idiot in front of the entire school?" she hisses.

"I'm here because I want to make sure you're okay, Cammi," I tell her.

"Well, newsflash! I'm not okay. I had an idea, you know. When I woke up yesterday, I thought: *You know what? I can live without being with Vin. Maybe we can still be friends. Maybe that can be enough.*

Maybe whatever we had can shift into something else," she says. "But that's not going to work for me. I can't look at you and not hurt."

Cammi walks past me. I follow her because I don't know what else to fucking do. Her words repeat in my head. *Maybe death will be less painful...*

I'm freaking out. I can't let her think like that.

Cammi walks out the back door, through the fence and into the park. The same path I took her down the first day I spoke to her. The day all of this started. I should have kept watching her from a distance. I knew getting close to her would only end in disaster.

Nothing good ever happens in my world. People like me shouldn't be loved. She shouldn't love me. If loving me is destroying her, I need to find a way to make her hate me.

Cammi sits down at the same tree and pulls something out of her bag. Not something, a fucking blunt.

"Where the fuck did you get that?" I ask, reaching out and snatching it right out of her hand. "Is this why your eyes are red? You're fucking high?" I'm yelling. I'm fucking furious. Whoever the fuck gave her this is going to be dealt with.

"What's your problem? You smoke all the time," she says.

"My problem is you don't smoke, and this isn't the answer, Cammi," I tell her.

"Seems to numb me pretty good. I want it back." She holds out a hand, like there's actually a fucking chance in hell that I'm going to give it back to her.

I shove the joint into my pocket and sit across from her. "I'm not giving it back. Whatever you're feeling, take it out on me. It's my fault. I get that. But I'm doing this for you, Cammi."

"No, you're doing it *for you*. You're running, Vin. You're giving up on fighting for your own happiness, and you know what the worst part of it is?"

"What?"

"You're letting them win. The monsters, they're winning," she says.

I can't argue with her, because she's fucking right. "I don't want to see you hurting," I tell her. "I can't do this, Cammi. We need to find a new way to coexist and you need to stop trying to mask your pain with fucking drugs." I know I'm the biggest fucking hypocrite in the world right now.

"I wouldn't have to mask the pain if you didn't cause it, Vin. You have the power to take it all away. Tell me you've changed your mind. That it was a momentary lapse in judgement and we can just go back to being us." Cammi looks at me with so much hope in her fucking eyes.

"Let me drive you home. You don't have to be here today," I tell her.

"I tried. I love you, but I guess it wasn't enough. For that, I'm sorry. I thought if I loved you enough, you would see that you were worthy of being loved. I'm sorry I couldn't be enough." Cammi pushes to her feet. "Don't follow me. Being around you isn't helping me right now," she says, and then I watch her walk away.

"Wanna tell me why we're heading to the bleachers?" Dash asks.

"Because some fucker gave Cammi pot and I want to know who it was. So I can cave their fucking heads in."

"Wait... Why is Cammi smoking pot all of a sudden? What the fuck did you do?" Marcus chimes in.

"I had to break up with her," I hiss, hating the words as they fall from my tongue.

"You dumped her? What the fuck for? Even a blind guy can see how much that girl loves you, man," Dash says.

"It doesn't matter. What matters right now is finding out who supplied her, and making sure it doesn't fucking happen again." I walk under the bleachers and all the stoners turn to face me. "Who the fuck supplied Cammi today?" I ask, anger vibrating off me.

They share a glance, none of them saying a single word to me.

"I asked a fucking question. If someone doesn't answer me, I'm going to assume it was all of you." I remove my blazer and hand it to Marcus. I then proceed to roll up the sleeves of my white school shirt. I fucking hate this uniform, but I don't want the hassle of buying a new one because I got blood all over it.

"It was me. I thought she was getting it for you," Hunter says.

"You thought fucking wrong." I snap right before my right fist connects with his jaw. The fucker falls to the ground. Doesn't even try to fight back. "Any of you sell to her again and I'll make sure you're drinking through a fucking straw. Got me?"

"Got it." I hear one after the other stutter in my direction.

Satisfied that they're not going to give Cammi any more weed, I grab my blazer off Marcus and walk out.

"So... you gonna tell us what happened with Cammi or not?" Dash asks.

"Not," I grunt.

"Okay, cool, man. Whatever. But you know, if you need to talk, we'll listen," he says. "In the meantime, I vote we go to my house. Party for three."

I can't think of a better idea. I should go home first and check on my brothers. "I'll meet you there."

The moment I walk back into the building, I know she's here. I glance to my left and see her standing at Elena's locker. *Fuck me.* I shrug my blazer back on and keep walking. Forcing myself to brush right past her. Pretending she's not there. Pretending she doesn't fucking exist. I need to make her hate me. It'll be easier for her if she does.

Chapter Twenty-Two

Cammi

I packed a bag as soon as I got home. I can't be here. I cannot go to school every day and see him. I have an aunt in Sydney. I'm going to go and stay with her. Finish out my school year online. I've got it planned out. I just need to get my parents on board with the idea.

Which is why I'm now standing in front of them with a fully packed bag and printed-out plane ticket. I might have already called my aunt, who was thrilled to have me. My mum doesn't want me to go. But as soon as my dad found out I had my heart broken by a boy, he was all for me getting away for a while. I think his enthusiasm has more to do with putting distance between me and *that boy* than it has to do with healing my heart.

I still haven't given them a name. I don't want them to have a negative opinion of Vin. He's not a bad guy. He's lost and confused right now. But he's a good person deep down. I know, in his mind, he's doing what's right for me. I'm not going to try to convince him that he's not anymore.

I got the message loud and clear when he walked right past me in the hall and acted like I didn't exist. It's going to be easier for both of us if I remove myself from the equation. As effortless as Vin made it look to ignore me, I know it wasn't. I saw the way his pinkie finger tapped rapidly along his thigh, the way his chest rose and fell quicker than it normally would.

He can pretend like it doesn't hurt better than I can. Then again, he's had a lot of years to build a mask of indifference. I've never had to look at the person that my body craves and not be able to touch them.

How do you come to terms with the fact that you love the one person responsible for hurting you in the worst way? If I could hate Vin, I still wouldn't. Because the love I feel for him, the connection we have—despite him trying to cut through it and destroy it—is something I will always treasure.

I get it. I'm probably a sucker for punishment at this point, and some would say I have no sense of self-worth. But they don't know... They don't know what it's like to be loved by him. To be the object of his affections.

When I was with him, it was like I was wrapped in a big fluffy blanket and nothing could ever get to me. I felt more loved than I ever have, more desired. Vin made me feel like I was truly something special, his own personal saint.

It's the kind of love people spend their entire lives dreaming about finding, and I was lucky enough to find it so young. Now I just have to spend the rest of my time here reminding myself that it is better to have loved and lost than to never have loved at all. At least, that's what people say. I'm hoping those people are right.

"Are you sure?" my mum asks, pulling me from my thoughts.

"I'm sure. Besides, it will give me a chance to get used to Sydney before uni starts next year," I tell her, trying to put a positive spin on the whole thing.

"I don't like it. I was meant to have at least four more months with you," she says.

"I'm only going an hour and a bit away," I remind her.

"On a plane, Cammi, *an hour and a bit* on a plane," she corrects me.

"I'm sorry. I just can't stay here." I can feel my bottom lip tremble.

"Okay, whoever this asshole is, Cammi, he doesn't deserve your tears. And if you give me a name, I'll tear him a new one," my dad says.

"Thanks, Dad. Can you give me a ride to the airport instead?" I quickly change the topic because no way in hell am I giving them Vin's name.

The De Bellis family is notorious around Melbourne, and if my parents knew I was mixed up with them, that I'd witnessed my boyfriend kill someone, they'd have me on a flight to some isolated country with a new identity.

"Sure. Come on, let's go before I change my mind," Dad says.

"I'm going to say goodbye here. I won't be able to not get on that plane with you if I go to the airport." Mum wraps her arms around me. "Whatever you need, you call me. I promise, it doesn't feel like it now, but it will get easier," she whispers.

I want to ask her how she knows that, how someone who is still with their high school sweetheart could know anything about the heartbreak I'm feeling right now. I don't do that. I know she means well, and she really would do anything for me. Like let me leave home so close to the end of senior year.

"I know. I'm going to be okay. I promise," I tell her.

The ride to the airport was quiet. My dad kept looking over at me with so many questions in his eyes. I'm thankful he didn't ask any of them. Now, I'm standing in the airport about to go through security, and he looks like he's about to burst into tears.

"Thanks for bringing me. I'll call you when I get to Aunt Stacey's." I wrap my arms around my dad.

"I hate seeing you so hurt, Cammi. Let me at least break one of his knees," he grumbles.

"I'm okay. Promise. I will be at least." I smile at him. "Go and make sure mum's not falling apart too much back at the house. I expect she's baked at least two dozen cookies by now."

217

"And probably cupcakes," Dad adds. "Call as soon as you get there. Love you, Cammi."

"Love you too, Dad." I kiss his cheek, then turn and walk towards the line for security.

An hour later, I'm sitting on the plane about to turn my phone onto flight mode. Before I do, I open Vin's contact and type out a message to him.

ME:

> I wanted to let you know that I'm leaving. I can't continue to walk through school acting like everything is okay. Today was hard. Tomorrow won't be any easier. I'm taking myself out of a situation that's not good for me. You will probably say you don't care, but we both know you'd be lying. I love you, Vin. I will always love you. I wish things were different.

After hitting send, I switch off my phone. The only reason I let him know I was leaving was because I know he'll look for me when he notices I don't show up to school. He will no doubt stress about where I am. The last thing I need is for him to show up on my parents' doorstep.

Leaning my head back against the seat, I close my eyes. *I can do this. I'm going to be okay. I'll make sure I'm okay. I could really use a joint right now.*

My eyes open at that thought. *Nope. I'm not going there.* I liked it, the couple of times I tried it. But right now, I just need to get through this one day at a time.

I smile when I see my aunt with a huge sign covered in rainbow glitter, my name scrawled across it. "Aunt Stacey, did you think I wouldn't know who you were?" I ask her.

"Pfft, you'd never forget me, baby girl. I make it my life's mission to be unforgettable," she says.

She's not wrong. My Aunt Stacey is a free spirit. Never married. No children. She's the most spontaneous person I've ever known. And I wouldn't change a single thing about her.

"Okay, I've gathered all the supplies. Ice cream, matching PJs, and more junk food than we could consume in an entire year. Tonight, it's me, you, and *The Notebook*," she says.

I smile. I love my aunt. She's not going to bombard me with questions. She's just going to be there. Which is exactly what I need right now.

"I couldn't think of a better way to spend my night," I tell her.

I don't turn my phone back on until I'm in bed, my stomach so full of junk I feel sick. But when I see the barrage of text messages and missed call notifications coming through from Vin, I feel even sicker. I scroll up and start reading through them.

> **VIN:**
>
> What do you mean you're leaving? What are you doing, Cammi?

> **VIN:**
>
> Cammi, what are you talking about?

> **VIN:**
>
> Where are you? I'll come and see you. Don't do anything rash.

> **VIN:**
>
> Cammi, message me back. Answer my call. Just tell me you're okay? I'm going out of my mind here.

I send him a quick reply.

> **ME:**
>
> I'm okay. I had my phone off. I'm in Sydney with my aunt.

After I press send, I plug my phone into the

charger. I don't know if I want him to keep messaging, or to just leave me alone. What I do know is that I'm tired. And now that I'm lying here in the dark, I finally let the tears fall freely. I finally let myself fully feel the hurt.

Chapter Twenty-Three

I'm back here. He kept his word and brought me back here. I really should have known better than to think he'd change his mind. It's been a year. Every month for a whole year, my father has made me strip naked, then shoved me into this room.

I know what happens next. They're coming for

me. Sometimes I wait for hours, others minutes. I don't want to be here. The thought of what's about to happen sends a fresh wave of panic through me.

I try the door handle, and to my surprise, it actually opens. He forgot to lock it. He never forgets to lock it. It has to be a trick, one of my father's sick mind games. He did this on purpose.

Does he want me to try to escape or does he want me to stay put?

I don't care what he wants. If I see a way out of this room, I'm leaving. I don't look back as I start running down the hallway. I can hear their screams. The screams and cries of the other children stuck in this hellhole. I want to find a light and burn this place down. Maybe if I can get outside, figure out where we are, find the address, I can come back and set it alight.

If I did that, though, they wouldn't get out. The other kids. They'd die in here. And it'd be my fault. Although death might be welcomed. If it came for me, I'd open my arms and let it take me away.

I manage to get to a door that I hope leads to outside. My palm touches the handle, and then I'm yanked back.

"You got farther than I gave you credit, boy," a deep voice whispers as an arm wraps around my waist and my back is pressed up against a man's chest.

"Run, little boy, run. I like to chase." He drops his arm and I quickly turn around, but there's no one there. I'm alone.

Turning back to the door, I open it and I run. The sticks and stones dig into the soles of my feet, but I don't stop. I reach the edge of the backyard that leads into the bordering bush. Without thought, I run between the trees, my pace slowing down as I navigate over fallen tree trunks, huge rocks, and whatever else is scattered around the dirt.

My chest burns, but I can't stop. I need to keep going. Just when I think I've run far enough, I collide into a tree. My chest scratches against the bark, and a heavy—a very heavy—palm pushes against my back.

"I told you I like it when you run. And you delivered. I knew you would. Now tell me, boy, is this tight little ass of yours going to deliver too? Is it going to choke my cock good?" the deep voice hisses in my ear as those same heavy hands spread my ass cheeks apart.

I sit up in bed while a scream tears through my lungs. My chest heaves as I try to get my bearings. I'm at home. *I'm not there. I'm not there.* I look around my bedroom, at all the familiar things. *This is my space. I'm okay.*

Spotting my tin on my shelf, I drag myself up, grab it, and swipe my phone from the bedside table before walking straight out to the balcony. My body falls to the ground, and the cool night air against my sweaty skin sends chills through me. Lighting up a blunt, I tap my phone open to her message thread.

> CAMMI:
>
> I'm okay. I had my phone off. I'm in Sydney with my aunt.

She's really gone. I've driven her out of fucking town. I want to fly to Sydney and drag her back. I can't do that to her, though. I can't force her to be around me. She's right. It does fucking hurt seeing her and having to pretend like I don't care. Because I do. I do care. Way too fucking much.

Before I can talk myself out of it, I send her another text.

> ME:
>
> Are you awake?

I don't expect her to reply, but when my phone lights up with her picture on the screen, my heart skips a beat. She's calling me. I click the answer button and bring the phone to my ear. I don't say anything, just listen to her breathing.

"Vin? Are you okay?" Her sweet fucking voice breaks the silence.

"No," I answer.

"What's wrong?"

I shouldn't do this to her. I'm meant to be letting her go, letting her start over without me. She needs to hate me, and here I am, leaning on her for comfort when it's the last thing I deserve to take from her.

"They're back," I tell her. "You're not here... I can't... I tried to sleep and they came back."

"The nightmares," she says. It's not a question; it's a statement. She knows what I'm talking about. She doesn't know what the nightmares entail, although I'm sure she can take a good guess now that she knows what happened to me.

"I shouldn't have called you," I tell her.

"Technically, I called you. And I want you to call me, Vin. It doesn't matter what time or what you need. I'll always answer," she says.

"I don't know who else to talk to. There is no one else I want to talk to," I admit. I know I could call up Dash or Marcus, and they'd be here in a heartbeat to hang out and do whatever to occupy my mind. But all I really want right now is to wrap myself in Cammi, and I can't fucking do that because I sent her away.

"You can talk to me. I'm not going to lie. It hurts, Vin. I'm hurting, but I will always be here for you, no matter what," she says.

"I'm sorry," I whisper. "I don't want to hurt you, Cammi."

"I know," she whispers back.

"Why are you awake?" I ask her.

"Couldn't sleep," she says.

"How long are you staying in Sydney?"

"I'm not coming home. I'm going to stay here. Finish the school year out online and then start university next year." She sounds like she's reciting a speech. She's got it all planned out.

I don't know what to say. I want to tell her to come home. That I need her. But that'd be fucking selfish and counterproductive. "I hate that you felt like you had to leave."

"Me too," she says. "Vin?"

"Yeah?"

"Go back to bed. I'm going to video call you." She hangs up, and straight away a video call request pops up.

"Hey." I try to smile when I see her face, but my

heart fucking hurts. Her skin is blotchy, and I can tell she's been crying.

"Hey," Cammi repeats.

I push to my feet, walk back into my bedroom, and lie on the bed. "Maybe we could try this friend thing out?" I suggest. She is my best friend after all. She's the first and last person I think about every day.

"Mhmm. Sure," Cammi agrees but I can tell it's not what she wants. It's not what either of us wants.

"Close your eyes. I want to tell you a story." I wait for her to do as she's told before speaking up again. "There was a boy, a rebellious, lost boy. He thought he had everything under control. He thought that he was handling life just fine. Then God gave him a saint..." I see Cammi smile, and by the time my story ends, she's asleep. "I love you, Cammi," I whisper and disconnect the call.

Standing against the wall opposite her locker, I glare at every fucker who dares to look at me. I'm in the mood for a fight and the first idiot who wants to take me on is going to cop the brunt of my anger. I'm pissed at myself. And at her. She's really gone. I was hoping it was all a bad fucking dream, and she'd show up at her locker this morning. I know better than to hope for shit, but I really wanted her to be here.

"You can stare all day long. She's gone. Because of you. Whatever you did to her, I hope you're happy with yourself because you fucking broke her." Devon, one of Cammi's friends, stops in front of me.

I don't respond to her. What the fuck can I say? She's right. I did break Cammi. The one good fucking thing I had in my life, and I broke it. I always knew I would. It's why I stayed away from her for so long, why I watched her from a distance for years. She doesn't know just how long I wanted to talk to her, how long I wanted to touch her. I never told her.

I had her, and now I've driven her away. The monsters won, and I let them. I should have fought harder. But I can't beat them. Sometimes you just have to learn to live with them.

"You're pathetic. I'm glad she's gone, so she doesn't get drawn back into your bullshit, Vin. Leave her alone. She's going to heal, and then she's going to find a man worthy of her," Devon hisses.

Her words are like a knife to the heart. *She's going to find a man worthy of her.* Fuck no. I can't have her. But like fuck am I going to let anyone have what's mine either. The thought of Cammi being with someone else makes me physically ill.

"Haven't you got something better to be doing with your time?" Dash throws back at Devon. *When did he even get here?*

"Nope," she replies.

"Find something then. And remember who the fuck you're talking to while you're at it," he grunts.

"Fuck you." Devon looks from Dash to me. "And fuck you too. Or better yet, do the world a favour and go get hit by a bus."

I raise an eyebrow at her. She might be one of Cammi's best friends, and that has given her a lot of freedoms others don't have when it comes to talking to me. But I will not be talked to like this by anyone. "Did Cammi tell you why we broke up?" I ask while taking a step in the girl's direction.

She takes a step back, shaking her head as I take another step forward until she's pressed up against Cammi's locker.

Then I lean in, keeping my voice low. "She watched me kill a man with a steak knife. She stood there and watched and wanted to help me. She didn't question why I killed him. She didn't run to the cops. She wanted to help me." I watch Devon's face pale. "Whatever is happening with Cammi and me is none of your fucking business. She is mine. She will always be mine, no matter how far she runs. What we have is unbreakable. Trust me, I've tried," I tell her and then step back.

Without sparing the girl another glance, I turn and walk out of the building. I shouldn't have even fucking come here today. I'm not worried that Devon will tell anyone what I said. Who would believe her anyway? Probably everyone, but there's no evidence, and I know Cammi would never speak a word against me.

By the time I get to my car, Dash is right behind me. "Where we going?"

"Cinque," I tell him. My brothers and I own a distillery a short drive from town. It's the best place to get fucked up on both whiskey and weed.

"Let's go then." Dash opens the passenger side door of my car and gets in. No questions asked.

Chapter Twenty-Four

Cammi

Two months later - November

It's over. I've finally graduated high school. Although it's very anticlimactic when you graduate online and there is no ceremony or after parties. My mum tried to convince me to return to Melbourne for graduation. I couldn't do it.

I still cry myself to sleep on the nights I'm not talking to Vin. We speak at least three times a week. It started off with him calling me every night and sending me messages throughout the day. Over the last few months, the number of messages has lessened and the calls are quicker.

We're both hurting, and I'm not sure if talking to him is helping or just delaying the inevitable. I'm going to have to find a way to move on from him. I just can't bring myself to let him go. The ache in my chest is still going strong. I'd go home in a heartbeat if he said he wanted to get back together. I've stopped asking him. There's only so much rejection one person can take. And although I understand why he's saying no, that doesn't make it any easier.

I've appreciated the time away, though. I love being with my aunt and honestly it's refreshing. After the third week of listening to me cry myself to sleep, she booked me an appointment with a therapist. I'm doing weekly visits. I go along with the advice the therapist gives me during our sessions, and some of it *is* good advice. But when she tells me that my relationship with Vin is toxic and codependent, I dismiss her. She's also told me that if I want

Vin to heal and recover from his own trauma, I need to give him the space to do so.

Which is why I've limited the phone calls and messages. I don't know if it's working. Vin has been going through a lot. His brother got sentenced to *years* in prison. And now Gabe's girlfriend, Daisy, is leaning on Vin for support. He's helped her move, go off the grid so no one can find her. Oh, and she's pregnant and Vin promised her not to tell anyone. Although I'm not sure I count, considering he called me straight away, freaking out and not knowing what to do. He's a great brother, even if Gabe doesn't know it. Vin has been there for Daisy, flying back and forth between Melbourne and Adelaide, making sure she has everything she needs.

A knock at the front door has me putting my bowl of cereal down, along with my self-pity, and dragging my body off the sofa. I glance at the old band shirt and pyjama shorts I'm wearing. I probably shouldn't be answering the door looking like a bum. But whoever is knocking is persistent and won't stop. So I pull the front door open and freeze.

My eyes blink and blink again. I must be seeing things. My mouth goes dry. I can feel my hands start to shake. I've seen him on the phone during our video chats, but seeing Vin on my doorstep is something else.

"Cammi? Say something. You look like you've seen a ghost," he says.

"How? Why? What are you doing here, Vin?" I ask, snapping out of my stupor.

"It's graduation. I have a gift for you," he explains. "And I didn't want you spending graduation alone, so I... ah... I brought the party to you."

"You brought what party to me?"

"Your graduation party. I flew your friends here. They're waiting at The Merge for you. To celebrate with you," he says.

"The Merge?" I've heard of the nightclub. I haven't been there, though. I don't really leave the house all that much. The thought of going out to a nightclub isn't high on the list of things I want to do. "Can you tell them you couldn't find me? I don't want to go out." I turn and walk back into the house, leaving the door open.

Vin follows me, shutting it behind him. "Are you okay? What's wrong?"

"Nothing's wrong. I'm enjoying the party for one I have going on here." I wave a hand at the plethora of snacks spread out across the coffee table. Reaching for my bowl of cereal, I bring a spoonful of the sugary goodness to my mouth. "I'm completely fine sitting here alone. I'm pretty good company," I say around a mouth full of food.

"You're the best fucking company, Cammi." Vin sits next to me on the sofa. He's so close I could reach out and touch him. I could move just an inch and be pressed up against him. His scent surrounds me. "If you don't want to go out, that's cool. We can stay in. Party for two." He smirks.

I turn and fully look at him. His sandy-brown hair is longer than it was a couple of months ago, and the loose curls hang over his forehead. Dark shadows cover his under-eye area. I already knew he wasn't sleeping well. I didn't know how *unwell*, though. I need to remember that he's not mine. I need to distance myself. I push up from the sofa and take my bowl into the kitchen.

"You don't have to stay. You should go and party with whoever came up with you," I tell him.

"I'd rather stay and hang with you." Vin follows me into the kitchen.

"Why?" I ask him. "Why are you here, Vin?"

"Because we're friends, and friends hang out," he says.

"You want to hang out with me? Do anything I want to do?" I question as an idea comes to mind.

"Anything within reason," he says cautiously.

I could ask him to kiss me right now. The thought has crossed my mind. And, boy, do I want him to kiss me... That's not what I'm going to ask, though. Because as much as I might want it, and I know he wants it too, he's still not in a place to accept that we can be more than friends.

"I want to sleep," I tell him. "I'm tired, Vin. I'm so tired. All I want to do right now is go to bed with you and sleep."

"Okay, where's your bedroom?"

I point behind him and start making my way towards the room. "It's a little messy," I warn. There are clothes and books everywhere. The bed is unmade. Without glancing in his direction, I climb onto the mattress and pull the blanket over myself. "I want you to hold me, Vin, so I can sleep. Please."

I'm not lying. I am bloody tired, but I also want him to get some quality sleep. And I'm hoping that I can give that to him, like I used to. Vin yanks his shirt from over the back of his head and tosses it on the floor before lying down next to me.

"Vin? Can you wrap your arms around me?" I ask, knowing full well he won't touch me if I don't.

"Are you sure? Cammi, I don't want to give you the wrong idea," he says.

"I know where we stand, Vin. I just really want a cuddle," I tell him. "I don't sleep well. And you and I both know you don't either, so let's just sleep while we can."

"Okay." Vin holds out his arm and I crawl into him, resting my head on his bare chest. There's new ink I haven't seen before. I don't know what it is. But the design has a pointy arrow shape on the top and something similar to wings coming out of the sides.

My fingers trace around the black edges. "What is this?"

"It's the symbol for a saint," he says.

"My therapist says cuddling releases oxytocin and that's why we like it so much and why it helps me sleep better," I hum. "And then I looked up the psychology of cuddling. Apparently, it makes you less likely to look for a partner in other people."

Vin's hand, which was dragging absently up and down my arm, stops at the same time I hear him hold his breath. "Are you looking for a partner in other people?"

I snort, literally snort. "No. But if cuddling stops you from looking elsewhere, then I might just glue myself to your side." I laugh, trying to pass it off as a joke.

"I'm not on the market, Cammi. If I were, you'd

be the first and only person I'd call," he says. "Close your eyes."

"Can you tell me a story?" I ask him. He's told me the same story over and over again for the past two months. I love hearing it, even if the ending is a fantasy that's probably never going to happen.

I wake up alone. He's gone. If it weren't for his scent still on my pillow, I'd think I hallucinated that he was even here. I don't want to get out of bed. I'm content to sit here and wallow all day.

"Cammi, there's... ah... You should just come and see this," Aunt Stacey calls out.

Either she's burnt something. Again. Or she's found the dress of all dresses. Also, again. She's what I like to call a shopaholic. She's obsessed with finding the next best outfit, or shoes, or bags.

I get up and walk out to the living room and realise it's neither of those things. Aunt Stacey is standing in the middle of the room surrounded by a million red roses—well, maybe not a million but there are a lot of them here.

"There's a card," Aunt Stacey says.

"So open it. I didn't know you were dating anyone," I tell her.

"Oh, baby girl, these aren't for me. This says *Cammi*." She picks up a card that's taped to a small box.

My heart beats rapidly in my chest and my hands go clammy. *Did Vin do this?* I don't know anyone else who would do something like this. I take the card off my aunt and tear it open.

> To Cammi,
>
> Happy graduation. I'm so proud of you and everything you've achieved. You are destined for greatness.
>
> Love always,
>
> Vin

I peel back the lid to the box and my brows draw down. "Why would he give me a car remote?" I ask aloud.

"He what?" Aunt Stacey runs to the front door and opens it. "Oh my freaking god!" she squeals.

I push past her, stopping on the porch the moment my eyes land on the shiny, brand-new

Mercedes G-Wagon—complete with a red bow to accentuate the perfectly white paint job—now parked in the driveway.

Holy shit, he got me a freaking car? What on earth is he thinking?

"I can't accept this," I tell Aunt Stacey before heading back into the house.

"Oh, but you can, and you should." She sighs, still staring at the car.

"Nope, I'm telling him to come and get it. I don't want it." I storm into my bedroom and grab my phone. I slam a finger onto his name in my contacts and wait for him to pick up.

"Hey, you woke up," he says.

"Vin, what the hell? Come and get your car. I don't want it. What were you thinking buying me a damn car?" I yell into the phone.

"I was thinking that it's graduation and I wanted to get you a gift," he says.

"I don't want it. There is only one thing in this world I want and you can't give me that. Take it back. Friends do not buy other friends cars, Vin."

"Well, you've never had a friend like me before. The car is yours, Cammi. I'm not taking it back. I gotta go. I'm about to board the jet." He disconnects the call.

"Argh!" I scream as I throw my phone down onto the bed. I'll figure out a way to return this car to him, even if I have to drive it to Melbourne and leave it in his driveway myself.

I walk back outside and stare at the monstrosity. It is a really nice car. But honestly, even if Vin were still my boyfriend, I wouldn't want him buying me such extravagant gifts. I don't need them. I don't want to be that person. I like Vin for who he is, not what he can get or do for me.

My phone vibrates in my hand, and a message pops up on my screen.

VIN:

Keep the car. It's part of the story. Think of it as your white carriage. Also, I really want you to have it, Cammi. It makes me feel better knowing that you have a way to get around that's not on those filthy Sydney trains.

ME:

Okay.

I might have agreed to keep the car, for now, but that doesn't mean I'm not going to find a way to return it to him.

Chapter Twenty-Five

December

It was a mistake to go and see Cammi last month. I didn't want her to be alone, to celebrate graduating alone. Especially considering the only reason she ran off to Sydney was because of me. I didn't want to leave her. I wanted to stay. I wanted to give her—*us*—exactly what we both want.

I want *us* back. I've been fighting with myself since I saw her. Fighting to not go back and just do it. She's mine. I can't let her go, nor do I want to. I also don't know how to be with her without bringing her down.

I can't do it to her. I won't. I'll end up hurting her more than I already have. She's in therapy because of me. When she told me she was seeing a shrink, my first thought was that I was going to lose her completely. She's going to realise that I'm too fucked up of a person for her to even *want* to be with.

My second thought was: *I hope it helps her with her sadness.* Because she is sad. Again, shame on me for that. I just don't know how to fix it. It's almost Christmas now. She's coming home for a week. Well, to her parents' house. I know if she's that close, I'm not going to be able to stay away from her.

"Seriously, Vin, if you're going to come and hang out here at least pretend to be happy to see me," Daisy says.

We're sitting on her sofa watching a movie. I came to Adelaide, because it's almost Christmas and I didn't want Daisy to be alone either. Her stomach is getting huge. I wish I could tell Gabe or even fucking Gio that she's pregnant. Gabe should know. Maybe then he'd lift the fucked-up visitation ban he put on her.

Daisy wants to be the one to tell him, and since my dumbass brother won't put her name on the visitor's list, she can't go and see him to tell him he's going to be a father. I know our solicitor is working on an appeal, or some shit to get Gabe out on early release. I fucking hope it works too; otherwise, Daisy is going to be raising this kid alone. Well, not alone. Because I'll always be here but it's not the same.

"Sorry," I mumble under my breath.

"Spit it out. What's going on in that pretty little head of yours?" Daisy asks.

"You think I'm pretty, Daisy? Like prettier than Gabe?" I ask her with a smirk.

"No one is prettier than Gabe. Now, stop stalling, Vin. Out with it. What's going on?" Her tone is more firm.

I've never been one for therapy, never wanted to sit down and talk to some head quack. I will, however, talk to Daisy. Over the past few months, I've slowly been opening up to her about my past, about Cammi, about everything.

"Cammi is coming back to Melbourne for Christmas." I sigh.

245

"And that's a bad thing?"

"I don't know." I lift one shoulder into a half shrug. "I don't have the willpower to stay away from her if she's so close."

"Vin, you're a De Bellis. You have the means to go and see her anytime you want, and you choose not to. You have the willpower," Daisy says.

"I should stay away from her though, right?"

"Why?"

"Because the last time I left, it was hard—really fucking hard. What if I can't leave again?" I tell her.

"What if you don't leave? What would happen if you don't?" Daisy asks me.

"I'd end up hurting her more. Drag her down to my darkness again," I try to explain. "I don't want to do that."

"Then don't. You realise you're only hurting yourself *and Cammi* by keeping this distance between you? Does she even still want to be with you, Vin? How do you know she hasn't already moved on and found someone else?"

I glare at my sister-in-law. Oh, yeah, by the way, another secret no one else in the family seems to know about is the fact Gabe went and married Daisy before he got locked up. Fucking idiot didn't tell anyone.

"She's not moving on," I grunt.

"See *that*." Daisy points at me. "You either need to let her go or man up and be with her before she does actually move on." She shakes her head. "I get it. You're scared to bring her into the world you and your brothers live in. But do you really want to spend the rest of your life alone?"

"It's not the family business, Daisy. You know that. I'm fucked up. I can't even touch her without her specifically asking me to. No matter how much I want to." I run a hand down my face.

"Has she ever mentioned that it bothers her?" Daisy raises a brow at me.

"No." I fully believe Cammi is my ride-or-die girl. She would do anything for me, and I'd do anything for her. Which is why I'm torturing us both by keeping us apart.

"No one can decide what to do for you, Vin. But if it were me, and Gabe was staying away from me on purpose, well, I'd probably rip his balls off. But I get it. I get why he doesn't want me to visit him there. I don't like it and I'll forgive him eventually. But I understand. Which is the exact reason I'm waiting for him to get out." Daisy rubs a hand over her protruding stomach. "Well, that and this little guy."

"Yeah, you're married, Daisy. It's different.

Cammi and I just graduated from high school. She has her whole life ahead of her."

"Maybe, but if you know, *you know*. And from what you've told me, you both already *know*."

"What I *know* is that sometimes I wish Gabe found some ditzy chick who wasn't so smart." I laugh.

"No, you don't. I know I'm your favourite sister-in-law," Daisy says with a smirk of her own.

"Meh, I don't know. El made me chocolate chip pancakes yesterday," I say. And at the mention of her friend, who she hasn't spoken to in months, Daisy's eyes water up. Fuck, she cries so easily and over anything lately.

"How is El?"

"Pregnant and probably about to kill Gio's over-bearing ass," I grunt.

"I can imagine." Daisy smiles but it doesn't reach her eyes.

Two weeks later, I find myself climbing up the side of Cammi's house. I know she's here. I might have put a GPS locater on her phone that I never told her about way back when we were dating. Luckily for me, she hasn't upgraded devices. I push the window up and climb through.

"Ah, Elena, I have to go. I'll call you back tomorrow." Cammi stares at me while talking into her phone.

"He's there isn't he? Cammi, do not let yourself fall into that trap again. Kick his ass to the kerb," Elena replies through the speaker.

"I'll call you back tomorrow." Cammi throws the phone to the edge of the bed, her glare still narrowed in on me. "Why are you climbing through my window?"

"I was feeling nostalgic and, honestly, I wasn't sure your parents would let me in," I explain.

"My parents don't know who you are, Vin," she says. "I never told them."

"Oh." I don't know how I feel about that. Now isn't the time to unpack it, though. "I.. ah... have a Christmas gift for you."

"It's not a car, is it? Because I'm still trying to explain why 'a friend' gifted me a car worth over three hundred thousand dollars," she says while using air quotes.

"We are friends, Cammi. But, no, it's not a car

this time." I smile. "But tell me you don't like the car."

"It's nice, but I don't need it, Vin. I don't want you giving me extravagant gifts." Cammi shakes her head and then leans over the bed, reaching for something on the floor. When she sits back up, she's holding a small white package. "I got you something too."

I pull a rectangular box from my back pocket and walk closer to the bed.

"You can sit. Here, open mine first," Cammi says while passing me her gift.

I take the box and tug on the red ribbon before removing the lid. I look inside and see three crystals sitting on tissue paper.

"There white chalcedony crystals. They are supposed to help with nightmares and give you a more peaceful sleep. You can put them under your pillow."

I look up at her. She got me crystals to help me sleep. I don't believe for one second a few pretty stones are going to take away my nightmares. But the fact she thought of something like this—the fact she wanted to help me—has emotions clogging up my throat. "You got me something for my nightmares?"

"It's stupid. I can keep them. I just thought... if I

can't be there to help you, then maybe these could." Cammi reaches for the box.

"Cammi, it's not stupid," I tell her while tugging the gift closer to my chest. "Ask me." I look her dead in the eye. It's not going to be good for either of us, but I really need to kiss her right now.

Cammi's eyes widen before she says, "Vin, kiss me like I'm yours. Kiss me like it's the first time."

I drop the box I have for her on the bed and cup her face with my palms. "You forgot the *last time*." She always used to ask me to kiss her like it was the first and *last* time.

"I don't want there to be a last time," Cammi whispers as my lips press against hers.

My tongue slides into her mouth. *Fuck, I've missed this.* I feel like I've just come home after a really long time away. So does my cock. One touch and I'm hard as a fucking rock.

I pull back from the kiss way too soon. I see the want in Cammi's eyes. I don't want to go there. I know things aren't returning to the way they were, and I don't want her to think I came here for a fucking booty call.

"Open yours," I tell her, picking up the box and handing it to her.

Cammi pops the lid and runs her fingers over the

white gold bracelet. She smiles as she fingers the single charm in the centre. "It's the Eiffel Tower," she says, slowly removing the bracelet from the cushioning. "I love it."

"It's a start," I tell her. "I'm going to make sure it's filled with all the places in the world you've seen."

Cammi frowns. "But I haven't seen the Eiffel Tower."

I pull out the envelope that contains two first-class tickets to France for New Year's week. "This is the second part of your gift."

Cammi opens the envelope and gasps. "Tickets to France? We're going to Paris?" she squeals.

"*You're* going to Paris," I tell her.

"But there's two tickets. You don't want to come to Paris with me?" she asks.

"I want to go everywhere with you, Cammi, but I'm not going on this trip. I want you to take whoever you want. A friend, your mum, your aunt."

"Okay, I want to take my best friend. Hold on, let me message them to see if they're free," she says, setting the tickets down and picking up her phone.

Seconds later, my pocket pings with an incoming text. I pull out my own phone and stare at the screen.

CAMMI:

Some fool got me tickets to Paris for Christmas. You wanna come with me?

"Fool, huh?" I ask her with one brow raised.

"Well, if you think I'm taking anyone else with me, then you most certainly are a fool. We are going to Paris, Vin!" she says with so much excitement in her voice.

"I shouldn't have kissed you," I tell her. "I'm sending mixed messages and that's not fair to you. I want you to be happy, Cammi. I really do. I just can't give you everything you want, everything you deserve."

"Why do I feel like you're breaking up with me all over again?"

I can see the way her lower lip is wobbling as she tries to hold back tears. "I'm not. We're friends. Always will be."

"A friend wouldn't let another friend go to Paris alone," she whispers.

"Okay, I'll come," I say, despite my better judgment. I already know it's going to be torture being around her so much and not being able to touch her.

Chapter Twenty-Six

Cammi

January – Paris

I cannot believe I'm actually here. I'm standing in front of the Eiffel Tower with Vin. Who has been acting a little off since we landed in Paris yesterday. And when I say Vin De Bellis is acting off, I mean worse than normal.

I don't know what's wrong with him. Every time I've asked him about it, he's says he's fine or the jetlag is getting to him. I don't buy it. Vin runs on very limited sleep. I don't see him being all that bothered by the time zone change.

I was so excited when we landed yesterday I could barely sleep last night. Well, that and the fact that Vin was across the hall. He rented a two-bedroom apartment for us. And insisted on us sleeping in separate beds.

It hurts, knowing he's so close and not being able to touch him. To not be able to sleep curled up next to him. It hurts more knowing how much he's fighting to keep us in the friend zone. I'm not going to push myself on him, though. Whatever demons he's fighting have already caused me more pain than I ever thought possible.

I'll wait. I have faith that he will beat those demons. I'm just not sure how much of my heart will actually be leftover when he finally does.

"Vin, hold my hand," I tell him, and I can hear the excitement in my own voice. "We're at the Eiffel Tower. I can't believe we're here." Thankfully, Vin does take hold of my hand. I look over to him and he's staring at me. "Are you not impressed? It's stunning." I lift our joined palms while gesturing to the structure in front of us.

"It is," he agrees with a smile. "You look really happy."

"I'm at the most iconic, romantic place in the world with my favourite person *in the world*. What's not to be happy about, Vin?" I ask him.

"Favourite person, huh?"

I roll my eyes and tug on his hand. "Don't play stupid. It's not a good look on you. Now, come on. I want to get closer."

As soon as we're practically under the tower—which took ages, mind you—I turn to Vin and take a deep breath.

"I want you to kiss me like they do in the movies. Pretend you've just proposed, and I said yes," I tell him.

Vin doesn't disappoint. "She said yes!" he calls out loudly, and as onlookers cheer and clap, he wraps his arms around my waist and lifts my feet off the ground. His lips slam down on mine and he spins us around in a circle.

Just like they do in the movies...

Everything fades away, the noises, the crowd. It vanishes and all I'm left with is Vin. His arms around me and his tongue dancing with mine. This is what dreams are made of.

By the time he sets me back on my feet, I'm dizzy. My arms don't want to unwrap themselves from around his neck. "I don't want to let go, because I know when I do, we go back to... not this. Not us," I whisper. And a tear escapes, running down my cheek.

"As much as I don't want to, we have to, Cammi," Vin says.

I drop my arms and take a step back, forcing a smile on my face because I'm not going to let my own sadness bring this trip down. "I think champagne and cheese sounds really good right now. Let's find somewhere to eat."

"You okay?" Vin asks, falling into step next to me.

"Mhmm, I'm good. I'm in Paris. Nothing is going to ruin this opportunity," I tell him.

"Okay, food and then the Louvre?"

"Sounds like a great plan."

We find the cutest little café that overlooks one of the main streets. It's a great place to people watch. I really do love this city.

"I think I could live here," I tell Vin after biting

into a chunk of cheese that makes my mouth water. "The food here is amazing."

"It is," he agrees. "You could easily get into a school here if you wanted to."

"I think I'll see how Sydney works out. I like living with my aunt. And I'm getting used to the city," I tell him.

"Would you ever move back to Melbourne?" Vin asks.

"If I had a reason to, I would in a heartbeat." We both know I'm talking about him. "I have an idea."

"What?"

"What if, just for this week, we evoke the *friends with benefits* program?" It's been a really long time since I've been touched, since I've had an orgasm. I don't know if Vin has spent the same amount of time celibate, but I don't think he's been with anyone else either.

"Friends with benefits. What kind of benefits are we talking here, Cammi?" Vin aims a questioning brow in my direction.

"The orgasm kind," I whisper. "It's been a really long time for me, Vin, and there's only so much a girl can do for herself."

"Just so we're clear, it's been just as long for me," he states. "I don't want to lose the friendship we have, Cammi. I can't risk losing you completely."

"That's never going to happen. I promise," I tell him. "I get it. I know that when we go home, you'll be in Melbourne and I'll still be in Sydney. And we will go back to being friends *without* benefits."

"Okay," Vin says. "But you have to promise me, Cammi. Promise me that after we leave here, you're not going to hate me."

"I couldn't hate you even if I tried." I smile at him. "Now, can we reschedule the Louvre and go back to the apartment instead?"

After Vin pays the check, because he refuses to let me pay for anything, we head back to the apartment. Both of us are quiet. The anticipation of what's about to happen building within me. I haven't felt this level of excitement in a long time.

As soon as we're behind closed doors, I drop my coat to the ground before I reach for the hem of my sweater and lift it over my head. I step backwards towards the bedroom as I leave a trail of clothes behind me.

Vin's eyes fill with heat, lust, need. He tugs off his coat, letting it hit the floor, as those dark eyes of his roam up and down my body. I lose my bra, right before my shoes fly across the room as I kick them off my feet. Vin growls, audibly growls, as he takes in my bare chest. The back of my knees hit the bed while my fingers undo the button on my jeans and I slide the material down my legs, along with my panties.

Once I'm completely naked, I lie on the bed. Vin stands at the edge of the mattress, staring down at me. "You're so fucking beautiful, Cammi," he says.

"Vin, I want you to touch me. Everywhere. I want you to make love to me. I want you to kiss me. I want you to use my body for your own pleasure while giving me mind-blowing orgasms too." I don't know how much more explicit I can be in giving him permission.

"Open your legs," he says. He's statue still, doesn't move a muscle.

I spread my legs wide, my knees bent and forming a butterfly shape as my feet almost touch.

"Fuck. You're drenched. Look how much you're glistening for me, Cammi." Vin drops to his knees. "Touch yourself. Show me how you've been giving yourself pleasure."

I bring my fingers to my clit and start slowly rubbing small circles. My eyes close. There's something erotic about having him watch me touch myself. It feels good, but it's not what I want. I want him. "Vin, please, I need you to touch me."

"Where do you want me to touch you, Cammi?" Vin asks.

"Everywhere. I want your hands on me, Vin. I want your mouth on me," I moan as my fingers continue to explore, pleasure building throughout my body.

Then I feel his hands on my thighs. He's shaking. My eyes open and connect with his. I want to ask if he's okay, but then his fingers push my own away and run straight up the middle of my wet folds.

"Oh god." My head falls back again. And his mouth is on me, kissing up the inside of my thigh.

"Fuck, I've missed this," he says, following his words with a lap of his tongue right up the middle.

"Oh, shit. Yes!" I cry out. My hands twirl into his hair. They're only there for a moment before Vin grabs both of my wrists and pins them against the bed.

His tongue swirls around my clit. His mouth closes over me, sucking, and I'm gone. It's been so long since I felt like this. I can't hold it back as little fireworks go off inside my body.

Vin kisses his way up my torso. *When did he take off his pants?* I'm not about to stop whatever he's doing to ask him, though. His mouth latches on to one of my breasts and my back arches off the bed.

"Vin, please, I need you," I tell him. "I need you inside me."

He looks up and then moves until his cock is pressing at the entrance of my pussy. "Are you sure?"

"Yes," I tell him, my eyes connected with his. And then he slowly enters me. My hands grip his arms. "Yes, yes," I say again as he bottoms out inside me.

Vin slides out and slams back in again. His cock filling me up and stretching me out. "I love you, so damn much," he says and then claims my mouth with his.

He continues to slowly slide in and out of me while kissing me gently. His hands caress up and down my body. And I can feel it. His love. I don't doubt that he loves me. I never have. Which I guess is the reason I hold on to hope that one day we can have this again. For now, I'll take what I can get.

My legs wrap around Vin's back, and he adjusts my left leg, hooking his arm under my knee and bending it to my chest. I can feel him deeper in this position. I moan into his mouth while my fingers dig into the skin on his forearms. I can feel myself about to tumble over the edge again. It's building and so damn close. As soon as I explode, Vin pulls out of me, grabbing his cock and squirting his cum all over my stomach.

"Fuck," he hisses before falling next to me on the bed.

"Uh-huh," I mumble, catching my breath.

"That was..." He turns his head to look at me.

"So damn good." I smile at him. "Give me two minutes and we can do it again."

"Give me five." Vin laughs. He looks relaxed, more relaxed than I've seen him in a long time. It makes my heart swell with joy, and I can feel the shattered pieces slowly being glued back together.

"I love you too," I tell him after a few more moments of silence.

"I know," he says, and I can hear the hint of sadness in his voice.

"This *friends with benefits* week is going to be amazing."

"It's what comes after that scares me," he whispers.

"It's us, Vin. It will always be us, whether we have benefits or not." I roll over to my side. "Now, how about you help me shower, considering you're the one that made me all dirty?"

"I like you dirty," Vin smirks. "But a shower sounds good too."

Chapter Twenty-Seven

January - Paris

"**A**re you ready for me, boy?" The masked man walks into the room, a strap hanging from his hand. I already know I'm not walking out of here today.

My father will take me to a makeshift hospital until I'm not covered in the welts, cuts, and bruises this man is going to leave on me. I don't care, though. Hopefully, today will be the last day I have to endure a beating from a masked man.

Maybe today is the day I finally die.

I stare the stranger in the eyes. Ice-blue eyes. They're cold. Just like you'd imagined a monster's eyes to be. His body is huge, fat, and covered in faded tattoos.

It's temporary, *I tell myself. It's only going to last so long and then I can go home. I just have to get through it. Or die. I'm okay with either option.*

When I don't answer him, he snaps out an arm, slapping me across the side of my legs with the belt. "I asked you a question, boy. You deaf?" he yells. "No, I think you just like the punishment. Bend over and I'll give you a proper belting."

I don't have a choice. There is no way out of this room. Out of this nightmare. I don't willingly bend over, though. I never have and I never will. They can do what they want to my body. I will not make it easy for them or be subservient to their demands. If they want me to do something, they will have to force my body to comply.

Which is exactly what the man does. His hand

wraps around my hair and he yanks until I'm forced onto my knees. Then his foot comes out, kicking at my back and pushing me down. My hands land on the hard concrete. I don't cry out. There's no point. No one is coming to save me. I learned that much a long time ago.

I can only save myself. I haven't figured out a way to do that yet, but I will. If it's the last thing I do, I will kill one of these men. And then maybe all the others will think twice about coming for me.

The belt whips across my ass, and my skin burns with the contact. I still don't cry. My fingers clench as I stay down. Because if I try to get up now, it'll be worse.

"You got nothing to say, boy?" the man hisses. His foot kicks at my stomach and then his hands push on me until I'm flat on my back. He straddles my body, his palm wrapping around my throat, squeezing tight enough to restrict my airflow.

My lungs burn. But I don't move. Instead, I look at his neck and imagine that it's my hand wrapped around his throat, squeezing the life out of him.

"Vin, wake up." I try to turn my head, but I can't. She's not supposed to be here. Cammi. I can hear her voice. But I can't see her.

"Wake up. Vin, please. It's me. It's Cammi. Stop." Her voice sounds raspy. What's wrong with her?

"Cammi?" I choke on the words. My eyes open, and I see her.

She's on the bed, underneath me, and my hand is wrapped around her throat.

No! I shake my head. No! I jump off the bed and walk backwards, getting as far away from her as I can. "No," I say aloud. She wasn't supposed to be there. She shouldn't be here.

What have I done?

"It's okay. Vin, it's okay. You're safe," she says, scrambling off the bed before attempting to step closer to me.

I hold out a hand while shaking my head from side to side. "Don't. Don't come near me." I stare at the marks around her throat, marks my own hands left. I did that to her. *Fuck.* Tears burn my eyes. I can't... I don't know what to do. I need to get away from her. So far away. "I'm sorry. So fucking sorry," I tell her. "I didn't know." It's no excuse. I should never have laid a hand on her.

"This isn't your fault, Vin. I tried to wake you up. It's my fault. I should have waited for you to wake up on your own," she says.

I tilt my head and stare at her. She loves me

beyond fault. A fact I've always known. I never want to take advantage of that love, which is why I've tried to keep my distance. Because as much as she loves me, she *will* see past every single one of my flaws. Cammi will dive head-first into my darkness to be with me, a place she doesn't belong.

"It won't ever happen again," I tell her. "Pack your things. We're going home." I walk out of the room. I need to get her home, and then I'll say goodbye for good this time.

I have no idea how I'm going to do it. I just know I have to. For her. She's not going to get hurt by me ever again. The only way I can ensure that happens is if I remove myself from her life completely.

"What? Why? Vin. I'm fine. You're fine. *We* are fine," she says, following me out of the room.

"Cammi, I almost choked the life out of you and you're standing here telling me it's fine? It's not fucking fine. None of this is fine." My voice rises.

"I can't lose you, Vin. It was an accident. Please, don't do this," she says, tears falling down her cheeks.

"I'll arrange for a doctor to meet us at the airstrip. I'm booking us a private jet to get us home," I tell her.

"I don't need a bloody doctor. I need you!" she yells. She's angry. Good. She should be angry. I can deal with anger, a lot fucking better than I can deal with her sadness.

"Cammi, please. Just... let's just get home and then we can reevaluate." I have no intention of doing that. I know what needs to be done and I'm going to have to be strong enough for both of us in order to do it.

"I need you in my life, Vin," she says, her voice a lot quieter now.

"I know," I say, because I really do know. I need her too. But my urge to protect her against everything I am is so fucking strong I can't overlook it. And I can't unsee what I just did to her.

The jet touches down in Sydney, and it's not long before I lead Cammi over to the car I arranged for us. We're both silent as I drive her back to her aunt's place. Each of us knows what's coming, and neither of us is thrilled about it.

When I pull up outside the house, I turn in my seat to look at her. Cammi has tears running down her face, and I feel like the shittiest person on earth for ever making her cry. "Kiss me like it's the last time you ever will," I tell her.

"I can't do that because I don't want there to be a last time, Vin. I'll kiss you like I'm going to wake up tomorrow and you'll be knocking on my door, ready for another kiss from me." She leans in and presses her lips against mine briefly before she pulls back and forces a smile onto her face. "See you tomorrow, Vin." Then she gets out of the car and walks around to the trunk.

I follow her, pulling out her suitcase before turning back in her direction. "I'll bring it in for you."

"No, it's fine. I got it." Cammi takes the suitcase and starts wheeling it up the path to the front door, pausing at the halfway mark to turn around and look at me. "Vin, I really do hope I see you tomorrow," she says and then turns back around.

I jump into the car, and as soon as I see Cammi shut her front door, I drive towards the airport. I just need to get home.

My heart is gone. I left it back in Sydney. I have no idea what's pumping the blood around my body at the moment. I just know it's not my fucking heart. I walk through the front door and head straight up to my bedroom. Where I dig out my little tin, pick up a joint, and search around in my drawer until my fingers wrap around a lighter. I go out onto my balcony and fall into the seat.

I'm two puffs in when the doors open and Gio walks out. Usually, I'd try to hide the fact that I'm smoking weed. Right now, I don't fucking care enough.

My brother lowers himself onto the seat next to me and holds out his hand. He doesn't say a word. And I try not to act shocked when I pass him the blunt and he lifts it to his lips. "It's good," he says, blowing out a heap of smoke before passing it back to me.

"It's okay." I shrug.

"So, there a reason you booked a private jet to bring you home from France?" Gio asks.

"Cammi," I say.

"What about her?"

"I..." I can't even say the word. I fucking hurt her, put my hands on her and hurt her.

"You what?" Gio presses.

"I was having a nightmare. She tried to wake me up, and when I came to, she was underneath me and I was choking her," I admit. "I didn't know... I didn't know it was her."

"You're not responsible for what you do in your sleep. You're not even conscious. Anyone who knows you knows you wouldn't hurt a woman on purpose."

"It doesn't matter. I hurt her, Gio. Her neck was fucking red. I did it, asleep or not," I grunt, before inhaling another lungful of smoke.

"What does she say about it?" he asks.

I roll my eyes. "I could probably kill her mother in front of her and she'd find a way to forgive me, Gio."

"Sounds to me like she's a keeper then." He chuckles.

"She is. But I can't do it to her. I can't strap her down to a life filled with my bullshit. I will just keep hurting her."

"I'm no expert, but don't you think you leaving her *is* hurting her?"

"But she's alive. I could have killed her." The thought of draining the life out of Cammi's eyes makes me physically ill. I can taste the vomit at the back of my throat, ready to spill over at any moment.

"You didn't though," Gio says. "I don't know the

girl very well, but from the one encounter I've had with her, I can say that I like her. And I think she's good for you. You smoke less when you're with her and you hang out with those loser friends of yours less when she's around."

"Dash and Marcus are not losers." They are my friends. The two people who have always been there for me.

"Sure, they're not." Gio pushes to his feet. "Ellie expects you at the dinner table. Get ready for the inquisition. She'll want to know everything about Paris."

"Perfect," I groan. "Just how I wanted to spend my night."

"Better than sitting out here feeling sorry for yourself, little bro." Gio walks back through the door without sparing me another look.

I finish my blunt and walk straight into my bathroom. I need a shower. I can't go to dinner smelling like weed. I don't need that kind of lecture from El.

Chapter Twenty-Eight

A year later

If you've ever wondered if it were possible to die of a broken heart, I'd say it is. I'm just not there yet. I've been knocking on death's doorstep for a year and the fucker won't let me in. If he had, I wouldn't be here today to tell this story, so I guess it's probably a good thing.

Twelve months ago, I lost him. Completely lost the man I loved. After we returned from France, he wouldn't answer my text messages, wouldn't return my phone calls. And like the idiot I was, I kept calling and messaging. Every day. For six whole months.

I'd wake up with renewed hope that things were going to change. That he'd come to realise he needs me just as much as I need him. It was a really long time to hold on to that hope, but I thought our love could overcome anything.

Until somewhere along the six-month mark, I found myself sitting in the middle of a lecture and it hit me. It was really over. I don't know why it took so long. But when that knowledge came tumbling down on me like a ton of bricks, my heart stopped. Literally stopped.

One minute I was sitting in a lecture theatre; the next, I was waking up in an ambulance, being rushed to the hospital. The doctors never could find a reason as to why my heart gave in that day. My parents flew up from Melbourne, and I was made to undergo all kinds of medical tests.

None of it mattered. I knew why. And it was

because of him. Vin really did give up on us. On me. I've accepted that now. I'd love to say I've moved on, but I haven't. I can't imagine dating anyone. Maybe I'll spend my life like my Aunt Stacey. A free spirit. Alone.

I've made peace with it. With him. I hate what he did, but can't bring myself to hate him. I just have to remember what he did, how he left without even a backwards glance. I won't be hurt like that again.

Now that I'm back in Melbourne, I'm sure it won't be long before I run into him. Especially once classes start next month. I'm ready for it... I think. It's not like he's going to try to talk to me or anything. He's going to do what he's done for the past year. Ignore me.

"Okay, you're all set," the lady behind the counter at student services says to me, snapping me out of my thoughts.

"Thank you." I take the envelope full of useless information I'm probably not going to need.

There's still a month before classes start. I returned to Melbourne for my parents. They both came up to Sydney a month ago to tell me they were divorcing. I didn't ask why, nor did they offer up an explanation. It was a shock. I honestly thought my parents' relationship was solid. It wasn't until two days ago, when I came home to stay with my mum, that I found out my father had cheated on her with his receptionist.

My mum was in tears. She's still trying to come to terms with everything that's happening. I was just angry. So angry that my dad would do that to her. Why would he do that? I want to ask him. I have so many questions, but I can't bring myself to do it. I don't want to be caught in the middle of my parent's divorce, and I don't want to have to take sides.

Although, right now, I'm stuck with my mum. She is devastated and needs me more than Dad does. When I saw him yesterday, he looked overworked and stressed but he said he was fine. Thankfully, when I stopped by his office, he had a new *male* assistant. I don't know what I would have done if the woman he cheated on my mum with was still there.

As I walk out of the student services building, I bump into a chest. Arms reach out to grab me to stop me from falling. "Cammi?"

A familiar voice full of shock has me looking up at Vin's best friend.

"Dash." I smile and take a step back. Holding the large envelope against my chest, like it's going to protect me somehow. Wait... Do I need protection from Dash?

"You coming back to Melbourne?" he asks casually.

"Ah, yeah. My mum needs me here. So here I am." I have no idea what I'm supposed to say to him.

"Okay, well, I'll see you around then, I guess. Welcome back, Cammi." He smiles and steps towards the building.

"Dash?" I call out to him, and he turns to face me.

"Yeah?"

"How is he?" I ask, already regretting the question. I don't care how he is. I don't want to see him, and I certainly do not want to get caught up in the trap that is Vin De Bellis.

Dash appears to think over the question. "He's... okay. Although I have a feeling he's about to be a lot happier real soon." He winks and then turns before pushing through the door.

He's okay. Well, I'm glad he's doing okay. Not that I didn't think he would be. After all, he's the one that ended our... friendship, relationship, whatever it was. He ended it, not me. So why wouldn't he be okay?

I wish I didn't ask Dash. If only I could turn back

time, I'd act like I didn't care one way or the other how the hell Vin De Bellis was doing. Because I can't. And the more I remind myself that I don't care, the more there's a chance I might actually talk it into being. Like manifesting, I think. If you say it enough, it happens, right?

I park my mum's car in the driveway before grabbing the grocery bags from the boot. And why am I driving my mum's car? Because I returned the fancy-as-shit G-Wagon Vin bought me. About a month after France. I had it shipped from my house to his. I even left a letter in the glove box, hoping he'd read it and call me.

When I walk through the door, I find my mum on the sofa. "Hey, I'm cooking dinner," I tell her.

"You're cooking dinner?" Mum asks. "Who are you and what have you done with my daughter?" She follows me into the kitchen.

"Haha, funny. I cook," I tell her as I set the fresh veggies on the benchtop.

"What are you cooking?" Mum peers into the grocery bags.

"Chicken stir-fry. It's Aunt Stacey's recipe," I say.

"Actually, it's my recipe. Aunt Stacey stole it from me and claims it's hers," Mum corrects me.

"I've lived with you my whole life. I've never seen you make this." I pull a cutting board out of the cupboard.

"That's because your dad didn't like it." Mum gets a sad look on her face. She didn't cook something just because my dad didn't like it?

I remember how Vin used to take me out for sushi because he knew I loved it. He'd never order anything, but he was happy to just sit there and let me enjoy one of my favourite foods.

"You're doing it again." Mum points at me.

"Doing what?" I turn on the tap and bring the veggies closer to the sink so I can wash them.

"You're thinking about him. Whoever that boy is. You get this faraway look on your face. When are you going to tell me about him?" she asks.

"I did tell you about him. He was there and then he wasn't. The end." There really isn't anything else to say.

"That's not information, Camile. What's his

name? He clearly left an impact on you if he still takes up space in your head," Mum presses.

If only she knew how much space in my head and heart Vin takes up...

"It's not important. *He's* not important. He's not anything anymore." I shrug.

"I'm sorry. I really hope you find your one great love story. But I think, for now, you should focus on being young and free. You don't need to tie yourself down just yet. Live, laugh, party. Have fun, Cammi." Mum walks over to the fridge. "Do you know what chicken stir-fry pairs well with?"

"What?" I ask.

"Moscato," Mum says, putting the bottle on the bench and grabbing two glasses.

"Do you believe that people only get one true love in their lifetime?" I really hope that's not the case. Not for me, but I can't help but think about Santo at his fiancée's grave. He deserves to find that kind of love again.

Me? I have no interest in being hurt by love for a second time, so I'm steering clear of it for the foreseeable future.

"I think there are different levels of love, baby. Some loves are the great, all-consuming, soul-claiming types. Some are not as intense but still just as important," Mum says.

And some loves are forever, no matter how much you deny it. I think this to myself. Now is not the time to tell my mother just how much of myself I lost to Vin.

Chapter Twenty-Nine

I don't think I've ever appreciated the darkness that clouds my family until this past year. I've embraced it, used it as my personal therapy, I guess.

It took some convincing. But Gio finally let me work. He'd wanted to keep me out of the business and on the straight and narrow side of things. That shipped sailed a real long fucking time ago, though. So, eventually, he started giving me jobs, ones I could use to release some of my pent-up anger.

Truth is, with Gabe being locked up and Santo off his rocker, my big brother needed us to step up. Neither Marcel nor I complained about the work. We've always known it was coming. We've been groomed for this life since the day we were born. I know Gio copped it a lot worse, seeing as he was always destined to take over as boss. Although I doubt our father ever thought it would happen the way it did. At first, I was relieved. The day Gio killed the fucker, I felt free. It didn't take long to realise the old man's impact would stay with me forever.

I'm never going to be rid of the monsters. The nightmares continue to come every night, except they're worse now. Because now I'm choking the life out of Cammi, watching her body turn grey and lifeless beneath me. That nightmare almost became a reality twelve months ago. Which is the only reason I've managed to stay away from her. I will not be the reason she leaves this earth before her time. It's fucking hard living without her, but I know it'd be harder if I had to go on living knowing she *wasn't*.

Okay, hard is an understatement. It's been hell.

I've wanted to reach out to her, tell her how fucking sorry I am. How I wish I could be normal for her, wish I could fix my issues. I've even gone to a shrink. Once. I ended up punching the fucker in the face and walking out after he suggested I had to distance myself from my family. He said the fact that I was still moving around in the same world they do is part of my problem. I will never leave my brothers. That's out of the question. I would rather spend an eternity with the monsters than turn my back on my family. I'm not a danger to them. If I wasn't a danger to Cammi, I never would have left her either.

"Where's your head at?" Marcel asks me.

"Nowhere," I tell him.

"Good. Get it in the game. You ready?" he asks.

"I was born ready." I smirk before jumping out of the car. I open the boot and take out the baseball bat. "Let's fuck some shit up."

The thought of smashing shit makes me really fucking happy right now. Like I said, this is better therapy than any fucking head quack could offer me.

I walk up to the door of the shop, swing the bat back, and smash the bottom panel of glass. The sound it makes when it shatters is like music to my ears. Then I lift a boot and connect it with what's left of the frame, kicking it open.

"Was that really necessary?" Marcel asks.

"I thought so." I shrug as I step into the store. I don't know exactly what this guy did to piss off Gio. I don't bother questioning orders these days. I just follow them, happy for the chance to break shit. My bat comes down on the first glass counter, smashing through the top. I watch as the shards fall around the coloured gem stones beneath.

Cammi would love these. I shake the thought of her from my head.

"What the hell are you doing?" A man in his mid-fifties steps out from behind a counter. He's the only one here. We waited for the last customer to leave about ten minutes ago.

"You know, that's a really good question. Why don't you tell us why Giovanni sent us to pay you a little visit?" I ask while pointing the end of my bat in the fucker's direction. When he doesn't answer quickly enough, I swing and hit the side of another display case. "Cat got your tongue, Joe?"

"I... I... d...d... don't know," he stammers out. "Just stop, please."

"You got the cash you owe my brother?" Marcel chimes in, and I look over at him.

That's what we're here for? Money?

Makes no difference to me. I just like smashing

shit, which is exactly what I intend to do. I bring my bat down on the next display cabinet. This one is full of pink stones. I reach in and pick up a small heart-shaped gem and pocket it before stepping back towards Joe and raising my bat again.

"Wait." He holds out a hand, like that'll fucking stop me. "I have it. I have Gio's money," he says.

"Well, where the fuck is it?" This comes from Marcel. "Hurry up. I don't have all day and that one..." My brother gestures to me. "...can only be kept on so long of a leash before he gets impatient."

I smile and Joe's face pales. *Yeah, fucker, you should be scared. Real fucking scared.*

"It's in the back," he says.

"Let's go." Marcel follows Joe to the back while I stay behind to keep an eye on the door.

When I hear shit start to bang around, I walk over and peek inside the room. Marcel has Joe by the throat, the fucker's feet barely touching the ground.

"Let this be a warning. Next time, we won't be so forgiving," my brother says and then proceeds to punch the guy in the stomach before letting his body slump to the ground.

"I would have done that, you know."

"I'm aware." Marcel grabs a bag from a nearby

desk before tucking it under his arm. "Let's get out of here."

"What's he owe Gio money for anyway?" I ask once we're in the car.

"Loan repayment. He borrowed funds to open his little shop," Marcel tells me.

My hand reaches into my pocket, and my fingers rub the little heart-shaped gem I swiped. Cammi would love it. Not that I'll ever be able to give it to her.

My phone vibrates in the centre console of the car, Dash's name flashing on the screen. "You gonna get that?" Marcel asks.

"Nope, he can wait," I say, letting the call ring out, only to have it start up again. I snatch up my phone and slam on the green button. "What the fuck is so important you're blowing up my phone?"

"She's back," Dash says, and my heart picks up speed. No. He's not talking about Cammi.

"Who's back?" My words are slow, measured.

"Cammi. She's back in Melbourne. Saw her today at student services," he tells me.

She's back. She's here. In Melbourne. Where I am. She's supposed to stay far away from me. I can't be near her. Fuck. He could be mistaken. It might not be her.

"Yo, Vin, you there, bro?" Dash asks.

"Ah, yeah. You sure it was her?" I question him.

"Positive. She asked about you. Not in the way that would suggest she hoped the fiery pits of hell had swallowed you alive either. It was more the *I hope he's okay because I still care* kind of way."

"Riiight." I sigh. There is no way Camile Taylor still cares about me. I made sure she'd hate me. I ignored every single text message and phone call. She even returned the car, and when I found a letter in the glove box, I didn't write back.

"Well, I wanted you to know, so when you did see her around campus, you didn't think you were seeing shit. It's real," Dash says.

"How'd she look?" I ask him, regretting the question as soon as it's out of my mouth.

"Thought you didn't care." He laughs.

"I don't. Forget it." I'm about to hang up when his voice stops me.

"She looked thinner... and sadder," he says.

"Thinner?" I repeat.

"Yeah." He sighs. "I don't know, man. You should go and see her or something."

"I can't do that. Thanks for letting me know," I tell him before cutting the call.

"She's back in town?" Marcel asks, making no pretence that he wasn't listening in.

"Seems that way," I grunt.

"I know you have this whole martyr thing going on, Vin. But you gotta wake up and see that you're only hurting yourself *and her*. I might not have known the girl well, but the brief time I did spend with her, it was obvious how much she loved you," he says.

"*Loved*, past tense. And I never once doubted that. It's because of that love she was blinded to what being with me would really mean for her." I run a hand through my hair. I need to get out of this car. "Pull over. Let me out here."

"Here? Where the fuck are you going?" Marcel asks.

I pocket my phone and unclip my belt. "Out. I'll have Marcus or Dash come get me." We're already in the middle of the city.

Marcel pulls over before turning his glare on me. "Don't do anything stupid, Vin," he warns.

"Aye-aye, captain." I wave him off with a salute as I push open the door and step out onto the kerb.

I wait for my brother to drive off before I turn around and walk down the street. I know where I'm going. Ten minutes later, I walk into Marcus's new ink shop. He bought this place two months ago, much to his parents' disapproval. I love the joint, and he's a great fucking artist.

"Do you have an appointment?" He looks up at me from his sketchbook.

"I don't need one," I tell him, making my way over to the chair. I strip off my shirt and lie down, getting comfortable.

"Make yourself at home." Marcus chuckles.

"I need something."

"What do you want?" he asks, coming over and standing next to me.

"The Eiffel Tower. Right here." I point to a blank patch of skin on my left rib cage.

"You want the fucking Eiffel Tower?"

"That's what I said," I grunt.

"Fine. Give me ten." He goes off and starts sketching my design.

I like living in the fantasy. When shit gets too fucking hard, I go back to that moment when I kissed Cammi under the Eiffel Tower as if she'd just said yes to my marriage proposal. What I never told her was that I fucking wished it were real. I wanted nothing more than for it to be real, for me to be able to make her my wife.

I pull out my phone and swipe over my GPS

app. I haven't tracked her location in a long time. The little red light comes to life, hovering right over her parents' house. She's so fucking close, yet so far away. I could easily go and climb through her window, pretend we're back in high school, pretend that Paris didn't happen.

Except it did happen. When I close my eyes, I see her underneath me, my hands around her throat.

Fuck, I need this tattoo. It'll be a permanent reminder of everything I fucked up. And why I need to stay the fuck away from Cammi. I won't risk hurting her again.

Marcus comes back over and holds up a sketch on a transfer sheet. "You ready?" he asks me.

"Yep, go for it," I tell him. He places the transfer onto my skin before gesturing for me to have a look. "That's good."

He's drawn the Eiffel Tower with a pile of skulls and black roses around the base. It's fucking perfect. "Did you think it wouldn't be?" He raises a questioning brow.

"Never doubted you for a second, bro." I laugh. The sound of his gun whizzes to life, and I lie back and close my eyes, enjoying the sting of the needle against my skin.

Chapter Thirty

One month later

It's the first day of classes and my second year of university, but as I park my car on campus, my anxiety sparks to life. I'm not nervous

Kylie Kent

about the school itself or my course list. It's him. I'm fucking petrified of seeing him.

What if he's with someone else? Can I really handle seeing that? I wouldn't blame him if he were. It's been over a year since we last spoke. He could have been with a million women since then. Well, maybe not a million, but he's a De Bellis. Those guys don't exactly have to work to get women.

Just the thought of having to see him makes me nervous, while the thought of seeing him with a different girl leaves me feeling nauseated. I can't see that, but maybe I need to. Maybe if I see that, it'll be the final nail in the coffin, so to speak. The last straw. The push I need to be able to let go of him completely.

I like to tell myself that I've let go. That I'm over him. I'm not. How do you get over a love like that? I honestly thought I was one of the lucky ones. I found a guy who I thought loved me so intensely, so wholly, at such a young age. I thought we'd grow up together, and then grow old together.

What are the chances of seeing him anyway? It's a big campus, and we're not exactly studying the same subjects. I've been back in Melbourne for a month and I've yet to see him anywhere. Not that

I've ventured out a lot. If I'm honest, there was that tiny, minuscule part of me that hoped he'd reach out. I have no doubt Dash would have told Vin that we ran into each other.

But it's been radio silence. Not that it matters. I'm over him. I don't care, right? That's what any normal person would say after a year of waiting. And you know what the sad thing about it is? I still lie awake at night and wonder if Vin is sleeping, if the nightmares are still haunting him. Has he found another way to get a peaceful night's rest? How is he functioning and going on with life without me?

Because I'm struggling. I struggle every damn day.

I might have taken a little extra care in getting ready today, put on that little bit of extra makeup and did my hair up nice. It's for my benefit, not his, though. I'm probably not going to see him, but on the off chance that I do, I want to look my best. I don't want him to see how much he's broken me. I might love him, but I'm not going to let him break my heart twice. Once was enough.

My phone vibrates in my bag, and I pull it out to see a message from my aunt lighting up the screen.

AUNT STACEY:

Good luck today. Remember you
are great. You are amazing!

Her words bring a small smile to my face. I've always had a close relationship with my aunt, but it's gotten stronger over the last year. I leaned on her, and she let me. She's helped me when I couldn't help myself. She saw me at my worst. When I couldn't get out of bed for weeks at a time, when I couldn't eat or keep food down, it was my aunt who held me in her arms and let me cry every night for months. And let's just say, if she knew who *he* was, she would have hunted Vin down and found a way to hurt him.

I type out a reply, thanking her, and then throw my phone back into my bag. I have five minutes to get to my first lecture. I make it just before the doors are locked, grabbing a seat in the back of the hall as quietly as I can. I do not need to draw attention to myself right now.

"Hey, I'm Scarlett."

I turn to see a friendly smile on the face of a cute redhead. "Cammi," I whisper back.

"You look stressed. Don't be. I've heard Professor Carter is easy," she says.

"Perfect." I return her smile. The class has

nothing to do with my nerves. But I appreciate her concern.

"You're new," she says.

"Just transferred from Sydney," I tell her.

"Oh, fun. Wanna grab coffee after class?"

"Sure," I agree because, so far, she seems nice. And, honestly, it'd be great to make some new friends. I have Elena still, but she's studying law, and I'm pretty sure none of her classes are anywhere near mine. Devon went to university in Queensland, and Lauren ditched uni altogether to open her own bookshop. Which is doing really well.

I do my best to listen to the professor's introduction. By the time the lecture is over, I think I finally manage to focus. I've had to teach myself how to compartmentalise. I can't spend all day thinking about him. So I let my mind drift for little spirts of time each day. Then I think about other things. I'll pinch my wrist, do anything to distract myself if he creeps into my mind too much. It kind of works.

"When's your next class?" Scarlett asks.

"Ah..." I pull out my timetable and check the clock on the wall before peering over at her again. "I've got an hour."

"Perfect. Come on. I'll show you the best coffee shop on campus," she says.

"Amazing. Thank you. Do you mind if I invite a friend?" I ask, already tugging my phone out of my pocket.

"Not at all." Scarlett picks up her bag and waits for me as I send Elena a quick message.

ME:

You free? Going to a coffee shop with a new friend.

ELENA:

Friend? Female or male? And which coffee shop?

I glance to Scarlett again. "What's the name of the coffee shop?"

"Japas," she says.

ME:

Japas. Female friend.

ELENA:

Meet you there.

Dropping my phone into my bag, I follow Scarlett out of the building. "Thank you," I tell her. "My friend Elena is meeting us there."

"What's she studying?"

"Law. Do you live on campus?"

"Yeah, you?" Scarlett asks.

"No, I'm staying with my mum for a bit." I plan on getting a job and an apartment soon. For now, I'm happy to stay and help my mother.

We make small talk as Scarlett directs us to the coffee shop. The whole time, I'm looking around the gardens and the walkways. I need to stop. I'm not looking for him.

I order a vanilla caramel latte and a muffin that I know I won't eat. But it looks good, and by the time we sit down, Elena walks in. "You have no idea how freaking glad I am you're finally back." She wraps her arms around me. "It's been way too quiet around here."

"I've been back for a month," I tell her, returning her hug.

"Yeah, but back at school. With me." She smirks.

"Back? Where did you go?" Scarlett asks.

I make quick introductions before explaining how I was in Sydney for my first year, leaving out the reason why.

"So, have you seen him yet?" Elena says right after our coffees arrive.

"Seen who?" Scarlett looks in my direction, her eyes full of intrigue.

"No one, and no," I answer both of them in one breath.

"*No one* sounds an awful lot like a someone." Scarlett laughs.

"Her ex," Elena clarifies. "He goes here."

"Have *you* seen him?" I counter.

"I try not to," she sneers, like the mere thought of Vin sends her into a fit of rage.

"What did he do? Cheat?" Scarlett asks me.

"No, he wouldn't do that." I don't want people talking badly about him. I know I'm meant to be the one hating him, and I do. Well, some part of me does. There's just a bigger part that loves him.

"He broke her heart. And ghosted her," Elena says.

"Has he... Do you know if..." I can't even bring myself to ask the question.

"No," she says. "From what Marcus tells me, he hasn't touched a single person."

He hasn't? Why not? "You still talk to Marcus?" This is news to me.

She looks away and shrugs. "Every now and then," she says before asking, "How's your mum?"

"Nah-ah, do not even try to change the subject. What's going on with you and Marcus?"

"Nothing. He needed help with his shop and he asked me. That's it. There's nothing to tell." Elena looks everywhere but at me as she speaks. "So, back to Vin? What are you going to do when you see him? Kick him in the balls? Chop them off?"

"No. I'm going to be mature and walk right past him if I have to. I'm not going to let him have any more of an impact on my life." I don't believe my own words. I guess we're both lying now.

"How long has it been? Since the breakup?" Scarlett asks me.

"Three-hundred and ninety-eight days," I tell her.

"Oh, so... a while," she says.

"I love him more than I love myself," I attempt to explain.

"Love or *loved*?" Elena presses.

"Same thing." I shrug.

"No, they are two very different things, Cammi. You love him still or you loved him once. See? Two different meanings." This comes from Scarlett.

Again, I lift a single shoulder. "Do you ever really just stop loving someone? I feel like if that were possible, you probably weren't really in love with them to begin with." I need to get out of here. I can't sit around talking about him. I'm supposed to not be thinking about him at all. "I have to get to my next class. I'll catch up with you both later."

"Sure, thanks for the chat," Scarlett says.

"I'll come with." Elena jumps up from her seat. And as much as I want to be alone, I can't bring myself to tell her I don't want her to come with me. Besides, she knows this campus. She might come in handy in helping me find where I'm actually going. "Are you okay? Really, Cammi. Don't lie to me," Elena asks as soon as we're out of earshot.

"I'm trying to be," I tell her.

"Okay, whatever you need, all you have to do is ask. I'm here for you, Cammi. Always." She wraps her arms around me.

"I know. Thank you." I've never really confided much about Vin to my friends. I don't know why. I guess I just want whatever we had to stay between us. Private. I don't want them tainting my opinions of him or what we shared with their own. I meant what I told Scarlett. I really did love him more than myself. Do I still feel that way? I'm not sure.

"Shit," Elena hisses. "Ah, Cammi, let's go this way," she says, pulling me in the opposite direction.

"Why?" I ask her, looking around at the almost-empty field we're walking across. And that's when I see the reason. "Vin." His name is a whisper on my lips.

My feet stop, my legs buckle, and my heart picks up speed. I can't move. I'm frozen in place. Staring into the darkness of his eyes. My head starts to spin and my chest starts to ache. I bring my hand up, rubbing at the spot where it hurts most, but it does nothing to alleviate the pain.

"Elena? It's happening again," I manage to get out before I feel myself falling.

Chapter Thirty-One

Cammi. She's here. Right fucking in front of me. Ten steps and I could be close enough to touch her. I don't dare move. Afraid if I do, she'll disappear. I knew there was a chance I'd see her on campus. I didn't expect to run into her so soon, though.

She's staring back at me, her hand rubbing at her chest. Her breaths laboured, heavy. Something is wrong... What the fuck is wrong with her?

My feet start moving towards her, and when I see her fall, I run. Catching her just before she and her friend both hit the ground.

"Cammi?" Her body is limp in my arms, her lips turning blue. I carefully lay her down flat, in case she needs CPR, before looking up at Elena. "What the fuck is happening? She's not breathing!" I yell out.

Fear. I've known it, lived within its embrace for more years than I care to remember. But nothing prepared me for this kind of full-on terror. I search for a pulse. There isn't one.

"Fuck! Call a fucking ambulance," I tell Elena.

"Already on it," Dash says.

I drop my palms to her chest and start compressions. "Cammi, do not fucking do this," I curse under my breath as I pump while counting to thirty in my head. My mouth closes over hers and I breathe air into her lungs twice. Checking for her pulse again. It's still not there, so I go back to compressions. "Where are they?" I yell at Dash, who has dropped to his knees on the other side of Cammi.

"I don't know, man. Let me help," he says.

"Don't fucking touch her," I growl as I keep

pumping. My mouth closes over hers again. I thought I knew what it was to be stuck in a nightmare. Those were fucking picnics compared to this. "Please, please," I whisper as I check for a pulse for a third time, cursing in relief when I finally feel one. "Fuck!" Placing my fingers under her nose, I test her air flow and can feel a light wind as she exhales on her own. "She's okay. She's okay," I repeat over and over to myself.

I can hear the sirens. And then everything happens so fast. The paramedics come. I vaguely hear Elena explain what happened. I'm in a daze until I hear her mention that it's not the first time.

My head spins in her direction. "What do you mean it's not the first time? What the fuck is wrong with her?"

"Like you care what happens to her," Elena hisses at me.

"We can take one person on the ambulance," the paramedic says as they lift Cammi onto a stretcher.

"I'm coming." I glare at Elena, daring her to challenge me. Thankfully, the girl's not dumb. She backs down.

"I'll follow you. Come on, Elena, I'll give you a ride," Dash says.

I follow the paramedics in the back of the ambulance, my eyes glued to Cammi. She hasn't woken up. She's got all sorts of shit connected to her body. "What's wrong with her?" I ask the paramedic as soon as we start moving.

"She's stable. We'll know more once they run some tests at the hospital," he says. "I need some information. Her full name?"

"Camile Taylor," I tell him, then add, "De Bellis." If I have to lie to make sure she gets the best fucking treatment possible, I will.

"De Bellis?" the guy parrots, looking up from his paperwork to stare at me.

"That's what I fucking said," I grunt. "Make sure only the top fucking doctors are treating her." I pull my phone from my pocket and call my brother. I can't deal with this. I don't know what to fucking do.

"Vin?" Gio answers.

"I need you to meet me at the hospital," I tell him.

"Which one and what happened?" he asks. I can hear him moving already.

"It's Cammi. She... I don't know what is fucking happening, Gio." My free hand is running through my hair without me even realising I'm doing it.

"I'm on my way. Which hospital?" he asks again.

"The Royal Melbourne, Mr De Bellis," the paramedic says into the speaker.

"I'll be right there." Gio cuts the call.

Fuck...

When I look back down at Cammi's face, her eyes are open and she's staring right back at me. "Am I dead?" she asks, her brows turned down.

"No," I answer her.

Cammi turns towards the paramedic and then back to me again. "Why are you here?"

"Cammi, your heart just fucking stopped. I had to perform CPR on you. Where else would I be?"

"Anywhere but with me. I'm sorry you had to do that."

I don't know what to say to her. She's sorry? She's fucking sorry I wasn't going to sit by and let her die? What the fuck is happening?

"What's happening, Cammi?" I repeat aloud. "Elena mentioned something about this happening before?"

"It's nothing," Cammi says, her eyes looking everywhere but at me.

"Miss De Bellis, if you could provide us with any background information on your condition or past conditions that would be helpful for us to know how to treat you," the paramedic tells her.

"It's Taylor. My name is Cammi Taylor. Not De Bellis. And I'm fine. They couldn't find anything wrong with me before and they won't now. Did my heart stop?" she asks.

My head is spinning. This has happened before, and I had no idea. She could have died, and I wasn't there.

"When was the last incident?" the paramedic questions her.

"Seven months ago," she tells him before turning back to me. "Where's Elena?"

"She's following us to the hospital," I say, "with Dash."

"I don't need a hospital. I'm fine. It was a momentary weakness. That's all," Cammi says.

"Miss De... Taylor, you've experienced some sort of arrythmia. We can't release you until a doctor has run some tests," the paramedic explains.

Thank fuck. Like I'm going to let her walk out of the hospital without finding out what is going on with her and how to fix it.

I follow the hospital attendees as they wheel Cammi into a private room in the ER. The paramedics relay all the info they have collected to a doctor before disappearing through the door.

"Miss De Bellis, I'm Dr Hart, the attending cardiologist. I hear you've experienced a similar cardiac event in the past?" An older guy with a pair of huge black-rimmed glasses introduces himself.

"It's Miss Taylor. And, yes. Once. But I'm fine, really. They've already done all the tests up in Sydney. They couldn't find anything," she says. "Can I go home now?"

"Fuck no," I cut in before turning my glare on the doctor. "Find out what's wrong with her or I'll make sure you can't get a job at as a GP in this town."

"Vin." Cammi's eyes widen as she glances between us. "He doesn't mean that. I'm sorry."

"He does mean that," my brother's voice booms as he walks into the room. "Giovanni De Bellis." He holds out his hand to the doctor. "What's happening with my sister?"

"Mr De Bellis, I'm Dr Hart. I'm going to run a few tests and see if I can find out what's going on with Camile's heart."

"Thank you, Doctor. Money is no object. Run every test and call in all the specialists. Whatever it takes."

"I'll be right back. I'm keeping her overnight while we run through a list of possible causes."

"*She* is right here and *she* gets a say in this," Cammi says.

I step closer to her bedside before whispering, "Just let them do the tests. Please, Cammi." I'm not above begging her to stay and let the doctors do what they have to do.

"Fine," she grits out between her teeth. "But cut out the whole *I'm a De Bellis* bullshit. We both know I'm not and you don't want me to be."

"Thank you," I say, ignoring that last part, because nothing could be further from the truth. I can't give her my last name. That doesn't mean I don't want her to have it. I turn to Gio. "Thanks for coming."

"Of course. What happened?" he asks me.

"She just fell over. Had no pulse and wasn't breathing. I gave her CPR until the paramedics arrived," I give him the *CliffsNotes* version.

Gio steps around me to speak to Cammi. "This has happened before?"

She nods her head. "Once. But it's really not a big deal."

"Your heart stopping is a big fucking deal,

Cammi," I tell her, my voice louder than I mean it to be.

"Vin." Gio cuts me a glare, and my mouth snaps shut. When he looks at Cammi again, his eyes are softer than I'm used to seeing them. "Ignore him, sweetheart. He's a little... distressed right now. When did it happen before? What hospital did you go to?" Gio asks her.

Cammi lists off everything she can remember. My brother thanks her before stepping outside the room, telling us he is going to speak to the staff.

"You don't have to stay," she says to me.

"I can't leave." I mean that. I physically can't walk out of this room. What if her heart stops again and I'm not here?

"Sure you can. You've done it before. You even made it look easy."

I see the hurt in her eyes. So much fucking hurt. "You think it was easy?" I laugh. It's not funny. And the sound is more manic than amused.

"It couldn't have been too hard." Cammi looks away from me, staring at the wall on the opposite side of the room.

"You know what's hard? Waking up and finding yourself, your own hands, choking the life out of the woman you love. That's fucking hard. Seeing that same woman on the ground without a fucking heartbeat pounding in her chest," I tell her. "I can live with you hating me, Cammi, but you need to be alive to do that. I can't live if you're not."

"And I can't do *this*, Vin," she says. "I need you to go. I can't..." She shakes her head while tears drop down her cheeks.

"I can't leave until I know what's wrong with your heart and how to fix it," I explain.

"I know what's wrong with my heart. You broke it." Her words send a dagger through my own chest.

"I'm sorry." I drop my head, leaning it on the edge of the mattress as I sit in the chair next to her bed.

"Me too," she whispers back.

"Cammi? You doing okay?" Elena's voice is followed by the sound of her rushed footsteps.

I don't bother looking up. I can't face anyone right now. I just need to know that Cammi is going to be okay, that whatever is wrong with her heart can be fixed.

"I'm fine. Everyone is overreacting," Cammi says.

"Why is *he* here? This is *his* fault."

The implication has my head snapping up and my glare aiming in Elena's direction.

"Elena, stop," Cammi hisses from beside me.

"Why? It's his fault. You were fine until you saw him, Cammi," Elena argues.

"What is she talking about?" I ask, looking from Cammi to Elena and back again.

"Nothing," Cammi says. "Elena, I have to stay here tonight. Can you get me some supplies? And where's my phone? I need to text my mum."

I pick up Cammi's bag and dig through the contents until I find her phone and hand it to her. The girls continue to talk and I tune out whatever it is they're saying, waiting for Elena to leave. When she finally does, I turn to Cammi. "Is it my fault?"

"Is what your fault?" she asks me.

"Your heart stopping?"

"Vin, I know all you De Bellis men think the world revolves around you, but my heart stopping has nothing to do with you. So, no, it's not your fault."

I can tell there's something she's not saying. I really don't have a right to continue to question her about it, though. "Why don't you rest?" I tell her.

"When was the last time you slept?" she asks me. "Not just for an hour here or there, like really slept?"

"France."

Cammi blinks. I don't think she was expecting that answer. "Put your head down here. Sleep, Vin."

"You're the one in the hospital and you're worried about me sleeping? Fucking saint," I tell her. I have no intention of sleeping anywhere near her. I never want to wake up with my hands on her again.

"Just rest your head. Close your eyes with me," she offers.

"I can't. I'm scared," I admit quietly.

"I know," she says.

Chapter Thirty-Two

Cammi

I can't believe it happened again. I thought for sure it was going to be a onetime thing—my heart stopping. It's scary. Although I put on a brave face and pretend that I'm fine, I'm not. I have no idea why my heart is giving out on me.

That's not true. The only common factor is Vin.

Did he really break my heart to the point of making it stop beating altogether?

Yes. The first time it happened, I was happy to blame it on my heartbreak and overbearing sadness. Now, I don't want him to be the reason. The look on his face was one of pure horror. He really has it in his head that he's going to hurt me. Or kill me.

And that's why he ghosted me. That's why I've been lost without him for the past year. I don't want to give him more of a reason to blame himself. He has enough shit in his head to deal with without having to worry about me.

Besides, he made the decision that I wasn't his problem a year ago. Which is why I don't understand why he's here right now. Although, if it were the other way around and he was in a hospital bed, I wouldn't want to be anywhere else either.

Why is love so hard? It's almost like a cruel joke, a payment for the sins committed in a past life or something. I can't think of another reason why God would give you a love you can't hold on to.

Vin fell asleep about ten minutes ago, his head resting on the edge of my mattress. His brother walks in with the doctor, and I bring my finger up to my lips. "He's asleep. Don't wake him up," I whisper.

Gio looks at Vin and then back to me. "He told me what happened in France."

"That wasn't his fault. He was having a nightmare," I say.

"I know. Told him the same thing." Gio sighs. "But he's stubborn and will always blame himself for it."

"Ah, Miss Taylor. I have your records from Sydney. It seems all the tests they did six months ago came back clear. I'm going to run a few more, just to make sure you haven't developed any complications that might not have shown up last time," the doctor says.

"Okay, but I'm fine. Really."

"I have a theory. You're young and we usually see this in much older patients, Ms Taylor." Dr Hart pauses, waiting for me to look up again.

"What?" I ask, curious.

"What were you doing the first time your heart stopped? Where were you?"

"I was in class." I keep my voice quiet, trying my best not to disturb Vin.

"What were you thinking about? When you were in class," Dr Hart presses me.

"Ah..." I look from Vin to his brother. I don't

think this is a conversation either of them should hear.

"I need to know, Miss Taylor," Dr Hart tries again.

"I was... um... I was thinking how it was over, like really over. And the realisation that I'm never getting him back hit me."

"What was over?" Dr Hart asks.

"My relationship. My boyfriend left me six months prior to that. Six months is a really long time to wait for someone to change their mind," I whisper. "I had hope, and then all of a sudden, that hope disappeared, and reality kicked in."

"Okay, thank you." Dr Hart scribbles something on the chart in his hand.

I take that moment to look over to Gio. The same man who is usually so stoic gives me a little smile and a nod. No idea why or what it means.

"And today. What are you doing?" Dr Hart says.

"I was walking across campus. I'd just finished having coffee with my friends. And then..."

"And then what happened?" Dr Hart urges me to continue.

"I saw... him," I say, then quickly add, "But it's not his fault," when the doctor's gaze falls to Vin, who appears to be sleeping. At least I hope he is. And I hope he didn't hear me.

"No, it's not," the doctor agrees. "We need to run some more tests, but I think you are suffering from a condition called takotsubo cardiomyopathy."

"What is that?" Gio asks the question before I can.

"It goes by a few different names. But, basically, it's when somebody experiences sudden acute stress, which weakens the heart muscles. And, in some cases, it can shut the organ down completely," Dr Hart explains.

Gio is typing something into his phone, while I have no idea what to say. "So you're telling me my heart stopped because I was stressed?" I attempt to clarify.

"Like I said, we need to run some more tests to confirm this theory, Miss Taylor. But, yes, you experienced severe emotional stress, which in turn caused your heart to stop."

I look at Vin. Thankful he hasn't woken up. "He can't know," I whisper to Gio, who looks to the doctor.

"Broken heart syndrome?" he asks, waiting for Dr Hart to nod before turning back to me. "He's going to hate himself more, but you can't hide this from him."

"Actually, I can. In case you missed the memo, we're not together. I don't need to tell him anything that concerns me," I spit out, my voice rising with my panic.

Gio smirks, opens his mouth, and then shuts it again when his brother's head lifts off the bed. "What's wrong?" Vin asks me.

"Your brother's an ass," I tell him. "And I think you should both leave."

Vin chuckles. "He is an ass, but he usually means well." He looks from me to Gio. "What'd you do?" he questions his brother before focusing on Dr Hart. "Wait... Did you find something, Doc?"

"We're keeping Miss Taylor overnight for observation. And we'll schedule some appointments for her to come back and see me for further testing."

"Why? What's wrong with her heart?" Vin says.

"Isn't it obvious? It's broken," I tell him. His face drops, and I feel like a bitch.

"You need to rest, Miss Taylor, and avoid stressful situations." The doctor shoots me a pointed glare before exiting the room.

"I'll give you two some space. Gabe and Daisy

are out in the waiting room. Daisy wants to see you," Gio directs to Vin, who nods in return.

"Your brother is out of prison?" I ask.

"Yeah, he is," Vin says. "What did Gio say that upset you?"

"Nothing," I lie. "Why don't you go home? Your family is worried about you. Go home."

"Sure, I'll go home," Vin agrees, and I sigh in relief until he adds, "When you get released and can come home with me."

"That's never going to happen. I don't know what you think is going on here. But *this*..." I gesture between us. "...isn't a thing." I give myself an internal high-five for having the strength to say those words out loud. I can't allow myself to fall back into the Vin effect.

Broken heart syndrome. I knew I had a broken heart. I didn't know it was an actual medical condition, though. And now that I have some sort of confirmation that the reason my heart stopped is because he left me, I don't want to become reliant on him again. I might not actually survive the second time.

"I don't care what is or isn't going on between us, Cammi. I care about your heart and making sure it doesn't stop. If I have to follow you around to make sure you're okay, then I will," he says.

I laugh. Where was this concern for me a year ago when I really needed him? Anger is building in my chest, quickly replacing the heartbreak. How dare he just waltz in like nothing happened? Maybe Gio is right. I mean, he's an all-powerful crime boss after all. Who am I to argue with him?

"You want to know what the doctor said, Vin?" I hiss, venom dripping from my voice.

Vin's back goes straight, and his eyes connect with mine. Unwavering. "What did he say?"

"He thinks I have broken heart syndrome, a condition where your heart weakens under severe emotional stress. Do you want to know what happened to me that caused my heart to break, Vin? The one person I thought would always be there for me *left*. The one person on this earth who I need—not just want but *need* —left. He left, and I was fucking devastated. Beyond devastated. I needed him and he wasn't there. So, yeah, my heart is quite literally broken. And I can only think of one person who's responsible for that happening."

By the time I'm finished yelling at him, my cheeks are wet and I feel like I've just let out a lot of stuff I was holding in. I've wanted to yell at him for so long. I've wanted to confront him, to shake some damn sense into him.

Vin's face is pale, and his eyes are watery with unshed tears. "I... did... this?"

I've seen Vin scared. I've seen him angry. I've seen him happy. Now, he looks downright broken.

"It's not your fault." I try my best to backtrack, because some insane part of me still wants to protect him.

"It is. I stayed away so I wouldn't hurt you, Cammi. I didn't know that by doing that, I was hurting you more. I was killing you," he says.

"You aren't killing me."

"I've weakened your heart. It's my fault. I did this. Fuck!" Vin jumps up from his chair and starts pacing.

"It's not your fault, Vin," I repeat.

He looks over at me briefly and then curses under his breath as he grabs the chair and throws it aside. It hits the wall with a loud crash, which has the door slamming open and Gio walking in with a gun raised.

I ignore the crowd of people rushing into the room, push up from my hospital bed, and walk over to Vin. I need to help him. I can't let him spiral because I was a bitch and told him something I should have kept to myself. "Vin, I need you to hug me. I want you to hold me like you're never going to let go of me ever again. Please." I brace myself for the rejection I'm sure is going to come.

Vin takes the one step towards me, closing the distance between us. His arms wrap around my back and he tugs me close to his chest. And I feel it. He doesn't want to let go. But that doesn't mean he won't. "I'm sorry," he whispers while burying his face into the crook of my neck.

"Me too," I tell him.

I don't know how long we stand there like this. But by the time I pick my head up and look around the room, the only person left is Gio. He's leaning against the wall, his ankles crossed and his hands in his pockets.

"I shouldn't have said that," I tell Vin. "It's not your fault."

"It is," he says. "I won't let it happen again. I promise."

I shake my head. I can't take any promises from him. I don't want them. I don't need them. Now that he seems calmer, I take a step back. "I will be okay. It was just a moment of weakness. I'm fine now. We broke the ice, right? We've seen each other, and now we can move on. If I see you around campus, I won't be so worked up." I smile, but it's hard. I know seeing him anywhere is going to be difficult, but I need to do this. I need to maintain the distance. To protect myself.

"Cammi, I'm not going anywhere." Vin picks up the chair, sets it back on its legs, and then just sits.

"It's okay. I'll leave," I tell him, walking right past Gio and towards the door.

"You can't fucking leave. You just had a heart attack. You need to get back into bed," Vin calls after me.

"Vin, why don't you go see Daisy and Gabe? I'll stay here with Cammi," Gio says.

"What if her heart stops again?"

"I'll be right here. I won't let anything happen to her." Gio puts a hand on Vin's shoulder. "Just give her a moment. She needs to relax. And right now, you're not helping."

"Fine," Vin grits out. He looks to me, like he's trying to gauge my reaction. "I'll be back, unless you want me to stay." He appears almost hopeful. And so much of me wants to tell him to stay. I can't, though.

I shake my head and walk back over to the bed. If he's leaving the room, then I guess I don't need to.

Chapter Thirty-Three

W hen I walk out to the waiting room, every fibre of my being wants to turn around and go back. I'm so fucking confused as to what I'm supposed to do here. I need to know that Cammi's heart is still beating. I thought I'd be fine if I saw her, that I'd be able to continue on without her. The past year has been hell, but I've survived.

Now that I've seen her, spoken to her, I need her more than ever.

I slept for an hour at her bedside. I tried not to fall asleep, but she gives me peace. Just being near her creates a calmness I can't find anywhere else. I still think she's better off without me. I don't trust myself not to hurt her. I also don't trust her heart not to fucking stop.

It's a *stuck between rock and a hard place* kind of deal. If I go back to not being around her, I risk not being there if she collapses again. What if she's alone? I can't let that happen.

"You look like shit," Gabe says, wrapping his arms around me in a quick hug.

"Yeah," I agree, because I probably do look like shit. What am I supposed to look like? I just found out I'm the reason Cammi's heart is weak. I broke it, both emotionally and physically. I will never forgive myself, and I'm going to do everything I can to make sure she's never in a stressful situation again. I just need to figure out how to do that.

"What happened? Do they know anything yet?" Daisy asks, Luciano sitting on her hip.

I pluck my nephew out of his mother's arms and

bring him to my chest. "Hey, little man. Miss me?" I kiss his chubby cheeks. I fucking adore my nephew. He's the coolest baby ever.

"Vin, what happened?" Daisy repeats, using her no-nonsense tone on me.

"I broke her heart." It's the truth. "The doctor thinks she has something called broken heart syndrome, and I caused it. I'm the reason her heart stopped today *and* six months ago."

"No. You're not lumping the blame of her heart condition onto yourself." Daisy shakes her head.

"Why not? I caused her so much emotional trauma that her heart physically weakened to the point of stopping. Who else is to blame for that, Daisy?"

"Vin, it's not your fault. You can't control how her body reacts to something," Gabe tells me.

I shrug. I know they mean well, but the blame's on me, and I'm not going to make excuses. I did it. I chose to break her heart, thinking it would be the one thing that'd save her. Little did I know, by doing that, I was slowly killing her.

I can still see her lifeless body on the ground, feel her lips as I breathed air into her lungs when she couldn't do it for herself. I hold Luciano a little tighter, needing something good to clutch on to. This baby is that. He's the essence of innocence and I aim to never let him lose it.

"I appreciate you coming, but I'm fine. I need to get back in there," I tell Daisy and Gabe. I've already been gone too long.

"You need to hand him back if you're sending us home." Daisy points to Luciano.

I look down at him. No one can resist his cute-as-fuck face. "Mind if I take him to meet Cammi?"

"Are you using my son to try to win over a girl?" Gabe laughs.

"No." I shake my head. "Maybe. But look at him. You can't stay mad when you see this face." I hold Luciano out. He smiles and giggles at me.

"Sure," Daisy says.

"I'll have Gio bring him back out in a sec," I tell them before turning around.

When I step into Cammi's room, I find her in the hospital bed again. Whatever she and Gio were talking about stops as soon as they hear me come in.

"Hey, mate." Gio smiles and kisses Luciano's tiny forehead. Then he looks to me. "I'll be outside. I have some calls to make."

I wait for the door to close. "Whose baby is that, Vin?" Cammi asks and her face pales.

"My nephew, Gabe and Daisy's kid." I hold him

out so she can get a full view of him. "Cammi, this is Luciano."

"Oh, he's cute." She sighs in relief.

"Wait... Whose baby did you think it was?" Surely she didn't think he was mine.

"I wasn't sure." Cammi looks away.

"I want you to be sure, Cammi. There hasn't been anyone else since the day we skipped class together and went to that park," I tell her. "There won't ever be anyone else."

"You don't owe me any explanations, Vin. You're single. You have been for a long time now. It's fine," she says.

"No, it's not f... *fudging* fine." I quickly correct myself. "You are the only woman I want. I was a fucking—fuck! Fudging idiot. I know that now. I thought I was doing the right thing for you, Cammi. You have to believe me. There isn't anyone but you."

Her eyes bore into mine. "I believe you," she says.

Now it's my turn to sigh in relief. Thank fuck she believes me. I don't want her to think I'd ever be with anyone but her.

"So, *fudging*, huh?" She smiles.

"Yeah, Daisy has a thing about me swearing in

front of the kid. And, honestly, she can be a little scary." I laugh.

"He really is cute. He looks like a De Bellis already." Cammi glances from Luciano to me.

"He's the best. Gio and El are about to pop one out too." I can't wait for another nephew to spoil.

"You like being an uncle?" Cammi asks.

"Love it," I say.

"You should take him out. This room is depressing, Vin. It's no place for a baby."

"Hold on." I walk to the door and find Gio standing just outside. He's on the phone but walks towards me. "Can you take him to Daisy?"

He nods and I pass him Luciano before heading back over to the chair next to Cammi's bed. I hang my head. I don't know how to fix this, how to fix us. How to fix her heart. And then an idea hits me.

I look up at her. "Ask me."

"W... what?"

"Cammi, ask me." I almost add the word *please*. She knows what I want her to say. I can see the indecision all over her face.

"No," she says. "I can't."

Ever felt like you've been slapped by a tidal wave made out of bricks? Yeah. Not fucking pleasant. I've really fucked up here. She's never said no to me before. "You can," I tell her.

"I don't want to," she clarifies. "I can't do this again, Vin. I can't. I can't." She repeats herself while shaking her head from side to side.

"It's okay. You know I'll never force you to do anything you don't want to do."

"But you did," she says, a single tear running down her cheek. I want to reach out and wipe it away. I almost do but I hold back. She doesn't want me to touch her. "You forced me to let you go, Vin. I didn't want to. I was so attached to you. I didn't want to let you go and you made me. I held you above everyone else in my life. I wanted to be to you what you were to me, but I wasn't enough for you. You said you would never hurt me. You promised. And you hurt me in a way no one else could."

"I know." I close my eyes, trying to find the right thing to say. "You were enough, Cammi. Me leaving was because of my own issues. It had nothing to do with you not being enough for me. You aren't just enough. You're more than that. I hate that I can't be the kind of guy you deserve. I hate that I let them win. I hate that I lost control, that I hurt you so damn much. I hate that even after all this time, after I've watched my brothers kill every single one of them, they still win. The monsters aren't going anywhere near you, Cammi. And I can't figure out how to erase them."

"Your brothers found them?" Cammi asks.

I nod my head. "Gio wasn't going to stop until he hunted 'em all down."

"Good. I think I might have just found a reason to actually like him." Cammi smiles. "I can't go back, Vin. I love you more than I love myself, but I need to put myself first this time. I can't let you back in. I won't survive when you try to leave again."

"What if I can guarantee I'll never leave?" I ask her.

"That's not something you can do." Cammi looks away.

"Marry me," I blurt out, and it's clear both of us are shocked by my words.

"What?" Cammi's eyes are wide as she returns her gaze to meet mine.

"I mean it. Marry me. I will never leave your side again, Cammi." I need to figure out a way to make sure I don't hurt her while I'm sleeping, even if that means having separate bedrooms. I will figure out a way to keep her safe. I have to.

"You're serious." Her words are a statement, not a question.

"I've never been more serious about anything in my life," I tell her. "I've known since we were fourteen that I wanted to marry you, Cammi. I just never thought it would ever be possible."

"Fourteen?" she parrots.

"I might have watched you from afar for longer than you know.

"I knew." She smirks before it drops into a frown. "Marriage isn't a guarantee of a forever."

"It is if it's us."

"My parents thought that too, and now they're in the middle of a divorce. I don't think marriage is forever," she says.

Fuck, I didn't know about her parents. "You know that what we have isn't like what others have, Cammi. Whatever this connection is between us, it has always been more. I know you feel it."

"Maybe, but you left, Vin."

"I was scared," I tell her. "I was fucking terrified of what I did to you, and you didn't hold me accountable, Cammi. You were ready to just forgive me, make excuses where there shouldn't be any. I was scared of what I'd do to you, of the kind of life I'd force on you if we continued."

"What's changed? Why now? Because I had a

small heart issue today? I don't want to be with you just because you think I'm weak."

"You are the strongest person I know. You are the most forgiving, the most beautiful creature, inside and out. You're not weak, Cammi. I want to marry you because I love you. I will love you until I take my last breath. And probably even longer. Just say yes. We can work on everything else. I'll do whatever it takes. You want to go to therapy together? I'll go."

I can see the wheels turning in her head. I'm not above getting on my hands and knees and begging her for another shot. I need her to believe in me like she used to. I need her to believe in us.

"Believe in us, Cammi. You know it's always going to be us. When it comes down to it, neither one of us is complete without the other. There isn't a universe out there where I exist without you."

Chapter Thirty-Four

Cammi

I want to throw caution to the wind and say yes. I want to be back under the Eiffel Tower and have Vin's proposal be real. But I don't need all the fancy romance. All I've ever needed is him and here he is, handing himself over to me. Forever.

Or at least for as long as a marriage might last. I

do think that the connection Vin and I have is intense. It runs deep within my veins. I'm just not sure I can trust him to actually stay. If I say yes today and he wakes up tomorrow or even ten years from now and decides that he's made a mistake, would I survive?

Would I survive the next ten years without him if I say no, though? I'm not sure. I know I'll always wonder *what if*. It's been complete and utter hell this past year having to live day by day knowing he was living a separate life, without me. Knowing I couldn't talk to him, cuddle with him. I really just want to cuddle with him.

I shuffle over on the bed. "I want you to lie down with me, Vin. I want you to wrap your arms around me and make me feel safe the way only you can," I tell him.

He's asking me to believe in us. I want to. I really, really want to.

Vin silently climbs onto the bed and pulls my body up against his. I rest my head on his chest. The rhythm of his heartbeat soothes me. He is the one haven I let myself completely lean on, and then he ripped it out from under me.

"I've been so lost without you. I don't know what to do anymore, Vin," I whisper.

"Do what your heart is telling you to do, Cammi. I love you. I will love you no matter what your answer is," he says.

Right here, in his arms, I feel like I can breathe again. I feel... free. "Is this real?" I ask him.

"I fucking hope so," Vin says.

"If I say yes, what does that look like to you? Us being married?"

"It looks like the second part of the story," he tells me. The story. Vin used to tell me the same bedtime story over and over again. It was our story.

"Tell me part two," I urge him. Because I need to know.

"When the sinner found his way back to the saint, he became alive again. So much so that he never wanted to go back to the depths of hell. He wanted to stay in the light that surrounded the saint. So he did. He married her, worshiped her every day for the rest of his life. He earned her forgiveness, and together they healed. The sinner and the saint had a lifetime of adventures. They travelled the world and made so many memories. Good ones, while the bad one served as lessons on mistakes they'd never repeat." Vin's words speak to my heart. I want that happy ending.

"Yes." The one word escapes my lips. I'm scared.

So damn scared. But I won't let fear stop us from having our life together.

Vin's body stills beneath me. "Yes?" he repeats.

I roll over onto my stomach to look up at him. "Yes. This is when you kiss me, Vin. Kiss me like you proposed and I said yes, because you did and I did."

Vin's lips descend onto mine, his touch so soft, tender. His palm cups my cheek as his tongue pushes into my mouth. I feel everything in this kiss. I doubted his love. There were moments I thought I had made it all up in my head, and he wasn't in love with me like I was with him. But this kiss... After this kiss, I know he loves me.

Vin pulls back, and his eyes connect with mine. "I love you. I promise I'm not going to fuck this up again."

"I hope that's a promise you can keep." I rest my head back on his chest.

"I'm going to do whatever it takes to keep you safe, Cammi. You and our heart," he says.

"Our heart?" I ask him.

"Your heart is my heart. I'm not going to live without you ever again. I was so fucking scared, Cammi. And I've been scared before, but I would willingly go back into that room with the monsters if it meant your heart would continue to beat."

I try to picture what he saw. How I dropped onto the ground, my body lifeless. I couldn't imagine if the roles were reversed. "I wouldn't want you to do that, Vin. Besides, the monsters are all dead now. Right?"

"Right."

"The nightmares?"

"They're different now," Vin says.

"What's different?" He's never really told me what they were about before. And I never asked. I have an imagination. I know what his father did to him, what that man let *other men* do to him. I don't need Vin to tell me more than that to know what's haunting him.

"You're there. In the room," he whispers. "And I can't stop myself from choking you."

I look up. "That's not real. You would always find a way to stop yourself." I know he would.

The door opens and Vin's brother walks back in. He looks at Vin in my bed and smirks. "I spoke to Dr Hart, Cammi. You can go home tonight if you want. You'll have to come back for some follow-up appointments. I'll have the family doc come and stay at the house to keep an eye on you."

Unwrapping myself from Vin's hold, I climb off the bed and step towards Gio. I throw my arms around him. I feel him tense, and then he places a single palm on my waist. "Thank you," I tell him.

"It's nothing really," Gio says.

"Not for breaking me out of here. Thank you for killing the monsters." I keep my voice low so only he hears it.

"You don't need to thank me for that. Just don't give up on him," Gio tells me.

I'm trying really hard not to run. My heart is guarded right now. I said yes, and I meant it. I do want to marry Vin. That's not to say that I'm not going to be waiting for it to fall apart. Maybe if I'm prepared for it to happen, it won't hurt so badly when it does. And I might just survive it.

I'm nervous. Being in Vin's bedroom is a little overwhelming, if I'm honest. Nothing has changed. It's still the exact same bedroom I remember. Right down to the little metal tin that sits on his dresser. I have no interest in what's inside it anymore.

I liked it, but I don't think it's the answer for my kind of pain. Also, the reaction Vin had when he saw me smoking was hypocritical as hell. It was the fact he thought his influence made me smoke that *made me* stop, though.

I don't like when he blames himself for everything. I blame him for breaking my heart, but I also blame myself for letting him. Did I fight hard enough for us? I don't think I did if I'm being honest. I never came back to Melbourne. I never confronted him.

I wonder if things would have been different if I did. If I had fought harder, maybe we would have been able to work through our issues sooner. Not that we're through them now by any means. My biggest hurdle is going to be forgiving him, which I'm not a hundred percent sure I'm ready to do.

"Do you want a shirt? Hoodie?" Vin asks. "I mean, if you want to use the shower or something..." He scratches the back of his neck. He's nervous too.

"Do you want me to leave?"

"No," he answers without hesitation. "I want you here, Cammi."

"Okay, a sweatshirt would be good," I tell him and watch as he heads for his closet. Then again, I could use a shower. "Actually..." I wait for Vin to turn back around before adding, "Can I have that one?" I point to the one he's wearing. If I'm going to wear one of his hoodies, I want it to smell like him, not washing detergent.

Vin reaches behind his head and pulls the hoodie off before handing it out to me. He's shirtless. Right in front of me, shirtless. I can't move my eyes away from his skin. Skin that's now covered in so much ink. So much more than he used to have. One in particular catches my eye.

"The Eiffel Tower?" I question him while staring at a black-and-white image of the structure sitting on a bed of skulls and black flowers.

"Yeah, it's where you first said yes." He smiles.

There's something else that happens when I'm perusing his body. A part of me I considered long since dead suddenly wakes up. With a vengeance. "Vin?"

"Yeah?"

"How do you feel about helping me shower?"

Vin's eyes instantly heat. "Are you sure? We don't have to rush anything, Cammi. And, well, we've never been good at just taking showers..."

"I'm sure." I pull my shirt over my head. And then turn around and walk into the bathroom. "But it's okay if you don't want to."

"Oh, I want to." Vin follows me. He reaches into the shower and turns it on. Memories of us in this bathroom fill my mind. Good memories. Hot memories.

We both work fast at getting undressed. I step into the stall, letting the hot water fall over my body. Vin steps in after me. He doesn't touch me. He just stares. "I'm going to fix what I broke, Cammi," he says.

"Vin, I want you to kiss me. I want you to touch me. Everywhere. I need... I need you... I need to feel you inside me."

Vin reaches out, trailing the tips of his fingers across my collarbone and down the middle of my chest. "I've missed you so fucking much," he says. I doubt he missed me as much as I've missed him though. I don't say that. I need to keep some thoughts to myself. And that's one of them.

"Please," I practically beg as his fingers skim over my lower stomach, heading towards where I really need them.

"Are you really sure you want this, Cammi? No regrets?" Vin asks.

"The only thing I will regret is if you don't touch me right now. Please don't make me wait any longer." I moan when his fingers finally slide through my folds. I'm so wet, so ready for him.

It's him. He does this to me. I didn't have a libido

for the past year. And now, all of a sudden, I feel like I'm on fire. My hands land on his chest, moving up and across his shoulders, then down to his arms.

"Oh god." My knees wobble when Vin rubs his fingers over my clit.

"You're so wet." He pushes those two fingers inside me. "Fuck," he hisses as he pumps them in and out.

Our lips find each other. And my arms circle around his neck, while his free arm wraps around my back, holding me both upright and in place as he fucks me with his mouth and fingers.

"I need you to come for me, Cammi. Come. Show me," Vin growls. He pulls back, his eyes roaming all over my face. He's always loved watching me when I come.

Who am I to deny him what he wants? I grind down on his hand. I can feel it. I'm so close. Moving my hips in rhythm with his hand, I find my groove and chase that feeling until I dive right over the cliff. I scream his name and my knees give out, but he keeps me upright, supporting my entire weight.

"So fucking beautiful," he says.

Chapter Thirty-Five

I think this is the closest I've ever been to feeling like a kid on Christmas day. I literally have my single wish right here. In my arms. Cammi. Watching her come apart in pleasure is the best fucking thing I've ever seen. It's like coming home after a really long time away.

My cock is rock fucking hard, and I know this is going to be embarrassingly quick after twelve months with just my hand for company. "I should apologise now," I tell Cammi as I lift her and she wraps her legs around my waist.

"For what?" she asks, her back hitting the tiled wall.

"For this being really quick. It's just, ah... been a long time."

"Vin, I don't care. Just fuck me already."

Pressing her body harder into the wall, I shift her weight and free my hand. Then I line up my cock with her entrance. "You want this, right?"

"Yes," Cammi groans and uses her legs to push herself down onto me. "Oh god."

She so fucking tight, so good. And then a thought hits me and I stop. "Wait." I don't know if we should be doing this. "We should wait. Talk to a doctor first. What if it's not safe, Cammi? What if it's bad for your heart?" Fuck, I need to be more careful with her. I can't let us get lost in the passion if it's going to impact her heart.

"I swear to God, Vin, if you don't start moving, I'm going to go insane. My heart is fine. I'm fine. I promise," she says. "I'll tell you if I start feeling *not fine*."

"Okay." I begin to move again, slowly. I can't fuck her roughly. I'm too fucking scared of hurting her. So instead, I take my time. My lips trail up and down her neck. "I love you," I whisper into her skin as my cock slides in and out of her cunt at a gentle pace. I fucking love being inside her.

"Please," Cammi moans.

"What do you need?" I ask her.

"You. Always you," she says.

"You have me," I tell her before capturing her lips with mine. I can feel myself on the edge. I need her to come again. I might be quick. Like I said, it's been a really long fucking time. But I'm not an asshole. I want her to find her release before I combust.

Moving my mouth away from hers, I kiss my way down her neck. "Are you going to show me again, Cammi?"

"Mmm." Her head falls back against the tiles. My hips circle as I grind against her. And then her legs tighten around me. "So close," she moans.

Picking up my pace slightly, I feel her pussy clenching, pulling me in every time I slide out. Until she squeezes me so damn tight I have to pull out while she's still coming. My own release spilling all over the outside of her cunt.

I rest my forehead against hers. "Are you okay?"

"Best I've been in a really long time," she says breathlessly.

I haven't been able to stop looking at her. She's fucking beautiful and she's here. In my bedroom. "You need to eat," I tell Cammi for the third time. I've been trying to convince her to come downstairs for dinner.

"I'm really not hungry, Vin. You can go eat with your family. I'll just... stay here." She motions a hand around the room.

"Cammi, when was the last time you ate?" I've been with her basically all day. She didn't touch the food they gave her at the hospital.

"This morning. I had a muffin at the café," she says. "I'm fine, honestly."

"What if we go to that sushi place you used to love?" I suggest, and Cammi screws up her face.

"I don't feel like eating right now."

I don't know what to do to get her to eat—actually I do. It's manipulative as fuck but I think it just might work. "Fine," I say, sitting down on the bed and making myself comfortable.

"What are you doing?" she asks before climbing on next to me.

"If you're imposing some kind of hunger strike, I'm joining you. I'm not eating until you do." I fold my arms over my chest.

"That's ridiculous, Vin. You need to eat."

I raise a single eyebrow at her without saying a word. We get trapped in a staring match. I'm stubborn as fuck, and when it comes to her well-being, I'll be more stubborn than ever if it gets me what I want.

"You're really not going to go and eat?" she asks.

"Nope. You wanna watch a movie?" I offer, reaching for the remote.

"Fine, I'll eat. Come on," Cammi huffs out.

"Glad you finally saw things my way." I smile at her as I climb off the bed.

Just before we walk out of the room, I reach down and clasp my hand around hers. I watch her face as I do, waiting for any indication that she doesn't want me to touch her.

Cammi turns and smiles at me. "It's okay."

I breathe out a breath I didn't know I was holding. I can do this. I can get past my messed-up fuckups and try to be better for her. I don't want her having to spend a lifetime having to ask me to touch her. Kiss her. Make love to her. I get that it's not normal.

"Wait." I skid to a stop in the hallway, my eyes honing in on her lips. "I... ah..."

"Vin, I want you to. I always want you to," she says.

I bend forward and meld my mouth with hers. "I really want to be better for you."

"I don't need you to be anything but yourself, Vin. All I need is for you to stay. Don't leave me again." Her words cut me deep.

"I was a fucking idiot, Cammi. Trust me, I'm not going anywhere," I say as I lead her downstairs.

My brothers are already sitting at the dining table, along with El, Daisy, and Zoe—Marcel's new girlfriend. Gabe has Luciano on his lap. This family really is growing fast.

I pull out a chair for Cammi. She sits down but doesn't let go of my hand. Her grip is tight, and I have to force myself to remain calm as I claim the seat next to hers. I try every fucking thing I can think of. Counting to five, looking over at the adorable face of my nephew, but I can feel myself starting to sweat.

Not now. Fuck, I can't even sit at a dining table

five minutes after I told her I was going to be better for her.

"What's wrong?" Cammi whispers while looking across at me.

My fingers clench and unclench. "Nothing," I tell her, forcing my tone to remain neutral.

And then she lets go of my hand. "Sorry," she says, "I didn't..."

"It's okay. It's not your fault," I tell her before turning my attention to the table. "Everyone, this is Cammi and we're getting married."

"You're what now?" Eloise asks.

"Getting married," I repeat.

Cammi is silent next to me. I kind of put her on the spot with this one, but I've been dying to tell someone.

"You're nineteen, Vin. You can't get married. You're still a kid," Eloise says.

Cammi looks like she wants to say something, but she doesn't. She looks to me instead. "Are you okay?" she mouths.

I give her a nod, then return my attention to my sister-in-law. "El, I wasn't asking for permission." I might have forged some adoption papers back when I was still in high school. That doesn't give her the mother title, though. As much as I love my brother's wife, accepted her as family, I'm not going to let anyone talk me out of this.

"You sure you want to marry into this family?" Daisy looks to Cammi while waving a hand around the table. "I mean, Vin's amazing and honestly I think he's going to make a great husband. But you get all of this too. Just so you know."

"I don't think this family is as bad as the rumours lead you to believe," Cammi says.

"Yeah, and what was I doing the first time you saw me?" Santo chimes in.

"Grieving," Cammi answers vaguely.

"I was digging up the grave of my dead fiancée," he clarifies. "And just so we're clear, *we*." Santo points to Gio, Marcel, and Gabe before finally aiming a finger at me. "...are usually digging graves to hide bodies, not to retrieve them."

"Okay, so do you want me to like order shovels or something?" Cammi asks, causing everyone at the table to burst out laughing.

"Can I keep her?" Zoe asks. "I like her."

"No, she's mine. Find your own friends," I'm quick to reply.

"When and where is this wedding happening?" Gio asks, finally breaking his silence.

Cammi and I look at each other. "We haven't gotten that far into the planning yet," I tell him.

"Okay." He nods, just once, which is his way of giving his approval—*blessing* even.

"Seriously? Just okay, Gio? They're nineteen!" Eloise reminds him.

"Babe, calm down. He's going to do this with or without us. And I'm not missing another one of my brothers' weddings," Gio says while glaring at Gabe.

It's a sore spot that Gabe and Daisy got married without telling anyone. I get why they did it. What I don't understand is why Gabe kept it a secret for the whole year he was locked up. I guess if he knew Daisy wasn't actually in Melbourne, a fact we all kept from him, he might have come forth with that info.

"What do your parents think about this?" Eloise asks Cammi.

"They don't know yet," she says.

Fuck, I didn't think about that. Her parents probably hate me already. I would if I were them. If I had a daughter and some prick broke her heart the way I broke Cammi's, I wouldn't let him anywhere near her again.

"I understand your concerns. We are young. But we're also not," Cammi tells Eloise.

"I know. I... Just, why rush? Why not wait until after you graduate?" Eloise suggests.

"Why wait?" I counter.

"Because... I don't know. Just because." Eloise throws her hands in the air, and her eyes water. "Everything is changing. You're going to move out. Marcel's gone, Gabe's gone, and now I'm going to be left with just his cranky ass." She gestures a thumb at Gio before turning it on Santo. "And his moody ass."

"Aw, you're going to miss me. I knew I was the favourite brother." I laugh. "And you married the cranky one so that is your own fault."

"I know." Eloise starts crying. She reaches out to swipe up a napkin. "Damn these stupid hormones."

"Yeah, we're never doing that," Zoe tells Marcel under her breath.

"Oh, we so are. More of you is exactly what this world needs," he replies with a grin.

As everyone starts chatting and the attention is finally off me and Cammi, I fill her plate with food before loading up my own. Then I lean into her ear. "If you don't pick up that fork and eat, I won't either."

"Is your family always this... much?" she asks me.

"Always. Sorry."

"Don't be. I think it's amazing." Cammi smiles as she grabs her fork.

Chapter Thirty-Six

Cammi

"No, no!"

I wake up with a start at the sound of Vin's scream. I reach out, about to touch him, and then stop and gently climb out of bed. I can't wake him up. Last time I did that, it broke us. I won't make that mistake again. Instead, I move to the sofa and sit down. I don't know what else to do, so I just sit here and watch as the man I love is terrorised by a nightmare of his own making.

Tears fall down my cheeks. I want to help him. I want to jump into his brain and eradicate every single one of the monsters haunting him.

I jolt in my seat when Vin bolts upright in the bed, his eyes roaming around the room with a crazed urgency. Until they land on me. "Cammi?"

"Sorry. I didn't know what to do," I tell him as I get up and approach the bed.

"I woke you up?" he asks.

"I didn't know what to do," I repeat. "I need to know what to do."

"Come back to bed." Vin pulls the blankets aside. "I don't need you to do anything. Just be here."

I climb onto the bed. "Want to talk about it?"

"No." His response is firm, quick, before he adds, "Sorry."

"How often does it happen?" I ask him.

"Every night." Vin rolls over. "They never used to come when I slept next to you until that one time in France."

"Are we really that broken that I don't bring you

that peace anymore?" I say the words that plagued my mind the entire time I watched him from that chair.

"You do. You are the only thing that brings me peace. They're not the same. Like I said, they're different now. Because you're in them."

"It's not real," I whisper.

"I know," Vin replies, but I don't think he does know. I think he's waiting for his nightmares to become a reality.

I want to be able to help him. I just have no idea how. "We're not too broken, are we?"

"No," he says. "I think we're perfect. *You* are perfect."

"Mmm, my parents are going to freak out, you know," I tell him.

"What happened with them? Why are they divorcing?" Vin asks.

"My dad cheated on my mum with his secretary." I sigh. "I really thought they were the real deal. They were young like us. They loved each other, but it wasn't enough."

"My father killed my mother when I was only a few months old. He told me..." Vin says, then stops. "When he would take me to that house, he'd tell me that it was my fault. He had to kill her because of me, that I was being punished for it. That's why he took me there."

I don't say anything. I don't want to interrupt him when he's opening up. So I listen. Fighting the tears that want to escape. Vin doesn't need that right now. All he needs is for me to listen.

"He said that I wasn't really his. That my mother cheated on him and I was the result. It's why he killed her..."

"That wasn't your fault, Vin."

"I don't even know if it's true," he says. "What would they say if they found out I wasn't really their brother?"

"Vin, oh my god. No." I move closer to him. My hand lands on his cheek, my thumb caressing his skin. "Your brothers love you. Even if it were true, you're still their brother. You all have the same mother. And I don't think they'd care."

"I don't know." He shrugs.

"Do you want to find out?" I ask him.

"I don't know."

"Well, if you do, we can do it without them knowing," I suggest. "We can do a sibling DNA test. I'm sure it wouldn't be hard to get a sample."

"Maybe. But what if it's true?"

"Like I said, it won't change anything. Your

father was an evil bastard, Vin. Whatever he did was on him. Not you. And you know what? If your mother cheated on him, I don't blame her."

"Yeah." Vin closes his eyes. "Are you worried about that? With me?" he asks. "Because I'll never do that to you."

"I believe you. I'm not worried about you cheating on me, Vin. I'm worried about you leaving me," I say, because it's the truth.

"That's my fault. I own that, Cammi, and I will do whatever it takes to make you find faith in me again."

"Do you have classes tomorrow?" I ask.

"Yes, but I'm not going," he says.

"Why not?"

"Because I'm not leaving you. I'd rather follow you around and make sure you're okay." This man really believes he's going to become my shadow. I almost laugh, but he's so serious.

"I appreciate the concern but you can't do that. I have classes too, Vin. I need to go to them, just like you need to go to yours."

"I could switch courses." He offers his idea of a solution.

"You think you can just waltz into second-year architecture?"

"I know I can. I'm a De Bellis. We always get what we want," he says.

"Do you...? Have you...?" How do I ask if he works for his brother? I understand that they're family, and I've seen Vin do some horrific things. But I've never asked him if he works for the family. "Are you in the mafia?" I blurt out. "Like I get what your family does, what your brothers do. But do you do that?"

"Babe, I've been a made man since I was thirteen. Our father made sure we all were."

My heart rate picks up. "That's dangerous." I don't want anything to happen to him.

"It is, but it isn't at the same time. Being a De Bellis earns you a certain level of respect. I'm not a street thug, Cammi." He smirks.

"Okay. Just don't die on me," I tell him.

"Ditto," Vin says.

"So, this is happening again?" Elena asks, handing me a cup of coffee.

"It is." I smile, blissfully happy, albeit scared to death.

"Are you sure, Cammi? He really fucked with you last time," she says. "I don't want to see you hurt like that again."

"Neither do I, which is why I'm giving him another chance. It's him or no one, Elena. There is no one else. I can't explain it."

"Okay, I'm going to be here for you no matter what. But does he have to watch you like that? It's creepy." Elena directs her gaze to where Vin is leaning against a tree. He's staring in our direction.

"He's worried about me."

"So am I," Elena says. "Are you really sure you should be back here?"

"The doctor cleared me this morning, after Vin made him do a house call." I sigh. "Come on, lets lose him for a bit. There's something I want to do and you know the saying about asking for forgiveness rather than permission." I smirk. Vin would have a fit if he knew what I have planned, which is why I'm not telling him until after I've done it.

"What have you got in mind?" Elena asks with a mischievous smirk.

"Where'd you park? I'll tell you once you get us both off campus."

"Deal," she says, quickly pushing to her feet. I follow her to her car, doing my best not to look over my shoulder. I know he's following us. There is no way he's just going to go away on his own. I should feel bad for ditching him like this, but I don't. He'll survive.

"Okay, we're going to have to be quick," I tell Elena once I see her car. "Are you ready?"

"Ready," she says, already pulling her keys out of her bag. Then we both sprint for her car and jump inside.

I see Vin running after me when Elena is peeling out of the car park like a maniac. Seconds later, my phone rings. "Hello?"

"What the fuck, Cammi? You ran? You have a goddamn heart condition and you're out here running? Where are you going?" Vin yells down the line.

"I'm fine. I'll be back soon. I'm just running an errand with Elena. You should go to class, Vin. I'll call you later." I hang up the phone. I know it's a shitty thing to do, and I get that he's worried about me. I'm just not going to play along with his craziness. We don't need to be around each other 24/7. It's not healthy.

"Okay, where are we going?" Elena asks.

"Marcus's shop," I tell her.

Elena's gaze flicks to me, a grin playing on her lips. "You sure? Vin will hate it. Let's do it."

The minute we walk into Marcus's shop, his eyes land on Elena and he smiles wide. "I didn't know you were stopping in today, babe," he says to her.

"I'm not. She is." Elena juts her thumb in my direction.

"Oh, fuck no. Nope. Not fucking happening." Marcus shakes his head.

"What? You don't even know what I want yet," I tell him.

"It doesn't matter what you want. I'm not doing it. Because I don't have a death wish." He holds up his hands in surrender.

"Fine, I'll go to another artist then, and I'll be sure to tell Vin I had to go to a stranger because you refused to draw on me," I threaten.

"Elena, help me out here, babe." Marcus looks pleadingly at my friend.

"Just do it, Marcus. Vin's not going to kill you." Elena rolls her eyes.

"Probably not," I say. Because, honestly, I'm not too sure where his craziness ends. It's been a long time since I've been around him—although when I was with him last night, it was like no time had passed at all. We just fell right back into each other. "Look, all I want is three numbers. 9-9-9."

"Why? What do they mean?" Marcus asks.

"Completion, transformation, new beginnings. It's like one phase of my life is ending to make way for a new one," I explain.

Both Marcus and Elena are staring at me like I've grown a second head, until the door opens behind us. I turn, expecting it to be Vin, thinking he's reached a new level of stalker and somehow hunted me down. It's a different De Bellis, though.

Santo stares at me for a moment before he asks, "Vin getting more ink?"

"No, I am," I tell him. "Well, trying to, but this one here is too scared to do the job."

"Right. What d'you want?" Santo asks me.

"Three numbers. 9-9-9," I tell him.

"Where?"

"Right here." I point to my left arm. I want the numbers on my inner wrist, right near the base of my palm.

"Okay," Santo says before turning to Marcus. "Do it."

"Seriously? Vin won't like it." Marcus folds his arms over his chest.

"Vin won't like what?" Vin's voice comes from behind me.

I spin around and smile at him. "Did you follow me?"

"Yes," he says, his eyes flicking from me to his friend. "What won't I like, Marcus?"

"Your girl here is trying to get me to ink her. Your brother ordered me to do it when I refused."

Vin is quiet for a long moment. No one talks. Not a single sound can be heard. "No."

"What?"

"No, it's not happening. And you should know fucking better," he tells Santo.

"Her body, her choice, bro." Santo shrugs.

The words connect with Vin, because he is obsessed with getting my consent. "What do you want?" I explain my idea, the location, and why. Vin nods. "I'll do it," he says. "Come sit down. Marcus, draw up the template."

"Sure thing. Just take over the whole shop while you're at it." Marcus shakes his head.

"I'll come back. I can see you're busy," Santo says to Marcus. Then he returns his attention to me. "Cammi, call me if these idiots give you any more trouble."

"Thank you." When he walks out, I look up at

Vin. "I think I like him the most out of all your brothers."

"That's because he has a weird soft spot for you. Trust me, he's not nice like that to literally anyone else." Vin laughs before yelling out, "Marcus, draw two templates. We're both doing it."

"You're getting the same numbers?" I ask him.

"Yep."

Chapter Thirty-Seven

A tattoo. She was coming to my best friend's shop to get a fucking tattoo. And my brother was in here encouraging her. I'm not against tattoos. Obviously. I'm fucking covered in them.

What I am against is anything hurting Cammi or

putting her under any kind of stress she doesn't need. I know the doctor said she could go on with her day-to-day life. She's got a heap of follow-up appointments and more testing to do over the next couple of weeks. But I'm not convinced she's fine. People's hearts don't just stop for no reason.

I read about the condition the doc thinks she has. Broken heart syndrome. It fits, and it fucking guts me that I did that to her. Which is why, when she told me about the tattoo she wanted and the meaning behind it, I caved and decided to tattoo her myself.

It's three numbers. It's not a difficult design or anything. At least if I do it myself, I can watch her reaction and stop if I think the pain is getting to her. Personally, I don't think tattoos hurt, but I've seen grown-ass men cry in Marcus's chair.

Marcus hands me the transfer sheet, and I look down at Cammi's wrist. I can do this. I can reach out and touch her. She wants this. I tell myself that she's already given me permission to touch her.

I gently wrap my hand around her wrist. Both of us are quiet, our eyes connecting as my thumb traces small circles over her perfectly untouched skin. And then she smiles at me, that blindingly bright smile. The one I've been waiting for. I used to love seeing her smile. She smiled yesterday but it wasn't real. It was nothing like the one she's giving me now.

"You really want this?" I ask her.

"I really do," she says.

"Okay." I turn her wrist over and stroke the area she pointed out. "Right here?"

"Yes," Cammi confirms.

After I stick the transfer on her, I peel the paper back and we both look at the numbers now marking her skin. Marcus pushes a table over to me with his gun, a new needle, and a tub of black ink. "If it hurts, I'm stopping," I tell Cammi. "I don't care if you end up with half a number, babe. I'm not doing this if it's going to cause you pain."

"It's okay. It's not my first tattoo, Vin," she says.

I blink once. Then twice. I've seen every inch of this woman naked. She doesn't have any tattoos. I would have noticed. "You don't have any tattoos, Cammi," I tell her confidently.

"I do, actually. You just haven't noticed yet," she says *more confidently*.

My brows draw down in confusion while my eyes roam over her body. "Where?"

Cammi moves her head to the side and lifts her hair. And right there, behind her right ear, is my name. Vin, with a love heart around the letters.

I'm fucking speechless. "When did you get this?"

"After the first time my heart stopped, when I realised you weren't coming back. I wasn't ready to let go. This was my way of keeping you with me," she says. "It's stupid. You hate it." She drops her hair and shifts in her seat.

"No, it's not. I love it. I'm just shocked. How the fuck didn't I notice it before? And I'm pissed at myself for making you feel like that," I tell her.

"We're moving forward, right? No looking back?" Cammi asks.

"Right. Should we do this?" I pick up the gun. I'm somewhat more relaxed now that I know she's aware of what to expect pain-wise.

"Let's." Cammi places her wrist on the armrest for me. After attaching the new needle and dipping it into the ink, the gun whirrs to life, and I get started.

Cammi doesn't flinch. I keep watching her, waiting for any indication that she's uncomfortable. I can hear Marcus and Elena arguing about something in the back of the shop, but I tune them out.

"All done," I tell Cammi, wiping the area clean.

"I love it. Thank you." She holds up her wrist to examine my work.

"My turn." I hand her the gun, place the transfer on the exact same spot, and then position my wrist on the armrest. Cammi goes to hand me back the gun, and I shake my head. "I want you to do it."

Her eyes go wide. "I can't do that, Vin. I don't know how."

"You do. It's just curves and lines. Just like all those buildings you love to draw."

"But that's on paper. This is your skin. What if I mess it up?" she asks.

"Then I guess I'll have a fucked-up tattoo forever." I laugh. "It's fine, babe. I'll help." I place my hand over hers and guide her over the first number nine. Once I think she's got the hang of it, I let go. She digs a little too hard at times, and I bleed more than I usually would. But it's fucking perfect when she's done. "I love it. See? You can do anything, Cammi," I tell her.

"That was fun. Maybe I should ask Marcus if he needs an apprentice." She smiles at me.

"Or you could stick with becoming an architect," I suggest, the idea of her touching other men for a living not sitting well with me at all. Plus, I know the kind of clientele Marcus gets in here and Cammi doesn't need to be anywhere near those guys.

"You just said I could do anything." She lifts a challenging brow.

"Anything within reason. Anything that doesn't

involve your hands on other men." I know my words aren't going to go over great, but I'm not backing down. No fucking way is she working here. Not that Marcus would hire her. If he knows what's good for him, he sure wouldn't.

"That's stupid. What if I wanted to become a doctor? I'd have to touch people, Vin," she says.

"Do you want to be a doctor, Cammi?" I ask, knowing full well she doesn't.

"No, but that's not the point. I could, if I wanted to."

"I have no doubt." I stand and start cleaning up Marcus's station.

"Cammi, I'm really sorry to bust up this love fest, but I have class." Elena walks out of the back room and over to us.

"Oh, we're done. I'll come with you." Cammi jumps out of her seat. "Thanks for the tat, Vin. I'll catch you later?" she asks, stepping closer to me. "Kiss me goodbye and follow me back to campus if you must. If not, I'll be okay. Promise. And I'll call you when I'm done for the day."

I lean down and capture her lips with mine. "I'll see you later," I tell her. We both know I'm following her back to campus. I'm not ready to let her go.

Gio tells me I need to step back a little and let

her have some space. He also said I'd end up suffocating her and she'll hate me for it. I've given Cammi enough reasons to hate me already, and I'm counting my lucky fucking stars that she's finding a way to forgive me. To give us another shot when she has every right to steer clear of me.

I lean forward and press my lips against hers again. I never want to stop kissing her once I start. "I love you," I tell her as I pull back.

"I love you," she says.

After she walks out, Marcus turns to me with a grin. "Want me to fix that?" he asks, nodding towards my lopsided number nines. Let's just say drawing on paper and skin *is not* the same, despite what I told Cammi.

"No," I grunt. "It's perfect the way it is." Because Cammi did it.

"Suit yourself." He shrugs. "Are you good? With her and you doing... whatever it is you're doing again?"

Marcus was there when I left her. I was a fucking mess. I'll never tell her how bad I got, and I hope like fuck no one else does either. Not because I don't want her to know, but because she doesn't deserve to have that thrown on to her. I have no one to blame but myself for what I did to us.

"I'm better than good," I tell him.

"You worried about it happening again?" He's asking about me hurting her while I'm asleep, while I'm trapped back in that fucking room.

"I'd be stupid not to be," I admit. "I woke up last night and she was sitting across the room. She didn't want to wake me up."

"That's good. She shouldn't be waking you up," he says.

Marcus doesn't know what happens in my nightmares, just that I have them. I've never come out and told my friends what I went through, and I won't. "Yeah, I guess." I run a hand through my hair. "I asked her to marry me."

"You what?" He stops what he was drawing and drops his sketchpad onto his table. "What'd she say?"

"Yes." I smile.

"Jesus, fuck, Vin. I swear to God, if you fuck this up with her again, I'm gonna cap your ass myself. That girl is fucking nuts about you and that's a once-in-a-lifetime kind of thing. Probably once in ten lifetimes for the likes of you." He laughs.

"I know," I agree. Cammi is the one-off and she loves me. Fuck knows why, but she does. Even after all this time, after everything, she said yes.

"What's going on with her heart?" he asks.

"I fucking broke it," I grunt.

"I know that, but what happened yesterday?"

"Literally, I broke her heart. Doc thinks she has broken heart syndrome, something about extreme emotional distress weakening your heart."

"Makes sense. You left her and you two were weirdly attached to each other. I guess it's like ducks or swans." Marcus isn't making any fucking sense. But then again, it's not often that he does.

"Huh?" I question.

"They mate for life, and if one dies, the other never moves on. They have one mate and that's it," he explains.

"Oh. Guess we're ducks then." I jump up, deciding I've given her enough space. Cammi will be heading to her next class soon, and I want to try to catch her before it starts.

Chapter Thirty-Eight

Cammi

I look over my shoulder. He's not there. I kind of expected him to just appear when I parted ways with Elena. I've been hanging outside my next lecture for the last ten minutes.

I don't know where he went, but I can't stand around and wait for him any longer. So I turn and push through the door. As I sit down, my phone, which is already in my hand, vibrates and a message from Vin pops up on the screen. A body falls into the seat next to me, but I don't pay it any mind as I read the text.

VIN:

Something came up. Running an errand for G. Call me if you need anything. I'll catch up with you later.

He's running an errand for his brother. He didn't show up because he needed to do something, not because he didn't want to. I breathe out a sigh of relief. But as quick as that relief comes, it's gone.

What is he doing? Is he safe?

"You know, if you keep frowning like that, you're going to get wrinkles. Not that it'll matter. I'm sure Vin will be just as obsessed as always." The voice grabs my attention. Dash.

"What are you doing here?" I question him. "Wait... Am I in the wrong place?"

I'm ready to jump up and find my actual lecture when he responds with, "You're in the right room, Cammi. Relax. I'm here under strict orders to keep you alive and calm."

"Whose orders?" I ask stupidly, like there would

be anyone other than Vin asking Dash to babysit me. "I don't need a babysitter."

"Don't kill the messenger, babe." Dash holds up his hands in surrender. "I'm just looking out for my mate's interests. Which happens to be you."

"You're really just going to follow me around until Vin is finished doing whatever it is he's doing?"

"It's what friends do," Dash says.

"Okay, then." I pull out my laptop. I need to focus this year. I barely scraped by with passes last year, and I really want to improve my GPA.

Dash, thankfully, is quiet throughout the entire lecture. And as promised, when I pack up and walk out, he's right by my side.

"You know I'll be fine. You really don't need to follow me," I tell him.

"You should give yourself more credit, Cammi. You're a hoot to be around. Best company I've had in years." Dash laughs.

"Thanks." I roll my eyes at him.

"Cammi? Hey, how are you? I heard you had a... um... incident yesterday." Scarlett stops in front of me.

"Oh, hey. I'm fine. It was a blip. Everyone overreacted," I tell her.

"Is this the ex?" she asks, looking at Dash.

"Ew, god no," I spit out and then cover my mouth. "No offense," I tell Dash before returning my attention to Scarlett. "This is Dash, a friend of the ex —though I guess he's kind of the not-so-ex again."

"Oh, that's great," Scarlett says. "Well, I have to get going, but let's catch up again tomorrow."

"Sounds great. I'd love that," I tell her.

When Scarlett's out of earshot, Dash turns and walks backwards, watching her go. "Who is that? She single?"

"That's my new friend Scarlett, and I actually have no idea." I realise we spent the whole time yesterday talking about me. I'm officially a shitty person. I didn't ask a single thing about her. "How have you been this past year, Dash? Anything new going on in your life?"

"Do you want the honest answer or the version that doesn't make people uncomfortable?" he replies.

"The truth," I tell him.

"My mum passed away. My dad's drinking too much, and my little sister is determined to send me into in an early grave by way of heart attack," he says. "Shit... Sorry, bad choice of words. Make that a stroke." Dash waves a hand around. "Add onto that, the whole watching my best friend fall apart because he was a fucking idiot thing."

"I'm sorry about your mum," I tell him. "I didn't know."

"No one does," Dash says.

"What do you mean no one knows?"

"I didn't tell anyone. Marcus has had his own shit going on and Vin, well, he's been through a lot." Dash looks away as he says this. "So, where to next, princess?"

"Dash, that's horrible. And you're right. Vin was a fucking idiot." I smile.

"Anyone who walks away from you is a fucking idiot." Dash winks. "Now, back to this new friend of yours. Scarlett? When are we seeing her again?"

"*I'll* be seeing her tomorrow. Want me to find out her relationship status?"

"Please do." Dash nods.

"Okay, I need to go home. So, I guess I'll just see you later? I'm sure you have a lot of other things you need to be doing."

"Actually, I'm free. Let's go." Dash wraps an arm around my shoulders and starts leading us towards the car park.

"Okay, then. But don't say I didn't warn you. My mum will be home and she's... sad," I tell him.

"Sad? Why?"

"My dad cheated on her, left her, and now

they're divorcing." I check my phone but there are still no messages from Vin.

"He'll be fine, you know," Dash says.

"I know," I lie.

When Dash pulls into my driveway thirty-five minutes later, I send up a little prayer that my mother isn't on the sofa crying and eating a pint of Ben & Jerry's. She's getting better. I only find her like that maybe once a week now.

Unlocking the front door, Dash is right behind me. "Mum, I'm home." I call out. "I'm not alone, so I really hope you're decent."

"I don't." Dash chuckles, and then moans when my elbow connects with his stomach. "Argh, fuck."

"That's my mum, dude. Just... *no*." I set my bag down before leading Dash through to the kitchen, where I can hear my mum banging around. "Hey, what's going on?" I ask, finding the counters covered in everything that used to fill the cabinets.

"Oh, shit, I didn't hear you come in, sweetie." Mum blows at the loose hair covering her face.

"Ah, yeah. This is my friend. Dash." I point to Dash, who is now privy to the insanity of my mother.

"Oh, finally. I can't believe you're bringing a boy home, Camile, and he's so handsome. Hi, I'm

Katrina, Cammi's mum. You'll have to excuse the mess. Spring cleaning and all," Mum says.

"Mum, it's summer," I remind her.

"It's a pleasure to meet you, Mrs Taylor. Although I would have picked you for Cammi's sister, not her mother." Dash holds out a hand, charm wafting off him in waves.

"Oh, I like you." Mum smiles. "So, what are you two kids up to anyway?"

"Oh, no, Dash is a friend, Mum. A *platonic* friend," I emphasise.

"I've heard friends make the best lovers. They're always generous." Mum winks at me.

"Gross, Mum." I turn to Dash. "I'm so sorry."

"Don't be. She's not wrong," he says. "Although I like to keep my heart in my chest, so platonic is all we're ever going to be. Sorry, princess."

"I'm ordering pizza, Dash. You're staying for dinner?"

"I'd love to. Thanks, Mrs Taylor."

"It's Katrina," Mum corrects him.

"I'm going to go shower quickly. Mum, don't embarrass me," I plead before turning back to Dash. "And I warned you. So, well, you're on your own."

As the sky got darker, so did my mood. Dash refused to leave and he's currently sitting on my bed, while I'm curled up on the sofa, pretending to read a book. I can't focus on the pages. All I can think is...

It's happening again. He's not coming back.

I was a fool to think everything would be okay this time around. This is why I kept my heart guarded. It's going to hurt, but not as much. I hope.

I was the idiot, fool me once and all that. I wanted it so badly I jumped in head-first and hoped for the best. That's the thing with hope. It doesn't always work out. Times like this, I wish I was the saint Vin claims me to be. If I were, I'd perform miracles and make Vin mine. Really mine. I'd make his nightmares disappear, and I'd make sure we got the happy ending to our story.

"Cammi, you're thinking so loud I can hear you all the way over here," Dash says.

"I'm reading," I tell him.

"Some talent you have there, reading upside down and all." He laughs.

I look down at the book I'm holding and quickly

turn it the other way. "Don't be jealous, Dash. We all have talents."

"You know he's going to show up," Dash says.

"I know." The lie slips from my lips.

"Do you?"

"I want to," I admit.

"But you're worried." Dash nods. "Understandable. But trust me when I tell you that boy loves you, Cammi. More than loves you. He's downright obsessed."

"I know he loves me. It's not that, that I'm worried about," I tell Dash.

"What are you worried about then?"

Before I can answer his question, my bedroom window opens. Dash is about to get up off the bed when a foot pops through, and he relaxes back against the headboard with a smirk.

"Told you," he says to me.

Chapter Thirty-Nine

I love my family. I really do. But sometimes I wish they weren't so fucking needy. I've been gone all afternoon and night, dealing with a problem Gio needed fixing. I've finally made it to Cammi's house. I was going to message her, but it's late and I didn't want to wake her if she was asleep.

When I stop on the street, I see Dash's car still parked in the driveway. I'd asked him to keep an eye on her for me. I didn't expect him to still be here, though.

My hand reaches for the tree next to Cammi's window when my phone rings. I pull it out and press answer. "What's up?" I try to keep the annoyance out of my voice. Because Gio might be my older brother, but he's also the boss of the family. Which means no matter what I'm feeling, he's owed a level of respect.

"You good? Where are you?" Gio asks.

"Just got to Cammi's. Are you really calling to check up on me, bro?"

"Ellie wanted to know. How is she?"

"Ah, tell her I'm fine. I'm good. I haven't seen Cammi for hours. Is there anything else you need? I'm kinda busy," I tell my brother.

"Nope, Marcel said you went overboard," Gio says, and there's his real reason for checking up on me.

"I did what you asked. I delivered a message," I tell him.

"Usually, people need to be alive to spread the message, Vin. No one learns shit from a dead man."

"Huh, I'll keep that in mind." I know I'm being a

smart-ass. I might have lost my cool today, but I don't care. I needed to let off some pent-up anger and resentment. All directed at myself, because I fucking broke the woman I love. In trying to protect her, I nearly fucking killed her. A mistake I'm not going to make twice.

"You do that," Gio says, then cuts the call.

"Nice chat." I shake my head and pocket my phone. When I climb through Cammi's bedroom window, all that anger comes back to the surface and is directed right at my fucking best friend sitting on my fiancée's bed like he doesn't have a care in the world. "Move, asshole," I growl at him.

"Thanks for keeping my girl company while I was busy, Dash," he says while mimicking my voice before answering himself. "Oh, no worries, mate. Don't mention it."

"Thank you. I didn't expect you to still be here," I tell him, while moving my eyes over to Cammi. She's sitting on the small chair in the corner of her room.

"I'll leave you two lovebirds to it, then," Dash says. "Cammi, coffee date tomorrow. You, me, and Scarlett. Make it happen."

"Do I even want to know?" I ask the moment Dash walks out the door. Cammi shakes her head.

And then tears just start streaming down her cheeks. I fall to my knees in front of her, my hands itching to reach out and comfort her. "What's wrong?"

"I thought you'd changed your mind," she says. "I'm sorry. I just..."

"It's okay. I'm never changing my mind, Cammi. You and me, we are getting married. We are forever," I tell her.

Cammi's eyes bore into mine. "What are you thinking right now?"

"I'm thinking how much I want to pick you up, carry you to that bed, and hold you. I want to make this right, Cammi."

She doesn't say a word. She just looks at me and waits. I know what she's waiting for. She's waiting for me to do just that. To pick her up, take her over to the bed, and hold her. It's fucking hard for me to do anything without her explicit permission first. What if I'm reading this wrong and she doesn't want me to touch her? Then I'll be no better than the monsters in that room.

Fuck. I'm so fucking torn. I want to be able to do this. I want to be the kind of guy who sees his fiancée upset and can wrap his arms around her and comfort her without being asked to do it. She deserves that guy. Which is why I find myself standing up. I reach down and pick her up bridal-style. Sweat forms on my brows and my hands shake.

I can do this. One step at a time.

When I make it to the bed, I sit down and Cammi curls her body into mine. "I want you to, Vin. I always want you to," she whispers.

Her words ease my discomfort. But I did it. I fucking did it. And she doesn't hate me. "I love you," I tell her. "Let's set a date."

Cammi looks up at me. "Really?"

"Yes," I tell her. "I have something for you. It's not a ring. Yet. But we're getting you one of those tomorrow." I pull the little pink heart-shaped gemstone from my pocket.

"It's a rose quartz. It's beautiful, Vin," she says, clutching it in her palms.

"I saw it in a shop and thought of you," I tell her.

Cammi smiles wide. "Do you know what this stone symbolises?"

"No. Tell me."

"Unconditional love and infinite peace," she explains. Well, fuck. No wonder it made me think of her. "You bought me a stone that means unconditional love and infinite peace. This is better than any ring."

"Ah, I didn't exactly buy it," I admit. I'm not

trying to kill the mood, but I don't want her to think I just go shopping for stones. "I was doing an errand for Gio and saw it. It made me think of you. It was about a month ago."

"I still love it," she says. "I love you."

"I love you. Always. So, that date? When are you thinking? Sunday? Monday?" I ask.

"As in, next week?" She laughs.

"Yeah, I mean, we could probably swing something tomorrow, but it'd be a push."

"Um, no. How about June fourteenth?" she asks me.

"The day we first talked to each other." I remember that day like it was yesterday. "It's perfect." My eyes land on her lips, and my head moves to hers. My heart races as our mouths brush. This is a lot for me, to initiate kissing her, without her verbal consent. But I'm going to keep pushing myself. I'm going to be the best version of myself I can be for her.

"What did you have to do today?" Cammi asks.

"Just some errands for Gio. Nothing interesting."

"I'm sure it was, but you don't have to tell me. I get it." Cammi curls back into my chest.

"It's not that I don't want to. I don't want you to be implicated in any way. If you don't know, then nothing can come back on you," I explain. "Not everything I do is aboveboard."

"I know," she says. "Did you know Dash's mum died?"

I freeze. "What?"

Cammi sits up again. "He told me today. She died a few months ago. His dad is drinking and his little sister is going off the rails."

"Why the fuck wouldn't he tell me all that?" I comb an aggravated hand through my hair, my thoughts bouncing around inside my head.

"I'm not sure, but I thought you should know. I like him when he's not hitting on my mum."

"Dash hit on your mum?" Truth is, I'm a little bummed my friend met her parents before I did.

"Flirted, hit on. Same thing. But we should help him," Cammi suggests.

"Yeah. We will." Right after I kick his fucking ass for not telling me about his mum and everything else he's dealing with.

"You should get some sleep," Cammi says. "You want to stay here? You could meet my mum in the morning?"

"You think walking out of her daughter's bedroom and sitting at the breakfast table is the best way to meet your future mother-in-law?" I ask her.

"Good a time as any. Besides, she assumed I was dating Dash and got so excited at the thought." Cammi laughs.

"I'd kill him. Best friend or not," I grunt.

"Good thing you're the only person I'm interested in," Cammi says.

I didn't sleep. Usually I can sleep when I'm next to her. But I kept obsessing about what she said about Dash's mum being gone. And then me meeting *her* mother this morning. I know Mrs Taylor isn't going to like me. Nobody wants their daughter to end up with a De Bellis.

"Stop worrying. I love you and that's all I care about. I don't care if anyone else approves or not. I *am* marrying you, Vin," Cammi whispers as we make our way down the stairs the following morning. "Mum, we've got an extra mouth to feed," she calls out right before we enter the kitchen.

"I thought you said..." Mrs Taylor turns around and her mouth drops in shock. "You're not Dash."

"No, Mum, this is Vin. My fiancé." Cammi smiles so wide while looking up at me.

"This is Vin?" her mother asks.

"Yeah." Cammi nods.

"It's nice to finally meet you, Mrs Taylor. I'm Vin De Bellis. Cammi has told me a lot about you."

Recognition fills her eyes when she hears my name, but she doesn't mention it. "It's nice to finally meet you too. But if you break my daughter's heart again, I now have a face to match up with the name and I'll hunt you down and slaughter you like a pig."

"Mum!" Cammi gasps. "How did you even know it was him?"

"You have his name tattooed behind your ear, Camile. It wasn't hard to figure out." Her mother says, then turns to me. "Now, how do you like your eggs, Vin?"

"Ah, I'm not fussy, Mrs Taylor," I say, still shocked she's gone from threatening to gut me like a farm animal to asking me how I like my breakfast prepared.

"It's Katrina. So, fiancé? When did this happen?"

"Yesterday," Cammi says. "We realised Vin was an idiot and we're working through things."

"I was," I admit.

"This engagement, is it going to be long? Like, a

we'll get married in two years kind of thing or *we're running off to Vegas tomorrow* kind of thing?" Mrs Taylor asks.

"June. I want to get married in June," Cammi answers.

"Okay, sit down. Let me feed you before we figure out how you're going to plan a wedding in just a few months' time. How do your parents feel about all this, Vin?" Mrs Taylor looks to me.

"Ah, my parents are dead," I tell her. "My brothers and their wives will help, though."

"Oh, I'm so sorry," Mrs Taylor says. "What happened?"

I glance at Cammi. No way can I tell her the truth. "My mother died when I was a baby, and my father passed away a couple of years ago, when Cammi and I were still at school," I explain cryptically.

"I'm really sorry. Come on. Sit down and eat. Have you told your father, Camile?" Mrs Taylor sets a plate full of bacon and sausages on the table.

"Not yet," Cammi says. "But I will."

"Well, I guess, welcome to the family, Vin."

After Breakfast, Cammi comes back to my house with me. "Where do you want to live?" I ask her as I pull some clothes out of my closet.

"Um, I was going to get a job and then start looking for an apartment near campus," she says.

"You don't need a job, Cammi. Focus on school. We have enough money." She's not fucking working and studying full time if she doesn't have to. I have more than enough for us to live off.

"I'm not living off you, Vin," she says as if reading my mind. "I can work."

"I know you can, but you don't have to. And it's not living off me when it's *our* money," I tell her. "Oh, your car keys are in the top drawer by the way."

"My what now?"

"Your car keys," I repeat, walking out of the closet.

"You kept the car?"

"I couldn't get rid of it. It's yours. The car's in your name. It would be illegal for me to try to sell it, Cammi." I smirk.

"Yeah, because you're so worried about breaking the law." She laughs.

"I love that sound."

"What?" Her mouth slams shut as she looks at me curiously.

"The sound of you laughing." I walk over and press my lips against her forehead. "We're buying an apartment near campus. Anything else you want? Any must-haves?"

"All I want is you," she says.

"You have me."

"Thank you."

"Cammi, ask me," I tell her.

"Vin, kiss me like it's the first and last time you ever will." She smiles.

"How about I just kiss you like I'm going to love you every day for the rest of our lives?" I counter.

"I like the sound of that kiss," she says.

When my lips fuse onto hers, everything seems right with the world. By some miracle, I have her back. And this time, I'm never letting anything come between us. Not even my own demons.

Epilogue

June

When I opened the door to my hotel suite, I did not expect to find my future brother-in-law sitting across the hall. Gun in one hand, a stainless steel flask in the other. He looks up at the sound, the pain in his eyes so clear. I close the door, sit down in front of him, gently take the pistol from his hand, and set it beside me.

"What's going on, Santo? Why are you sitting in the hallway?"

"I needed to make sure nothing happened to you," he says.

My heart hurts for him. I can't pretend to imagine how hard weddings are for him. "Nothing is going to happen to me. I'm fine," I tell him.

"Doesn't hurt to be extra cautious," he says. "So, today's the big day. You sure you're ready to become a De Bellis?"

My smile is big and genuine. I've been waiting for this day for months. "Well, I get a pretty amazing brother-in-law out of the deal, so, yes."

Santo smirks. "Vin's a nervous wreck. Has been all night. He thinks you're going to suddenly wake up and run for the hills."

"Mmm, I'm happy to stay firmly planted in dreamland. I'm not running. Is he really worried?"

"It's Vin. He's always worried he's going to lose you. It's part of the De Bellis curse," Santo explains.

I've heard the brothers talk about the De Bellis curse, mostly Marcel. I don't really buy into it, though. They're not cursed. They had a really shitty father. That's bad parenting, not a curse. "Where are you sneaking off to anyway?"

"Vin's room." I shrug. "I couldn't sleep. And I figured he wouldn't be able to either."

"It's bad luck," Santo says.

"Maybe, but we don't need luck. We have love." No amount of bad luck can keep me and Vin apart.

"You're good for him. I'm really glad he has you, Cammi." Santo pushes to his feet, swiping up his pistol from the ground. "Come on. I'll walk you to his room."

"One day, I hope you find something like Vin and I have." I take his hand and let him pull me up.

Santo smiles. It's not a happy smile. "I had it, or at least I thought I did," he says cryptically.

"Is that empty?" I ask, pointing to his flask.

Santo hands it over to me. The shiny silver has the Cinque logo engraved on the front. I unscrew the lid and take a sip. I've become accustomed to the whiskey over the past few months. Vin has been doing a lot of work out of their distillery. Sometimes I'll go with him just to hang out. I'm not much help.

When we reach Vin's door, I wrap my arms around Santo. "Thank you." I return his flask and pull the key card out of my pocket that gives me access to the room.

"Anytime." Santo nods. He stands in the hall, watching me as I slip inside.

"Cammi? What's wrong?" Vin asks as soon as I step into the living room of his suite.

"I couldn't sleep."

"Yeah, me either," he says. "Wait... Why? Are you changing your mind?"

I laugh. "No. Do you really doubt my love that much that you'd think I'd change my mind?"

"It's not your love I doubt, babe. It's your sanity and whether or not it's going to come back." Vin smirks as he approaches me. "Ask me."

"Kiss me like it's the last time you're going to kiss your fiancée, because after tonight, you'll be kissing your wife," I tell him.

Vin claims my lips, his tongue pushing past the seam and swirling around. "Mmm, you taste like Cinque."

"Santo was in the hall outside my room," I explain.

"Why?"

"Making sure I was safe. He had a flask. Can we go to bed now? I really want to go to sleep, wake up, and then marry you."

Vin takes hold of my palm and leads me over to the bed. He's able to do little touches, like this one, or brushing his fingers along my arm or down my back, without asking permission. He still likes me to ask him before he kisses me, or before we do anything more intimate. I'm okay with that, though, because he's healing in his own time. And it's okay if he's never able to just grab me and kiss me. I'll always ask him. I'll always give him what he needs.

Everyone is here: Lauren, Elena, Devon, Scarlett, Daisy, Zoe, Eloise, and my mum. I'm not nervous because today is a dream. I'm marrying the man I love more than life itself. My heart couldn't be happier.

The cardiologist confirmed I have a weak heart and that deep emotional trauma or stress can cause it to stop. It hasn't happened again. Vin goes above and beyond to try to protect me from anything that could trigger a negative reaction. Although, as long as I have him, I know I'm going to be okay.

"You look beautiful, baby," Mum says, standing behind me. I'm wearing a traditional white gown. It was only about the hundredth wedding dress I tried on before I said yes. I just knew this was the one the minute I stepped into it. Although I've had to get it altered. I've put on some of the weight I lost over the year without Vin. Probably because he feeds me all the damn time and my appetite has returned.

"Thank you." I look around the room. My bridesmaids, Lauren, Devon, Elena, and Scarlett are all wearing matching pale-pink dresses. "You guys look so good."

"We're just the backup. You're the star today, Cammi. Are you ready to become a wife?" Lauren asks. "This is literally a fairy-tale wedding, right out of a romance book." She sighs wistfully.

"I'm so ready." I smile.

"We're going to go out and sit. You look beautiful, Cammi," Eloise says. After her emotional outburst over Vin's announcement of our engagement, she apologised. Blamed it on pregnancy hormones and then helped plan this event. She's been amazing. I'm not just gaining four brothers. I'm getting three sisters too.

"Thank you." I hug each of my new sisters and then turn to my mum. "Is he here?"

My mum's face drops. I asked my father to give me away. We've had our differences over the past few months. Mostly because he wasn't a fan of Vin's and tried to talk me out of getting married. I love my father, and I understand his concerns. But nothing is going to stop today from happening.

"I'm sorry. I can't get a hold of him," Mum says.

"It's okay." I smile. It's not. I really wanted my dad to walk me down the aisle. I wanted him to see how happy I was and get past his hang-ups over Vin's last name.

"I can walk down with you," Mum offers.

"No, it's okay. I'll do it by myself," I say. "I'm fine. Promise."

I'm standing at the doors, counting down the seconds until they open while waiting for the song that I chose to start playing, so I can take those few final steps to my forever. My happily ever after.

A figure steps up next to me, and I look up into my father's eyes. "Sorry I'm late," he says.

"It's okay," I whisper. "I'm just glad you're here."

"You're my daughter, Cammi. I wouldn't miss this day for anything. I love you." He kisses my cheek.

"I love you too." I'm trying to keep the tears at bay. "Are you ready?"

"I'm never going to be ready to give you away, but let's pretend I am," Dad says as the song starts to play and the doors open.

Epilogue

All four of my brothers are standing up with me. Everyone has asked if I'm nervous. I'm not. This is a dream to me. I'm marrying Cammi. She's going to be my wife. I couldn't think of a better way to live the rest of my life than by her side.

I don't think it's possible to love anyone the way I love this girl. She's not just my world. She's my entire fucking universe. Whatever the connection is that we have, it's been there since that first day.

She's my own personal saint. God knows I'm not deserving of a saint, and yet he gave me one anyway. I'm sure it was a clerical error or some shit, but I'm not going to point that out. I'm not giving her back.

All of Cammi's friends are standing on the other side of the altar. Waiting. Cammi made sure to keep her entrance song a secret from me. No one would tell me what it's going to be. So when the music starts and the doors open, I'm fighting back tears.

She's fucking breathtaking. The song "Kiss Me" by Dermot Kennedy starts playing, and I can see Cammi's lips moving as she sings the lyrics, her eyes never leaving mine. My heart pounds. Each step she takes feels like an eternity.

I want to run down the aisle, throw her over my shoulder, and bring her up here. I want to be married already. I don't want to wait another second for Cammi to be my wife. To start our forever together.

When she finally makes it to the altar, I step forward and shake her father's hand, although I know he'd do anything to stop this wedding from happening. If he could. That said, I do have some newfound respect for him. He showed up. I was fucking petrified that he wasn't going to. And I was dreading the devastation on Cammi's face if he didn't.

My bride has the biggest smile on her lips instead. "I love you," she mouths.

"I love you." I can't take my eyes off her. This is it.

The ceremony goes by in a blur, and the last thing I hear Father Thomas say is, "You may kiss the bride."

This is the part I've been dreaming about. I look down at Cammi's lips. Before she can open them to say the words she knows I need, I slam my mouth on hers. And I kiss her like it's the first and last time I'll ever get to. I always will, because I'll never take our time together for granted. I'll cherish every single minute I get to spend with this woman. My wife.

Do you want to know how the story Vin tells Cammi ends? Get the bonus Story Time With Vin here.

Also by Kylie Kent

The Merge Series

Merged With Him (Zac and Alyssa's Story)

Fused With Him (Bray and Reilly's Story)

Entwined With Him (Dean and Ella's Story)

2nd Generation Merge Series

Ignited by Him (Ash and Breanna's Story)

An Entangled Christmas: A Merge Series Christmas Novel (Alex and Lily's Story)

Chased By him (Chase & Hope's Story)

Tethered To Him (Noah & Ava's Story)

Seattle Soulmates

Her List (Amalia and Axel Williamson)

McKinley's Obsession Duet

Josh and Emily's Story

Ruining Her

Ruining Him

Sick Love Duet

Unhinged Desires (Dominic McKinley and Lucy Christianson)

Certifiable Attraction (Dominic McKinley and Lucy Christianson)

The Valentino Empire

Devilish King (Holly and Theo's story)

Unassuming Queen (Holly and Theo's story)

United Reign (Holly and Theo's story)

Brutal Princess (Neo and Angelica's Story)

Reclaiming Lola (Lola and Dr James)

Sons of Valentino Series

Relentless Devil (Theo & Maddie's story)

Merciless Devil (Matteo & Savannah's story)

Soulless Devil (Romeo & Livvy's Story)

Reckless Devil (Luca & Katerina's Story)

A Valentino Reunion (The entire Valentino Family)

The Tempter Series

Following His Rules (Xavier & Shardonnay)

Following His Orders (Nathan &Bentley)

Following His Commands (Alistar & Dani)

Legacy of Valentino

Remorseless Devilette (Izzy and Mikhail)

Vengeful Devilette (Izzy and Mikhail)

Vancouver Knights Series

Break Out (Liam and Aliyah)

Know The Score (Grayson and Kathryn)

Light It Up Red (Travis and Liliana Valentino)

Puck Blocked (Luke and Montana)

De Bellis Crime Family

A Sinner's Promise (Gio and Eloise)

A Sinner's Lies (Gabe & Daisy)

A Sinner's Virtue (Marcel & Zoe)

A Sinner's Saint (Vin & Cammi)

A Sinner's Truth (Santo & Aria)

Club Omerta

Are you a part of the Club?

Don't want to wait for the next book to be released to the public?
Come and Club Omerta for an all access pass!

This includes:
• daily chapter reveals,
• first to see - everything, covers, teasers, blurbs
• Advanced reader copies of every book
• Bonus scenes from the characters you love!
• Video chats with me (Kylie Kent)
• and so much more

Click the link to be inducted to the club!!!
CLUB OMERTA

About the Author

About Kylie Kent

Kylie made the leap from kindergarten teacher to romance author, living out her dream to deliver sexy, always and forever romances. She loves a happily ever after story with tons of built-in steam.

She currently resides in Sydney, Australia and when she is not dreaming up the latest romance, she can be found spending time with her three children and her husband of twenty years, her very own real life instant-love.

Kylie loves to hear from her readers; you can reach her at: author.kylie.kent@gmail.com

Let's stay in touch, come and hang out in my readers group on Facebook, and follow me on instagram.

Made in United States
North Haven, CT
02 February 2025

65281901R00232